I0551682

Selkies of Scotland

WHITE RAVEN SERIES BOOK 3

AnneMarie Dapp

SELKIES OF SCOTLAND
Copyright © 2021 by AnneMarie Dapp

ISBN: 978-1-955784-47-4

Published by Satin Romance
An Imprint of Melange Books, LLC
White Bear Lake, MN 55110
www.satinromance.com

Published in the United States of America.

Cover Design by Ashley Redbird Designs

For Great-Grandmother Annie McClain

"The heart of man is very much like the sea, it has its storms, it has its tides, and its depths, it has its pearls too."

— VINCENT VAN GOGH

Prologue

Jade sipped her flute of champagne, reclining comfortably against the velvet seat cushion, and watched the pale mid-November sky fade away.

"A girl could get used to this luxury," she sighed. It had been five weeks since their rescue and they were on their way to Scotland to visit Aidan's family.

Aidan gave her a wink. "That's what I like to hear!"

"I'm glad. It's just disappointing that I wasn't able to talk to Topusana. I was so hoping to learn more about the Comanche. I guess I'll be investigating my Scottish side first," she said with a sigh. "Anyway, I heard from Mary before we boarded. She has coverage at The Muse Gallery for the next couple of weeks. She volunteered to work at the antique store until I get back. She seems pretty happy to be staying at the cottage while I'm gone."

"Oh?"

"Yes, appears Deputy Rheinstein volunteered to continue checking in on her while we're away. They really seemed to hit it off. I'm happy for them."

"Paul's a standup guy." Aidan smiled. "I'm glad they've taken a liking to each other."

"Me too. Oh, I almost forgot to tell you about the portrait. Mary told me the painting is back to normal. Can you believe it? The man is alone and on land again. It's like the changes never happened."

I

"Really?"

"Yep. It's a relief. The portrait was really starting to creep me out. Seeing the imagery change was like watching an episode of 'Night Gallery.' So spooky. I guess that's one mystery we didn't solve. I still have no idea where the painting came from."

"Well, at least it's gone back to normal for now. Hopefully, it will stay that way. Maybe we'll get some answers in Tobermory. My family is excited to have us with them for the holidays."

"I still can't believe we're leaving the country." She sighed. "I can't wait to see your ancestral home in Scotland. Are you going to change into a kilt when we arrive?" He gave her a wink and his lopsided smile. "I'll do whatever my lass desires." She giggled, imagining him in formal Scottish dress.

Aidan studied her face with adoring eyes. "You're a beauty, love." He cupped her face, kissing her on the forehead. Afterward, he refreshed their glasses and placed the bottle back into the ice bucket. Once he handed her her drink, he raised his glass.

"I'd like to make a toast."

She raised her glass in anticipation.

"To mysteries, adventures, and the great land of Scotland!"

They gazed into each other's eyes and clinked their crystal flutes. Aidan squeezed next to Jade on the lounge seat and took her hand in his. They both smiled, watching Morrigan and Dougal curl up across the aisle. Their pets had become inseparable in the last five weeks, choosing to bed down together even when their owners were not.

Aidan leaned down and whispered in her ear. "I love you, Miss Mackenzie."

"I love you, too, Mr. MacFie."

His lips found hers while the plane bounced in the turbulence. Lightning lit up the cabin compartment. Her breath hitched as his fingers slipped down her shoulders, grazing over her waist and hips. They lingered for a moment, before clicking the seatbelt over her lap. She gazed into his warm eyes while dimples rose in the corner of his cheeks. "I'll always keep you safe, lass. Ye have my word." She smiled up into his brilliant blue eyes.

"I know you will, love. You always have."

Aidan reached his arm around her shoulders while they braced for the impending storm.

Jade leaned against his powerful body, realizing she'd finally found her place.

Chapter One

Jade Mackenzie raced toward the pounding shore. Tears blurred her vision while she attempted to find her way through the shadows. She watched the melted wax stream over the candelabra clutched in her shaking hands. A pinpoint of light flickered in the distance. She followed the vague glow highlighting a narrow passage within the mouth of the cave. Pausing by the entrance, she hesitated. Swarms of rats scurried up the walls, fleeing from the soft candlelight. She shuddered, imagining them watching her from the damp passages. Cold sweat trickled down the small of her back and her lungs tightened in response to the frigid air. She could hear women crying, and realized time was not on her side. After saying a silent prayer, she slipped into the darkness.

Jade gasped as she woke from her nightmare. The plane struggled in the storm, while Aidan embraced her.

"It's alright, lass. We've hit some turbulence, but our pilot's the best."

The stewardess, Mrs. Macleary, walked down the aisle with her beverage cart. Aidan and Jade both noticed her pale face and pursed lips.

A tightening sensation gripped Jade's stomach when she approached. The middle-aged woman pushed back a lock of salt and pepper hair behind

5

her ear with a trembling hand. She offered a tight smile, which did not reach her baby blue eyes.

"Mr. MacFie, the Captain asked to have a word with you."

Aidan gave Jade's hand a gentle kiss before following the stewardess back to the flight deck. When he was gone, Mrs. Macleary smiled down at Jade and took her flute. "Would you like another glass of champagne, Miss Mackenzie?"

"Yes, please." Jade returned the smile. "Is everything alright, Mrs. Macleary? Is this kind of turbulence normal?"

"Well, dear, we do have some terrible storms over Scotland this time of year, but rest assured, our pilot is well-equipped to handle these kinds of issues. Just make sure to keep your seatbelt fastened. We may be in for a bumpy ride. I'll be returning to my seat in a few moments. May I offer you anything else before I go?"

"Thank you. I think I'm good. The champagne is lovely. I have to admit flying is not my favorite pastime."

The stewardess nodded. "You'll be fine, ma'am. Just sit back and relax. You're in good hands."

"Thank you," Jade said, leaning back in her seat. After Mrs. Macleary left, Jade took a sip of champagne and closed her eyes. The plane continued its rough course while she whispered a prayer for their safety.

AIDAN REACHED THE COCKPIT DOOR WITH A FEELING OF UNEASE. ONCE inside, he took a seat next to the captain. "Everything alright, Johnathon?"

Johnathon Green was in his mid-thirties, with dark brown eyes and a shock of red hair. He shook his head slowly, glancing down at the instrument panel. "Aidan, I asked you to come up here because we're in trouble."

Aidan's brow wrinkled as he studied the captain's profile. "What's wrong?"

"We've been dealing with some challenging weather conditions for the past several hours, but that's nothing new. Storms in this part of the world are common. The problem is with the engine. The plane's equipment was triple checked before we left, but there's something wrong with the navigation system. Simply put, it's not responding well."

Aidan's mouth drew down in a tight line. "How serious are we talking, Johnathon?"

"I'll be honest, it's bad. It's almost as if someone's messed with the equipment right before takeoff. Look, I'm going to do everything in my power to land this thing, but you need to be ready for a rough descent. I'll announce over the intercom when we're getting close. Please make sure to fasten your seat belts and prepare yourselves."

Aidan patted the pilot on the shoulder. "I have confidence you will do everything in your power to get us home."

Johnathon gave him a strained smile, then focused on the instrument panel. "Thank you, sir."

৩১৩

JADE CAUGHT AIDAN'S OCEAN-BLUE GAZE AS HE MADE HIS WAY DOWN THE aisle. She knew something was wrong even before he took his seat.

"What's going on?"

Aidan hesitated a moment. She bet he was trying to explain the situation carefully without scaring her.

"The captain is expecting a rough landing."

Her steel-grey eyes searched his face, and she swallowed. "Oh, God. That's not good." He reached his arm around her slender shoulder, and she closed her eyes. "I'm here, darlin'. It's going to be alright."

The stewardess strapped into her seat behind the flight deck and made the sign of the cross.

Lightning lit up the cabin as the plane struggled to stay on course in the torrential rains. A sudden drop in air pressure cued the release of oxygen masks. Aidan pulled one over his mouth and nose before fitting Jade's. His fingers encircled her hand as the aircraft lost altitude.

They bumped and swayed for what felt like an eternity. When the wheels finally contacted the ground, the plane bounced and skidded over the asphalt.

Jade let out a cry as they sped over the tarmac. She felt the seatbelt pinching into her skin as she was thrust forward. Her wine flute flew across the room, shattering against the wall. Dougal and Morrigan's eyes flashed open while the private jet bounced across the landing strip. Jade tightened

7

her grip on the chair and said a silent prayer. When the plane finally slowed to a stop, she released her breath.

Aidan gently removed her oxygen mask, along with his own, before nuzzling her cheek. He winced at the coolness of her flesh.

"Oh, Aidan. That was terribly frightening."

"Sorry, love." He took her hand and raised it to his lips. "I think we're out of the woods now."

After several minutes passed, Captain Green made his way to the cabin to check on his guests.

Aidan removed his seatbelt and shook his hand. "That was incredible, Johnathon. You really saved the day."

"Thank you, sir. It was a close one. We'll need the engineers to check this plane from top to bottom once we've unloaded. There's no logical reason this happened without someone messing with the control system. I'll give the jet a complete once over, but we are probably going to want to get this officially investigated. I wouldn't be surprised if there was foul play involved."

Aidan nodded soberly and pulled out his cell phone, searching his contacts for their driver's number. "Collins, we're ready for the car. Thank you. See you in a few minutes."

Aidan slipped Jade's woolen coat over her shoulders before putting on his own. Once they were bundled up, he took her arm and led her down the stairs and into the frigid evening. She blinked, her eyes adjusting to the bright lights surrounding the landing strip. Beyond the spacious tarmac were acres of endless fields of heather. She inhaled the aroma of the sea, feeling at home.

The distant sound of pounding surf eased her agitated mind while she waited. Moments later, a Silver Dawn Rolls-Royce pulled up and their driver opened his door. Jade blinked in astonishment, admiring the lush interior and bouquet of flowers on the seat closest to her.

Aidan reached for the colorful arrangement and handed them to Jade with a bow.

"Welcome to Scotland, lass."

She let out her breath, gathering the gift in her arms, breathing in the fresh scent of roses and lilacs. Despite the safe landing, her hands shook when she lifted the bouquet to her nose. "Thank you, Aidan. They're beautiful."

He gave her a soft peck on the cheek and held the door while she climbed inside the vehicle. Dougal hopped in beside her. The Scottish terrier yawned before resting his fuzzy head on her lap. Aidan placed Morrigan's cage next to the driver's seat before opening his door. The white raven ruffled her pearly feathers and glanced toward the windshield with interest. Once inside, he took Jade's hand while she leaned back against the lush interior. She sighed, enjoying the comfort of the heater.

They drove along a cobblestone road, cutting through a lush hillside. As they drew closer to the MacFie Castle, Jade noticed a receiving line of formally dressed staff awaiting their arrival. Her eyes adjusted to the muted scenery. She marveled at the lavish grounds surrounding Aidan's ancestral home. Jade blinked in surprise, studying the rows of vintage streetlamps lining the road. It was as if they'd fallen back in time. Before she realized it, the driver parked inside the roundabout adjacent to the castle's main entrance.

She'd tried to imagine the grandeur of the MacFie Castle many times while listening to Aidan's detailed descriptions of his ancestors' home. Yet, nothing could prepare her for the sheer magnitude of the estate. This reality sunk in when she noticed over two dozen staff members awaiting their arrival. She studied their pressed uniforms and serious faces.

The attending personnel were skilled in a variety of disciplines. Many had worked for the MacFie family for decades, like their families before them. Several times Aidan tried to explain his generational legacy in Tobermory, but it was only now beginning to sink in. Her boyfriend was the laird to one of the most famous castles in Scotland. She felt her stomach tighten at the thought of meeting everyone. Would they see her as just a silly American tourist out of her element? Not making a fool of herself was suddenly her top priority.

Seeming to sense her unease, Aidan slipped his arm around Jade's tiny waist and planted a warm kiss on her rosy cheek. "I love you, Jade Mackenzie. I hope you enjoy my ancestral home. It's an honor to have you visit, darlin'."

"I love you, Aidan MacFie." Jade smiled up into his vivid blue eyes. "I hope I don't do anything to embarrass you in front of your employees."

"There's nothing you could do to make me feel different for ye, lass." He chuckled, placing his large hand on her knee. He then leaned over to whisper in her ear. "You could run naked through the castle, and I'd love you all the more for it."

"Naked?" She felt her face flush. Jade put her hand to her mouth and laughed. "That would get the staff talking."

"That's my bonnie lass. Your laughter is music to my ears."

Aidan felt her body relax under his arm and smiled to himself. He knew she was nervous but understood there was nothing to worry about. He'd already spoken to his employees and instructed them on Jade's vegan diet requirements and preferences. Many of the workers he'd known since he was a small child. They were like family, and he looked forward to seeing them again.

The grand estate towered over the sandy cliffside, like a mountainous mirage. There was an organic feeling about the castle, something she hadn't expected when she tried to picture it back in the States. Once they'd parked, the driver rushed to Jade's door and smiled. She thanked him before turning toward the steps of the castle. Looking up at the curious faces made her heart race. She felt a mixture of excitement and nervous energy, but she was eager to meet the staff and explore the grand home.

Aidan turned to Collins, instructing him to bring Morrigan into the first guest room on the right wing, along with Dougal.

"My pleasure, sir."

Her brows raised, not used to being waited on.

"Oh, thank you, Mr. Collins," Jade said. She felt Aidan's hand graze over the small of her back as they made their way toward the reception area. She had an overwhelming sensation of slipping back in time. Men and women of various ages waited in two rows leading to the stone steps.

A woman in her early sixties was the first to address the couple. The housekeeper's grey hair was pulled back in a tight bun. Her black and white uniform was neatly pressed. She curtsied when introduced. "Welcome, Laird MacFie. It's a pleasure to see you again."

"Thank you, Mrs. Flannery. I'd like you to meet Jade Mackenzie."

"Miss Mackenzie, it's a pleasure to make your acquaintance." The middle-aged woman offered a warm smile. "We hope you enjoy your stay at MacFie Castle. It's been my family's honor to help manage the estate over the past two centuries."

Jade's grey eyes widened. "That's wonderful! It's a pleasure to make your acquaintance, Mrs. Flannery."

"Thank you. If you have any special requests, I can help you night or day."

Aidan turned toward Jade. "Mrs. Flannery oversees our kitchen and housekeeping staff. She's an excellent manager. I can't imagine the estate running without her."

Mrs. Flannery's face softened in gratitude. "Thank you for saying so, Laird MacFie."

Jade's mouth fell open when she heard Aidan referred to as a laird. *I really have fallen back in time.*

"It's an honor to be employed by such a well-respected family. Your parents were the dearest people. God rest their souls. It's my privilege and duty to care for the new master of the house," Mrs. Flannery said.

"Margaret Flannery's been with us since I was a baby. She's more like family than an employee."

"It's a true pleasure to meet you, ma'am," Jade said, making a small curtsey in return.

Mrs. Flannery smiled in surprise and gave Aidan an approving look.

"Please let me know if I can assist you in any way during your stay. It's our aim to make your visit as comfortable as possible, Miss Mackenzie. My daughter is newly apprenticed. She'll be helping you with setting up your room tonight," she said with a proud smile.

Jade turned to the teenager standing by her mother's side. The young woman curtsied, her cinnamon curls falling over her freckled face. She grinned at Aidan, soft blue eyes peeking beneath thick lashes.

"Jade Mackenzie, this is Marcail Flannery." Aidan said.

The teenager's smile faded when she was introduced to Jade.

"Pleasure, ma'am," she said, just barely above a whisper.

Her mother glanced at her in surprise.

"Well, that's a first. It's not like my daughter to be at a loss for words."

"It's very nice to meet you, Marcail," Jade said, flashing a warm smile.

The young woman nodded but did not return the smile. Instead, she looked down at the ground, studying her black loafers.

Jade was puzzled by her aloofness, but didn't have time to dwell on it. Before she realized, she was ushered down the long row of servants and introduced one after the other.

After meeting the Flannerys', Jade was presented to their head butler, Mr. Jacob Allen. He was in his early seventies with a serious demeanor and few words. Shortly after, she met the head groomsman, Rusty O'Sullivan, and his apprentice Donavon Dunsmore. They smiled when introduced and offered their services in the stables. Jade turned to Aidan with wide eyes.

"I had no idea you owned horses!"

Aidan chuckled, enjoying her delighted expression.

"Well, it was a little surprise I was saving for ye. I know how much you love animals, darlin'."

Jade grinned, shaking her head.

As she walked past the waiting staff, Jade tried her best to remember their names and faces. She stifled a yawn; the long flight was catching up with her. Once they'd reached the end of the introductions, Aidan led Jade toward the yett, a set of latticed iron and cherry wood doors leading to the castle entrance. The head butler, Jacob Allen, and his assistants moved to open them. She listened to the sound of scraping metal on granite, intrigued and slightly overwhelmed.

Aidan gently placed his hand against the small of Jade's back and led her inside. Spiraling staircases swept toward the stone ceilings, while massive portraits covered every inch of the walls. Many of the paintings represented the MacFie ancestors. Jade blinked in wonder while passing through a grand parlor filled with suits of armor and ancient artifacts.

"As I mentioned before, my great-uncle rebuilt the castle in the eighteenth century. It's a miracle they were able to recover many of the priceless relics. Several portraits were re-commissioned after the fire. By the time the castle was repaired, my great-grandmother had successfully relocated to America."

Jade recalled the story. When she'd first heard of Aidan's great-grandmother belonging to a non-human race called the 'selkie folk', she was astounded. Little did she know it was only the beginning of the mystery of the MacFie legacy. Through a collection of diaries, his great-grandmother revealed her husband, Railbert MacFie, had been murdered in a savage attack in their private garden. The castle was set aflame before his great-grandmother, Edina, escaped to her brother-in-law's estate. He'd promised an oath to his sister-in-law to re-build the MacFie Castle and give her safe passage to the Americas. Once she arrived in the States, she was escorted to one of the uncle's private homes, located in an established Virginia colony. The Selkie Hunters continued their search for Aidan's great-grandmother for decades afterward. Her grandchildren eventually relocated to Monterey,

California. Jade was surprised to discover her own great-grandparents worked alongside the MacFie clan in the nineteenth century, overlapping their family's histories.

There was so much more to discover concerning his family's rich history. Jade stifled a yawn despite her excitement. She wanted desperately to explore every inch of the castle, examine every portrait, rare antique, and nook and cranny. Sadly, her body and mind had other plans. The long trip and rocky landing had zapped her energy.

Aidan, sensing her fatigue, pressed his lips against the back of her neck. His touch sent an electric current through her body. She sighed as his hands encircled her waist. "Tired, darlin'?"

"I feel like I'm in a lovely fairytale." Jade smiled up into his dazzling aqua-marine eyes. "I'm dying to explore your home, but I can barely keep my eyes open."

"I'm pretty worn out myself. I arranged to have your suitcases, Morrigan, and her supplies sent up to your room. Let's get you to bed."

Jade held her breath when he flashed his disarming smile. The idea of Aidan joining her made her heart skip a beat. She suddenly felt wide awake. He led her to a spiraling stone staircase on the right side of the parlor, leading to the master suite. Medieval candle sconces were set along the rising walls of the castle, illuminating their path.

Once they'd reached the top of the stairs, they followed a long hallway. Several portraits and framed photographs adorned the walls, along with antique tables filled with priceless antiques. She paused next to an eighteenth-century mahogany table set beneath an ornately framed ocean-themed painting. A large Georgian vase sat atop an embroidered tablecloth. Pink roses and lilacs filled the crystal.

"Oh, Aidan. This reminds me of the bouquet and vase you gave me the day of my antique shop's grand opening."

"You have a good eye, lass." He drew her in his arms, and she gazed into his loving eyes.

"It's part of the same collection. I thought you might enjoy some fresh flowers on your arrival."

"You're truly the most thoughtful man I've ever known."

He took her hand, then quietly led her to the end of the expansive hallway.

When they'd reached an ornate golden door, he turned a crystal doorknob. Jade found the expansive bedroom adorned with eighteenth century furniture amazing. A roaring fire sat opposite a lavish king-size bed covered by a cherrywood canopy and sheer forest-green curtains.

"This room looks fit for royalty."

"Glad you approve, my lady. The fire should keep you nice and toasty tonight. November in Scotland is positively frigid."

"I can imagine," Jade said, grinning when she noticed Morrigan perching on her stand near the opposite end of the room. Her beak was hidden beneath her snowy wing.

Dougal jumped onto the comforter and thrummed his tail against the lace-covered bedding.

"Oh, Aidan…this is such a lovely room."

"I'm glad my lass approves."

Jaded noticed her suitcases were placed next to an ornately carved wardrobe. The sound of footsteps echoed down the hall. Marcail cleared her throat before tapping on the other side of the door. Aidan opened the partition for the young housekeeper.

"Excuse me, sir, and miss. My ma instructed me to help Miss Mackenzie unpack for the night."

Jade looked at Aidan in confusion. "Oh, that's very kind, but I can take care of my suitcases."

The teenager's baby blue eyes rested on Aidan's while she played with a lock of her cinnamon-colored curls. Her fingers grazed over a string of pearls encircling her ivory neck.

"I've got my orders."

Aidan smiled gently, trying to put the girl at ease.

"Marcail, you don't have to be so formal. After all, I've known you and your mother for as long as I can remember. Why, I believe you were just entering kindergarten when I was a freshman in high school?"

Marcail glanced up in surprise, a slight smile on her pixie-like face.

"And I'll never forget that little teddy bear you carried everywhere." He ran his fingers over the back of his dark hair. "What did you call it again? Mr.…."

"Mr. Fluffy Bum," Marcail whispered. Her face flushed, recalling the memory. "I can't believe you remember that!" She placed her dainty hands over her face, surrendering to a fit of giggles.

Jade glanced back and forth between the two and smiled. Aidan winked at his girlfriend.

"I'm happy to see you smiling again, Marcail."

"Thank you, sir," she said, blushing to her strawberry-blonde roots.

Once the teenager managed to stop laughing, she straightened the hem of her apron and turned toward Jade.

"Miss Mackenzie, would you like me to start unpacking your suitcases before your evening tea?"

"Oh, that's kind, Marcail. I don't want you to have to wait on me. I'm sure I can put my things away myself."

"I have my orders to unpack and get you settled in for the night." Marcail frowned, not expecting to be turned away from her duties.

Jade, sensing the girl's distress, offered a smile. "Oh, well then, if it's not too much trouble, I'd love the help. To tell the truth, I can barely keep my eyes open."

"Very good, ma'am. I'll get started right away."

The petite maid gracefully made her way to a large cherry wood wardrobe in the corner of the room. Intricate carvings of forest creatures covered the furniture. The image recalled Jade's favorite childhood book, The Lion, The Witch, and the Wardrobe. It was a stunning antique.

Jade turned to Aidan. "I don't see your bags?"

He offered his familiar lopsided smile. "Well, lass, I have my room down the hall. I'll be close if ye need anything."

It was Jade's turn to blush, realizing she'd assumed Aidan would be staying with her.

Marcail turned from the wardrobe, a hint of a smile on her face, before turning back to unpack the suitcase. It was just a moment, but it made Jade uneasy. She didn't like the idea of being eavesdropped. She couldn't quite place it, but something about the teenager made her apprehensive.

"Well, I should let you get comfortable, darlin'. It's been a long day. I'm looking forward to showing you the castle tomorrow morning. If the weather permits, we can visit the garden as well," Aidan said.

"Oh, yes. I'd love to see the garden and the rest of the castle." Jade remembered the dream she had concerning his great-grandmother tending to her herbs and plants. She wondered if seeing the grounds would match her vision.

Aidan kissed Jade on the forehead while Dougal leaned against his boots. When he turned to leave, his pup followed.

"Don't forget, if ye need anything at all, I'm just down the hallway."

"Thank you." She searched her boyfriend's face, wondering why he didn't want to stay in her room. He gave her hand a squeeze before leaving. Dougal followed his master out the door.

After he'd left, Jade turned her attention to Marcail. She was busy unpacking her clothes and hanging her collection of woolen sweaters snugly inside the antique wardrobe.

"Thanks again for all your help. I really appreciate it." Jade said.

The young woman turned, nodded, but did not speak.

For the next half an hour, Jade sorted through her belongings, making herself familiar with the massive room. She discovered an attached master bathroom. Inside was a clawfoot tub with a gilded shower fixture. A white vanity covered with pink flower etchings was set in the corner. A crystal vase rested on top. Pastel-colored roses filled the container. She bent down and breathed in their sweet perfume.

"You really thought of everything, Laird MacFie," she whispered. Sighing, she placed her beloved pewter brush and comb onto the polished surface. The set was one of her most precious antiques, an heirloom passed down through the generations. Whenever she brushed her sandy-blonde locks, she imagined her great-grandmother enduring the long trek across the Oregon Trail. In Cathy Mackenzie's diary, Jade discovered her grandmother packed her family's heirlooms in a hope chest before traveling out west.

After she'd finished unpacking her toiletries, she went back to the bedroom. The crackling fireplace and lovely antiques immediately made her feel at home. When the last of her dresses were hung, Marcail closed the wardrobe.

"My ma should be here with some tea in a moment. Goodnight, ma'am."

"That sounds lovely. Thank you, Marcail."

She watched the teenager turn to leave. When the door closed, she sighed in relief. Jade moved toward the large bay window overlooking the Atlantic. There were several rows of kerosene lamps illuminating the shore, casting soft light across the roaring waves. The view was spectacular, and her mind wandered while watching the cresting surf. She blinked in surprise when several dark forms surfaced from the cascading sea. Jade moved closer to the glass, trying to get a better look. A pair of grey seals made their way onto the sand dunes, galumphing across the beach.

More than a dozen seals were onshore by the time Jade heard a soft knock on her bedroom door. She left the mist-covered window and went to answer. *Maybe Aidan changed his mind*, she thought, her heart racing. She opened the door to see Mrs. Flannery waiting in the hallway. Jade flashed a welcoming smile, trying to hide her disappointment. The housekeeper wheeled in a silver serving tray, along with a polished teapot and ivory-colored teacups.

"Good evening, Miss Mackenzie. Ye must be terribly tired, poor lass. And I just heard about the airplane nearly crashing over the coast. Lord have mercy! I'll be saying my prayers tonight for God's divine intervention."

Jade smiled, enjoying Mrs. Flannery's company. The mother, unlike her daughter, was warm and talkative.

"It was a bit of a scare. I'll make sure to take my Rosary beads tonight and give thanks."

Mrs. Flannery searched Jade's face to see if she was serious, looking her square in the eyes.

Satisfied, she patted her hand.

"That's a good lass. Many brethren are leaving the Church these days. It's nice to see there's some devout young ladies left in this world."

"Thank you, Mrs. Flannery. It's a comfort for sure. My mom taught me to pray the Rosary, and it's always given me peace when times have been difficult."

"That's lovely. Does your ma live in California as well?"

Jade bit her bottom lip and looked away. "No, she passed away earlier this year."

"Poor dear." Mrs. Flannery folded her hands together and shook her head. "I'm terribly sorry for your loss. Well, now, you just have a nice cuppa and get some rest. I'll be by in the morning with refreshments. Laird MacFie suggested you prefer coffee in the morning. He wants you to be comfortable during your stay with us."

"Oh, that's thoughtful, but I wouldn't want to make more work for you."

"It's no trouble at all. What do you prefer, lass? Coffee or tea first thing?"

"Well, I do love my morning coffee." She lowered her voice. "To tell the truth, I'm a terrible grouch if I miss my daily dose."

"I'm the same way, Miss Mackenzie! Coffee in the morning and tea in the evening. Oh, and Laird MacFie made sure to instruct us about your special vegan diet preferences," she said with her brows raised.

"Oh, that's perfect. Yes, I'd love a little almond or soy milk with my coffee if possible."

"Wonderful. You should know that the master of the house made sure to set up everything to your liking. He's a darling man. Been considerate since he was a wee lad. His parents raised him right. God bless their souls."

Mrs. Flannery poured a steaming cup of black Scottish tea along with a splash of almond milk.

"Sugar?"

"Please," Jade said.

She watched the steam rise as the metal spoon stirred against the porcelain cup. The faint sound of the sea echoed in the background. The housekeeper left the serving tray by the side of the bed and made her way to the door.

"Please let me know if I can be of any help during your stay, Miss Mackenzie."

"Thank you, Mrs. Flannery. You may call me Jade if it pleases you."

"Oh, that's considerate, child. However, we must keep to tradition. Please have a good night, Miss Mackenzie."

When the heavy door closed behind her, Jade moved back toward the bedroom window. A light sprinkling of rain covered the glass, and she could see the moon shining over the breakers in the distance. She looked forward to exploring the beach in the morning. Her thoughts turned to Aidan as she readied herself for bed. After slipping on a flannel pair of pink pajamas and matching slippers, she took a seat at the side of her bed and sipped her tea.

She let out a sigh, imagining Aidan down the hall. If she were honest with herself, she'd love for him to visit her bedroom in the middle of the night. Since their rescue from the Hunters, they'd confessed their love for one another. Up until the kidnapping, Aidan held back complete intimacy fearing his selkie nature would come between them. Yet, once he'd saved Jade from a near drowning, she knew nothing but love for the man. When they finally admitted their true feelings, Jade confessed she was a virgin.

Aidan's reaction had been a combination of shock and intrigue. Since the Hunters were arrested in the States, the couple spent plenty of time together getting to know one another. And although they'd enjoyed many intimate moments, they'd yet to take their relationship to the next level. She wondered if their trip to Scotland would finally allow their love affair to fully blossom. Jade placed her teacup back onto the silver platter and made her way into her adjoining bathroom. After brushing her teeth and washing her face, she padded back to bed. She kicked off her slippers and turned off the antique lamp next to the bed. Listening to the crackling logs in the fireplace and the wind striking the thick windows, she drifted off to sleep.

JADE WALKED TOWARD THE GLASSY WAVES BENEATH THE STAR-FILLED SKY. *Moonlight showered ribbons of light over the sea. She listened to a melody in the distance, a beautiful harmony which spoke of an ancient way of life. Selkies rose from the depths, swimming toward the mouth of the cave.*

Cries of pain and laughter intermingled.

A baby cried in the darkness, and melodious voices rose in answer. In awe, she watched the great pod near the shoreline. Two raven-haired beauties galumphed toward the cave; one carried a newborn baby in her arms. The witnesses sang, their lovely voices celebrating the newest clan member. But joy turned to horror as dozens of cloaked Hunters appeared outside. They ran toward the helpless mothers with harpoons in their gloved hands. The sound of their screams followed her into the darkness.

Chapter Two

Jade awoke to Morrigan's cries. Rubbing her eyes, she slipped on a satin robe and slippers.

By the time she'd checked on her raven, there was a knock on the bedroom door.

Marcail wheeled in her cart with a silver coffee pot, a plate of strawberry scones, and a bowl of mash.

"Good morning, Miss Mackenzie. I've brought up some coffee and scones. Laird MacFie instructed the kitchen staff to prepare some mash for your pet raven." She absently touched a strand of pearls encircling her pale neck while she studied Morrigan. The corners of her mouth turned down in a grimace.

"Oh, that's so thoughtful! Thank you, Marcail."

Sensing the girl's unease, Jade tried to help her relax. "I love your necklace. Pearls have always been my favorite."

The teenager nodded, looking down at the marble floor. She folded her hands behind her back. "Thank you, ma'am. Would you be needing anything else right now?"

"Thank you. This is perfect."

"Good day."

After the young woman left, Jade shook her head, puzzled by Marcail's strange demeanor, wondering if she could have offended her in some way. Perhaps she'd ask Mrs. Flannery the next time she saw her.

She poured herself a cup of coffee, along with a splash of almond milk, into the porcelain cup. Jade admired the ornate design of violets and clover. After she took a sip, she prepared Morrigan's mash. The raven opened her beak in anticipation for breakfast, finishing the meal in several eager gulps.

"Well, sweetie, we should make time today to enjoy some fresh air."

Jade made her way back over to the window and gazed out at the expansive sea below. She shuddered, thinking about her nightmare. She knew from experience that her dreams were often glimpses of the future. She hoped the images were just her overactive imagination. Even so, she'd make sure to mention it to Aidan. The thought of seeing him again filled her with longing.

She sat at the edge of her bed and reached for a strawberry scone resting on a porcelain plate. When she bit into the warm pastry, her eyes lit up. Her senses were overwhelmed by the delightful mix of fresh strawberries, cinnamon, and flaky dough. Jade had never been a fan of scones, finding them dry and tasteless. She closed her eyes while she took another bite. Once she'd finished, she gathered up the day's outfit and readied herself in the adjoining bathroom, enjoying the luxury of the marble floors and jetted tub and shower.

Afterward, she changed into a comfortable pair of jeans and woolen sweater she'd purchased for the trip. Aidan warned her how cold Scotland could be in November, and she wanted to be prepared. She was just finishing putting on her boots when she heard a light knock on her bedroom door.

Jade's mouth fell open when she noticed Aidan standing outside with a formal kilt and sporran.

Taking a low bow, he took her hand and kissed the top. A tingling sensation moved over her skin and her breath hitched.

"Good morning, lass."

She laughed as he slipped his fingers around hers.

"How did ye sleep?"

Jade hesitated before answering. "Very well. The room is gorgeous. I love the fireplace and the view of the ocean. And what service! Tea in the evening and coffee and Morrigan's breakfast served in the morning? My goodness, I knew you were a man of means, but Laird MacFie, I didn't realize you were a nobleman."

He chuckled, gathering her in his arms. His lips found hers and she melted into his eager embrace. When he reluctantly let go, she looked up into his vivid blue eyes, trying to decide if she should tell him about her nightmare.

Sensing something was wrong, Aidan's brows raised. "Are you sure everything's all right, love?"

"Well, I did have a rather strange dream last night."

"Oh?"

"Yes, but I think I'd rather discuss it after we eat. It was a bit disturbing."

"I'm sorry to hear that." Aidan knew from experience not to take Jade's dreams lightly.

After all, she'd uncovered his kidnapper's whereabouts by one of her visions.

"Well, if you're ready, I thought we'd take breakfast in the great room. There's a lovely view of the sea from the dining room table."

"Sounds beautiful. Oh, I had a strawberry scone this morning. I can't believe the difference from the ones in the States. It was heavenly!"

"That's bonnie. I'm glad you liked it, darlin'. I'm excited to show you everything Scotland has to offer."

"Well, I already like what I see," she said, eyeing his muscular legs beneath his kilt. She bit her lower lip, wondering if he was wearing anything underneath. The thought brought a flush to her cheeks.

"Do ye now?" Aidan's face softened when he admired her delicate features. It was taking everything in his power not to sweep her up in his arms and take her to bed. Instead, he held her against his chest, giving her a gentle kiss. The light taste of strawberries lingered on her lips. When he embraced her, Jade could feel the pounding of his heart against hers, and time stood still. Suddenly, breakfast was the last thing on her mind. Aidan looked down at her flushed face and smiled.

"I have a few things planned for us today. I hope you like em'."

"Oh?"

"I figured we could stop into town after breakfast. I think you'll enjoy seeing the shops and scenery. And I want you to buy whatever catches your eye. My treat," Aidan said.

"Oh, that's so thoughtful, but I brought money."

"I'm sure you did, love, but let me spoil you while you're here. It really would make me happy." He offered a boyish grin, and she couldn't say no.

"You're the most generous man I've ever known. I'm finding it hard to deny you anything. Do you realize that?"

"Really?" He chuckled, scooping her up in his powerful arms as if she'd weighed nothing.

"Better be careful. I might have to put your words to the test."

She laughed, loving the way his arms felt around her. "Promises, promises," she said with a wiggle of her eyebrows. "I think I'd like that."

"Oh, you would now?"

"Hm, hm…" Jade tilted her chin down, admiring his formal kilt. "So, will this be your regular attire while we're in Scotland?"

He smiled. "Ye asked me earlier if I'd be wearing Scottish garb and I figured I'd introduce you to all our traditions."

"I love it."

"So, about the sleeping arrangement last night…" Aidan said.

"Yes?"

He let out a sigh, biting down on his lower lip. "It took all of my strength not to visit your room."

Jade let out her breath, happy he was thinking about her before bed.

"Why didn't you?"

"It's a little complicated." He took her by the hand and led her to the couch by the bay window. When they took their seat, the sun's rays caressed Jade's sandy-blonde waves.

Aidan kissed her forehead and slipped his arm around her waist. "You see, my family's clan has been held in high-standing within the Tobermory community for centuries. They follow traditions which go back hundreds of years. So, I want to set an example for the staff…to show you all the respect you deserve."

He kissed the back of her fingers; a tingling sensation rushed up her arm.

"You're a true gentleman, Aidan. I appreciate your thoughtfulness, but I must admit you were on my mind last night. I might have considered sneaking into your room myself."

He chuckled and gathered her in his arms. Warm breath tickled the curve of her neck and she shivered.

"Mmm…that would have been a welcome surprise." His lips caressed the back of her ear as he pulled her closer.

She sighed as he held her against his defined chest. Snuggling close, she breathed in his fresh aftershave. Footsteps sounded down the hall, followed by a light tapping on the bedroom door.

Aidan kissed Jade's flushed cheek and headed toward the door.

"How are you doing today, Marcail?"

The teenager grinned while she considered Aidan's face and fidgeted with the sleeve of her blouse.

"Very well, sir." When she glanced over at Jade, her smile faltered.

"Are you done with your morning coffee, Miss Mackenzie?"

"Yes, thank you. It was delicious."

The girl nodded without looking up and proceeded to gather the tray and Morrigan's bowl.

Jade stared at the closed door and shook her head. "I can't help to think I've offended the young lady somehow, Aidan. She barely makes eye contact with me."

"Hmm…it's not like her at all. We've known each other since we were children and she's normally quite friendly. Would you like me to have a talk with her?"

"I'm not sure. It might just make things worse. It's awkward enough already. I'd hate for her to think I was talking about her behind her back." Her brow furrowed. "So, you've known Marcail since you were children?"

"Aye. She was just a wee bairn when we first met. The Flannerys' adopted their daughter when I was about ten.

"Adopted?"

"Yes, Mrs. Flannery and her late husband were unable to have children of their own. It's a funny story, though. One day, they just showed up at the castle with an infant girl. Everyone was surprised since neither one mentioned they were looking to adopt, but my parents were thrilled for them. My mother threw Mrs. Flannery a baby shower in the grand ballroom. It was a lovely affair. I believe Marcail's parents were in their forties when the adoption took place," Aidan said.

"Oh, I see. That's why there's a bit of an age difference between the two. Makes sense." Jade bit her bottom lip. "I hope I'm not prying, but I had some questions regarding some of your traditions."

She leaned back on the couch, trying to collect her thoughts. His touch warmed her body; and she shivered in anticipation.

"Of course. Ask away," Aidan said.

"Well, I was wondering why there's so many servants at the castle if you only visit a few times a year? Everything seems so formal. Believe me, I'm not complaining. It's like traveling back in time and you know I love history. Simply curious is all." Jade cocked her head to the side. "For example, Mrs. Flannery refuses to refer to me by my first name." Aidan slipped his arm around Jade's shoulder.

"Yes, that's true. I can see why this all must seem strange to you. Let me try to explain. I've been so excited to show you my family's estate, but there wasn't enough time to prepare before we left Pacific Grove," Aidan said.

"I completely understand. Life's been racing along since the night we escaped the Hunters. I still can't believe everything that's happened," Jade said.

Aidan closed his eyes for a moment and pulled her closer. "The thought that you could have been hurt by those monsters makes my blood boil. It's why it's so important we find out if the Hunters are hatching another sinister plan in Scotland."

"I feel the same way, Aidan. I can't stop thinking about how their leader nearly took your life. If Deputy Rheinstein hadn't shot him in the arm, and the seals hadn't crushed him, I can't imagine what would have happened." Jade placed her hands over her eyes while the images came to mind.

"It's alright, darlin'. I'm here and I'm never going to lose you again."

His lips found hers and she surrendered to his kisses. After a few minutes, she sat back and gazed into his loving eyes.

"You have the habit of making me lose my train of thought, Laird MacFie."

He leaned back against the couch, his ocean blue eyes sparkling in the morning light. "I'm sorry, lass. Please, ask your questions."

Jade tried her best to concentrate, but it wasn't easy. "All right, love. I'm going to try to focus."

Aidan chuckled, biting his lower lip.

"I think I was asking about your staff and why everything appears so formal?"

"Yes, you were. I'll try to explain. So, it costs an enormous amount of money to keep up an estate this size. The art collection alone is priceless. Gardening, landscaping, and general maintenance are substantial costs necessary to keeping the castle running properly. Since my family's estate is highly valued by the Tobermory community, we're able to host weddings, tours, and seasonal events throughout the year to help balance costs. We've been lucky to have dedicated employees running things for years. Generations of workers have dedicated their lives to the MacFie Castle.

"For example, Mrs. Flannery's ancestors have been working and living on the property for over two centuries. It's been their time-honored tradition to school younger generations into the miscellaneous disciplines of castle life. Many of the staff work their way up in various jobs, depending on their skill sets. Mrs. Flannery is a general manager overlooking the housekeeping and kitchen staff. Her daughter, Marcail, will most likely be following in her footsteps. She's currently apprenticing alongside her mother. Along with the managerial roles, there are individuals who work together to help organize and arrange special events such as weddings and private tours. Their salaries come out of a trust set up by my great-grandparents. It works rather well, allowing me a life in America without having to spend too much time on the day-to-day operations. Although, I do have executive say and final decision making."

"That's actually quite fascinating. It's lovely how it all works," Jade said.

"Yes, it's different than back in the States, but I think you'll get used to everything in time."

"Thank you for explaining," said Jade. "It makes a lot more sense now. I'm looking forward to learning more about the history and traditions of your clan."

"Speaking of which, are you ready for your tour, lass?" Aidan asked.

"Please!"

Aidan took Jade by the hand and led her out the corridor and down the hall. Taking his time, he described the estate's rich history of family portraits, priceless antiques, and medieval furniture. Several pieces displayed the MacFie family's crest, a grey seal surrounded by purple heather on a royal blue background.

After the detailed tour, Aidan led Jade into the great room. She loved the large tapestries hanging on the high stone walls. They reminded her of the framed tapestry she viewed in Aidan's penthouse. Across the dining hall was a massive wall of windows opening to a spectacular view of the coastline. He pulled her seat out and she sat opposite the forty-foot mahogany table. Three serving maids busied themselves preparing the lavish breakfast, arranging crystal bowls filled with fruits, granolas, and an assortment of vegan dishes.

"We have a nice greenhouse by the garden with plenty of fresh vegetables and fruit. I think you might enjoy seeing the grounds later," Aidan said.

"Oh? Sounds lovely. Speaking of gardens, I was thinking I might bring Morrigan outside today. She's been cooped up for the last couple of days and I think the fresh air would do her good."

"That's a wonderful idea. The weather is supposed to be in the mid-sixties. Should be clear by this evening. We're due for some heavy rains later this week. I was planning on going into town after breakfast. I'd love you to meet some of my family members. I'm sure we can be back in plenty of time for Morrigan's outing and still enjoy an early dinner."

"Sounds great."

After their lavish breakfast, the couple headed to town, escorted by their driver, Collins. In the soft daylight, Jade was able to view the colorful buildings and seaside surrounding the village of Tobermory. Their chauffeur parked in front of a brightly painted ocean blue and lavender colored building facing the Atlantic. Jade glanced up at the sign above the pub. The Seal Cave Tavern was open for business. She noted Aidan's clan symbol. The tourist hotspot was as old as the town itself, passed down from one generation to the next.

Aidan pulled open the heavy oak door, and the couple entered the pub. A grey-haired man and his daughter worked the bar, serving up beer and whiskey to their eager patrons. Although it was late morning, Jade assumed some Scottish residents were a bit more relaxed considering their indulgences. Two middle-aged fishermen gave Jade an admiring smile, their eyes lingering on her toned figure. Aidan gave them a stern look and they looked down at their bourbons.

The tavern's owner grinned when he spotted Aidan. The burly Scotsman was barrel-chested with ruddy cheeks and shoulder length grey hair tied back in a ponytail. He came from behind the bar, gripping Aidan in a bear hug. He smiled, but it didn't reach his eyes. Losing his wife to cancer the previous year had left its mark on the once boisterous pub owner. Aidan noticed he'd gained at least fifty pounds since they last saw each other. His formal kilt was wrapped tight around his large frame. The tavern brought in tourists from around the world. Many of his patrons traveled from different corners of the globe and enjoyed seeing the traditional costumes of the Scots. So, his uncle provided what they wanted and took their coins with pleasure.

"Uncle Brodie, it's wonderful to see you again," Aidan said.

"Aye, nephew! We've been waiting for your visit!"

"Yes, well, some unexpected circumstances led to this trip I'm afraid." Uncle Brodie noticed the young woman standing next to his nephew.

"I see. Could these unexpected circumstances have anything to do with this bonnie lass?"

"Uncle, this is Jade Mackenzie. Jade, I'd like to introduce you to my uncle, Brodie MacFie."

"It's a pleasure to meet you, sir."

"The pleasure's mine, darlin'. A Mackenzie with an American accent? Charming."

"Thank you, Uncle Brodie. It's my first visit to Scotland."

"Very good, lass! What do ye think of our country so far?"

"Oh, it's bonnie," Jade said.

"Aye, we have a quick study, nephew! You're going to fit right in, Jade Mackenzie."

"I wondered if ye might have a moment to talk about some…private matters, uncle?"

"Always have time for my favorite nephew. Let's have a seat by the window."

He turned toward a buxom, red-headed woman behind the bar. "I'll be back in a bit, daughter."

"Good to see you, cousin," she said, waving at Aidan with her plump hand clutching a soaked dishtowel.

"Good to see you! Jade, this is my cousin, Molly."

Jade reached over the counter and shook hands with the barmaid.

"Nice to meet ye." The fiery red-head smiled. "Could I get you two a drink?"

Jade smiled. "Would you have coffee by chance?"

"Aye, we do, lass. Aidan, what can I get ye?"

"I'd like the same. Thank you."

"I'll be right over with your drinks. Let me get a pot boilin'."

"Thanks, Molly," Aidan said.

Uncle Brodie led the couple to the back room of the tavern. They took their seats next to a window overlooking the Atlantic. Jade watched the colorful boats in the harbor. They moved across the churning sea while dolphins skimmed over the breaking tides.

Jade turned toward Aidan. "I had no idea there were dolphins nearby!"

"Aye, lass." Aidan chuckled, reaching across the table to take her hand. "Scotland is rich with wildlife. I can't wait to show you the village.

"I'm looking forward to it."

He watched his uncle study Jade with interest, sensing his curiosity. After all, it was the first time he'd brought a woman with him to Tobermory.

A few moments later, Molly brought a tray filled with coffees.

Jade stirred in a packet of sugar and blew away the rising steam.

Uncle Brodie raised his brow and leaned forward, resting his large hands on the cherrywood table. "So, what's going on, lad?"

"Simply put, the Hunters are back. And they're planning a massacre."

His uncle made the sign of the cross over his barrel-shaped chest. "Dear God. Tell me everything."

❈

FOR THE NEXT HALF HOUR, AIDAN AND JADE DESCRIBED HOW THE HUNTERS stalked the couple in Pacific Grove, Jade's near drowning, their kidnapping, the death of the Hunters' leader, and their eventual escape.

His uncle clenched his meaty fists. "Damn the bastards. God. I wish I was there. I'd beat the life out of their pathetic leader and his henchmen."

"I know you would, uncle, but we survived and learned some important information concerning the Hunters' plans. We came to Scotland to try to prevent more bloodshed."

"So, what do you know, nephew? Tell me everything. I've people who can help."

"The leader mentioned a Final Reaping before he was killed." Aidan took a sip of his coffee. He leaned back in his chair. "He said it would take place in Scotland. So, we wanted to see if we could get to the bottom of all of this before the Hunters made their next move. Figured we start with you to see if you have any information."

Uncle Brodie sat back in his chair and let out a deep breath. Before beginning his story, he turned and waved to get his daughter's attention. "I'm going to need something stronger for this discussion. Bring me over a scotch on the rocks, lass." Molly went to work preparing his drink.

Uncle Brodie turned to his companions, glancing down at their half empty mugs. "Would ye care for something a little stronger?"

"Thank you, but I better stick to coffee. I think I'll need my wits about me to figure this all out," Jade said.

"Yes, the same for me," Aidan said. "Maybe just a coffee refill."

After their drinks arrived, Uncle Brodie took a sip from his glass, studying the ebbing tides.

"So, is it true? Are there selkies in Scotland?" Aidan asked, folding his hands on the table.

Uncle Brodie pinched his lips together and leaned forward in his chair.

"Well, it seems that now that ye had firsthand experience with the Hunters, it's time for your formal education. I discussed this with my brother years ago. Your parents wanted to protect you from our…unusual history. But things have changed." Uncle Brodie sat back in his chair, studying the couple in the morning light. "You should understand that being half selkie and human keeps you on the fringes of the selkie way of life. The majority of the MacFie family are born without the necessary genetic material which allows the turning, but it often lies dormant for future generations.

"Your parents realized at an early age you were showing the tell-tale hybrid signs. Nephew, ye took to water immediately. From the first time your mother placed you in the tub, you were paddling like a natural fish. Your parents feared for ye, lad. It's why they kept the truth from you."

Aidan leaned forward, locking eyes with his uncle. "I came across my great-grandmother's diaries my senior year before discovering the family secret. It was all so confusing. My mother told me she was going to explain everything. But she died before she could." Aidan's blue eyes filled with tears, recalling his mother's final goodbye.

Uncle Brodie made the sign of the cross and his pale blue eyes glistened. "God rest her sweet soul. We'd talked on the phone the evening you discovered the diaries. She hid them away afterward."

"Do you know where?"

"Funny you should ask. Your father mailed the diaries to me shortly before he passed. I made sure to secure em' in a safe deposit box. Ye see, lad, your parents worried if you understood your true nature, you'd make it your mission to search for your kind. They feared it could lead to the Hunters taking notice. Do ye ken?"

Aidan nodded, the memories flooding back to the day he'd discovered his great-grandmother's diaries in his attic. "Do you still have the key to the deposit box? I really would like to look at them."

"Of course, lad. I have it in the back office. Let me go fetch it for you. The diaries belong to you. They were always meant to be passed down."

Once his uncle left the room, Aidan closed his eyes, overcome by the painful memories of his parents' death. Jade put her hand on top of his and gave his fingers a gentle squeeze.

A few moments later, Uncle Brodie returned with an envelope with a golden key inside. He scribbled the bank's address on the back.

"Thank you. This means a lot," Aidan said.

"Of course. You should have had access to the diaries a long time ago."

"So, uncle...are there more of my kind in Scotland?" Aidan's brow raised, waiting for an answer.

Uncle Brodie bit down on his bottom lip before answering. He whispered, "Aye. I've seen em'." Aidan exchanged glances with Jade.

"I'm sure some of the townsfolk have spotted them every now and again around the coves, usually at the birthing season," Uncle Brodie continued.

"The birthing season?" Aidan asked.

"Let me try to explain," he said, running his hand through his greying beard. "In the selkie community, there's an alpha male in charge of the pod. Since their cycles are aligned, the females often become pregnant simultaneously. This helps the mothers care for their children together."

Jade leaned forward. "So, selkies aren't monogamous?"

"No, they're not. The male cares for his multiple wives, provides protection, and hunts while the mothers tend to their young. Females raise their children communally. When it's time to give birth, expectant mothers seek dry land, usually inside a cave, or other protected area. It's a vulnerable time for em'."

Jade crossed her arms over her chest. "Selkie women don't mind sharing their husband? What happens if a female doesn't agree with this arrangement?"

Uncle Brodie chuckled. "Good question, lass." He glanced at his nephew and smiled. "You have a sharp one here, Aidan. I'll tell you what I've learned concerning the selkie community. The male in charge of a pod is known as a *bull*. And yes, females don't always want to share their mate. As you know, Aidan's great-grandmother married a human. She chose to leave her pod and enter a monogamous human marriage."

31

JADE RESTED HER HANDS ON THE TABLE. "I SEE." IMAGES OF THE PREVIOUS evening's nightmare flashed in her mind. "Uncle Brodie, do you know when these births take place?"

"I do, lass. The *Great Birthing* takes place between autumn and early winter, sometimes earlier. It can happen anytime between July and November."

Jade glanced at Aidan. "Well, it's the middle of November, so the timing is right."

"The Hunters' leader mentioned coming back for a final reaping of the selkie folk. Could this plan coincide with their birthing season?" Aidan asked.

Jade shuddered, biting down on her lower lip.

Aidan glanced over at his girlfriend. "Are you cold, darlin'?"

"No, I'm fine. It's just that I had the most terrible dream last night. It involved selkies."

Aidan leaned forward in his chair. "You mentioned that earlier today. Are you comfortable sharing?"

She glanced between the two men and nodded.

"It's a little hazy, but I'll try to describe what I remember." She leaned forward. "I recall walking along a moonlit beach. It was so bright I could see a tidal island and beautiful white sands. The scenery resembled the Caribbean, but I believe it was Scotland."

"Lass, it sounds like you're describing Kilvickeon Beach," Uncle Brodie said. "It's a lovely area."

"Kilvickeon Beach? Interesting." Aidan glanced at his uncle. "Might be worth looking into. Maybe we could visit sometime this week. See if it looks familiar to Jade."

"Let me know if you need directions," Uncle Brodie said.

The men turned their attention back to Jade. She closed her eyes, trying to remember the details of her nightmare. "I remember stumbling upon a cave. It was set deep within the outcroppings of limestone. Before I realized what was happening, I was standing at the entrance, peering into the darkness. I could hear cries of pain mingled with a beautiful melody. When I peered inside, I was dumbfounded. In the back of the cave were two dark-haired selkies. One held a newborn in her arms and…"

Jade rubbed her temples and grimaced. Aidan took her hands in his, looking into her grey eyes.

"It's alright. Take your time." Jade shook her head.

"I remember walking toward the mothers when a shadow fell over me. When I turned around, there was a mob of cloaked men carrying torches and harpoons. The selkies screamed when the Hunters rushed inside with their weapons. And there was blood everywhere..." Jade closed her eyes as the terrible images came to mind.

Aidan placed his arm around her shoulder.

"You must have been terribly frightened, darlin'. But you're safe now." Uncle Brodie glanced between the couple and shook his head.

"I don't know what this means. Hopefully, it's just my overactive imagination," Jade said.

"Don't be so quick to dismiss your feelings," Aidan said.

He turned to his uncle. "Her dreams are powerful. When the Hunters kidnapped me in Pacific Grove, her visions led to my rescue. Jade's a powerful seer."

"I've known folks with the gift." Uncle Brodie took a sip of his scotch. "I've no quarrel with taking dreams seriously, but you need to understand something, the both of you."

The burly Scotsman stood from his chair. Gazing out the bay window, he watched the boats sail by, seeming to wrestle something over in his mind. He turned his chair backward and straddled it, resting his arms on the back. He fixed Aidan and Jade with a piercing look.

"You're both young and inexperienced in the ways of the Hunters. I realize you've dealt with them firsthand. You should know how incredibly lucky you were to escape with your lives. Better think things over before you get involved with em' again. They have a powerful following in Scotland. If ye plan on kicking a hornets' nest, you're bound to get stung. Are you sure you really want to pursue this?"

Aidan shook his head. "They stalked me in Pacific Grove, and it sounds like they're planning on something terrible here in Tobermory. These people need to be stopped. If not, it's just a matter of time before they come after us again back in the States. And...I have questions that need answering."

"What questions, lad?"

Aidan released his breath. "I need to know if there's more out there like me. And if there are, I want to meet them. If we can find the main pod, maybe we can warn the selkie folk of the Hunters' plans."

His uncle chugged his drink, wiping his mouth with the back of his large hand. "There's a small group of us getting together tonight. Many of the members are descendants of the MacFie clan. Others simply want to be involved to help protect the selkie folk. We meet monthly to discuss news of the Hunters. We even have a mole working undercover. Appears there's a hive of Hunters living out by the edge of town by the old Finnley estate. There's been a lot of talk that something big is about to happen. Could be related to this *Final Reaping* you've been talking about. You may come to the meeting tonight, but you both need to understand it's a dangerous game you're playing. Once you're in, you're in for life."

Aidan looked into Jade's grey eyes. They both knew what the other was already thinking.

"We need to get to the bottom of this before it's too late," Aidan said.

Uncle Brodie ran his meaty fingers down his wiry beard. "Well, seeing you're both determined, I suppose ye can come back to the tavern after supper. Meeting starts at eight. Give the door three quick knocks," he said, tapping three times on the table. "Perhaps the older members can give some information concerning the selkie pod's whereabouts. Make sure to mention what their leader said about the *Final Reaping*. I imagine the Hunters are beside themselves trying to find a new master."

"I know this must be a lot to take in." He studied the young couple with a look of sympathy. "Nephew, before you get down to business, why don't ye take Jade around town. You'll have plenty of time for work tonight."

"Yes, I think that's a good idea," Aidan said.

Uncle Brodie stood from his chair and stretched. When his daughter was finished collecting their empty mugs, he took Jade's small hand in his large ones.

"It was lovely meeting you today, lass. I hope you enjoy a little sightseeing before we get down to more serious business."

"Thank you, Uncle Brodie. It's been a pleasure."

Aidan placed his hand against the small of Jade's back and escorted her outside. The day was surprisingly warm considering the previous night's storm. They walked together along the cobblestone streets, passing brightly painted houses along the seaside.

"Wow, that was an interesting chat with your uncle," Jade said.

"Yes, I didn't realize there was a secret group actively keeping vigil of the Hunters. Might make our job easier. The meeting should be interesting; maybe we'll get some new leads." Aidan studied Jade's silhouette as she gazed in wonder at the ancient architecture. She absently pushed back a lock of hair from her heart-shaped face. The sea-breeze fanned the loose sandy-blonde tresses across her slender shoulders. She pushed the strands from her eyes absently. Aidan admired her in the soft sunlight. She was a natural beauty, smart, and loving. He let out his breath.

For the next couple of hours, they could relax and spend time sightseeing. Once this mess was over, he'd finally be able to focus his attention on Jade. His hand grazed over her tiny waist, and he nuzzled her cheek. She breathed in the fresh scent of his aftershave and smiled.

"So, lass, what would you like to do on your first day in Scotland?"

"Oh, I figured we would be busy playing detective today." Jade's brows raised. "If we don't have to work right now, I'd love to see some of the shops. I'm in no rush to get back, as long as we have time to let Morrigan outside to stretch her wings."

"I think that's a good idea. We'll want to head home before tonight's storm anyhow. The last thing we need is to get caught in one of Tobermory's autumn downpours. You think it gets cold in Pacific Grove? Just wait."

"Glad I packed some heavy sweaters and coats." She buttoned up her pea coat. "I had the feeling it might get nippy."

"Aye, smart thinking." He took her small hand in his and they turned down a busy alleyway brimming with tourists. Jade watched a family of five leave a brightly painted candy store. Three small children giggled while they skipped down the paved road, licking their rainbow-colored lollipops with greedy concentration.

"How about we pick up some sweets before heading back?" Aidan said.

Jade grinned, leaning into his gentle embrace. "Sounds fun." She looked through the shop window and watched a teenage girl stirring a large vat of chocolate.

"I'm going to get in trouble in this one. You know, I can't say no to chocolate," Jade said. Aidan laughed and squeezed her hand playfully. "This is my favorite candy shop in Tobermory. Please get whatever you fancy."

"You're going to spoil me on this trip."

"That's the plan," Aidan said, grinning. Holding the door for her, Jade breathed in the aroma of savory fudge.

After exploring their extensive collection, Jade discovered a display with vegan truffles in the back of the store. She picked a couple of cartons to take back to the castle, along with some gifts for Katie and Mary. The sale's girl wrapped up the golden boxes and placed them in a paper bag while Aidan paid with cash. The couple checked out several more stores for souvenirs before heading toward the pier. Slivers of golden rays slipped through a band of storm clouds over the sea. The soft light illuminated a school of bottle-nose dolphins cutting through the choppy currents. Jade rushed over to the guard rail and looked over.

"Oh, they're lovely, Aidan!"

"I'm so glad to be able to share this moment with you, lass." He placed his arm around her shoulder and kissed her cheek.

"This is truly magical." Jade looked up into his aqua-marine eyes and sighed.

He took her in his arms, kissing her softly in the cool breeze. A rumble of thunder rolled overhead.

Aidan gazed down at her flushed face and grinned. "Aye, you're a beauty, Lady Mackenzie." He glanced at the darkening sky. "I'd love to stay longer, but it looks like today's storm's arriving earlier than expected."

"I believe you're right."

"We better head over to the bank and get back home," Aidan said.

"That's a good idea."

They hurried along the cobblestone streets while thunder rumbled in the distance. The Bank of Tobermory was on the opposite end of town between a nineteenth century hotel and a pastel-colored bed and breakfast.

Aidan escorted Jade up the steps and inside the impressive building. The bank was surprisingly quiet, despite the lengthy line of customers. One teller busied himself with an elderly woman, while a frazzled mother waited impatiently in line. Her red-headed toddler climbed beneath the velvet-covered rope, dividing the customers into two rows. The boy crawled over to one of the empty teller's windows and began pounding the barrier with his tiny hands. The child's ruddy-faced guardian rushed to his side, lifted him onto the counter, and struck the silver bell with her plump fist.

While the angry mother was being ignored by the bank employees, another customer in the back of the line was escorted to a private desk in the front. The client absently touched her smartly coiffed pageboy with a manicured hand. Jade watched the stranger with curiosity. The woman crossed one shapely leg over the other and surveyed the room while the teller pounded away at his keyboard. Within moments, a second employee rushed to her side with a mug of coffee.

Several minutes passed before a tall grey-haired gentleman noticed Aidan and Jade standing in line and motioned them over to his desk. He asked to see proper identification before disappearing into the back. The woman with the pageboy stood from her chair with a satchel in hand. When she walked past their desk, she smiled down at Aidan, flashing pearly white teeth.

Jade watched as she gracefully left the building.

Jade shook her head. *It wasn't the first time Aidan managed to catch the attention of a beautiful woman, and she imagined it wouldn't be the last.* Luckily for her, he never appeared to notice.

ॐ

NEARLY FIFTEEN MINUTES PASSED BEFORE THE BANK MANAGER RETURNED. With his narrow lips pinched together, he presented Aidan with a stack of papers. After his client signed the host of official documents, the manager raised two fingers over his narrow shoulder, gesturing for Aidan to follow him.

While passing the reception area, Aidan noticed a hooked-nose gentleman placing stacks of money into a steel vault. His three-piece coal-black business suit made a bold statement in contrast to his fellow employee's casual attire. A gold watch dangled from his pocket of his impeccably ironed trousers. Absently, the man pushed his wired-rimmed glasses toward the back of his nose. His beady eyes narrowed when he realized he was being watched. Abruptly, he turned his back toward the men making their way toward the vault of safe deposit boxes.

Something seemed off about the transaction, but Aidan couldn't put his finger on it. He walked along the aisle of steel boxes. Once he located the matching number from his receipt, he inserted the gold key. When it opened, he held his breath before retrieving the leather satchel. Inside were ten diaries stacked together, along with an envelope marked Aidan. His heart raced, eager to examine the contents. While placing the last diary into the bag, he noticed a sapphire-colored velvet pouch pushed toward the back of the safe deposit box. He wondered what it could be. He slipped off the velvet ribbon and reached inside. On top of the jewelry case was a small note.

. . .

"To my nephew, Aidan MacFie,

Your parents mailed these diaries for safe keeping along with your great-grandmother's wedding ring. Your mother wanted it passed down to ye. I believe she imagined you might like to give it to your future bride one day.

Love,

Uncle Brodie."

Aidan bit down on his lower lip, picturing his mother's face. It was difficult not to give in to the tears welling in his eyes. He flicked open the jewelry box, holding his breath.

A gold band flashed in the dim light. On each side were etchings of the family crest. The cushion cut; a five carat ring was surrounded by blue sapphires. He'd never seen anything like it, imagining its value to be priceless.

Carefully, he slipped the ring back into the box and placed it into the velvet pouch. Once it was secured with the diaries, he closed the satchel and headed toward the lobby. The elderly teller watched him stroll down the aisle, his beady eyes narrowing. Aidan glanced over his shoulder, but the senior citizen vanished.

"Everything alright?" Jade asked.

"Good question." Aidan took her arm and escorted her to the door. "I'll fill you in when we're in the car."

As they headed back outside into the amber light, an ebony hearse drove alongside them. Aidan noticed the open driver's side window. A cloaked figure behind the wheel glanced over at the couple. The driver's face was covered by a black leather mask. Although there were openings for the eyes, the mouth and nose were covered by dark cloth flecked with white paint. Pointy gashes were etched over the lower half, mimicking an open-mouthed grin. After taking a good look, the driver turned their attention back to the road and sped around the corner.

Jade tightened her fingers around her boyfriend's hand.

"Did you see the driver's mask?" Aidan asked.

"Yes. That's seriously creepy. What on earth was he wearing? Is this some strange Scottish tradition?"

"No, darlin'. I've never seen anything like it. And it's odd considering the hearse slowed down next to us and then left in a hurry when we noticed."

Lightning flashed above, and they made their way back to their car.

"I think I've seen that sort of mask somewhere before. I wish I could remember." Jade shivered. "Looked as if there were teeth painted over the bottom of it."

"It's definitely bizarre," Aidan said. He put his hand beneath Jade's elbow when they reached the Rolls Royce. Their driver opened the door for Jade. Once they were on their way to the MacFie Castle, Aidan scanned the road, making sure they weren't being followed.

The sound of thunder echoed in the distance. A heavy mist hung in the air, making it difficult to see if there were other drivers on the road. Once they were back home, Aidan took Jade's hand and escorted her up the front steps. Two staff members opened the large doors and welcomed them inside. Mrs. Flannery was heading up the staircase with fresh towels for the bedrooms. She stopped halfway up and turned.

"Aww, I was hoping to find you two. Was wondering if you'd like a snack before supper, Laird MacFie?"

"Thank you, Mrs. Flannery. Would ye mind bringing us a pot of tea in the garden? We're going to be out there in a few moments."

The housekeeper turned toward Aidan with raised brows. "Are ye sure, sir? Appears we're going to have some rain from the looks of it."

"Oh, it was my idea." Jade smiled. "I hope it's no trouble. We're trying to get my pet raven a bit of air before the storm hits. There's just a little drizzle right now. We're hoping it will hold off for a while."

"Makes sense, Miss Mackenzie. I imagine your pet probably feels cooped up since the flight. It's mighty thoughtful of you. I'll be right out with your tea." She smiled and climbed the staircase.

Aidan called after her. "Oh, one more thing, Mrs. Flannery."

She paused, glancing over her shoulder. "Yes, sir?"

"Do you happen to know if there are any special events going on in town today? Perhaps a costume parade or festival is planned this weekend?"

"Not that I'm aware of, Laird MacFie."

"Thank you." He bit the corner of his lip. "We saw something rather unusual near the bank and weren't quite sure what to make of it."

"Oh?"

"Yes, when we were on the way to the car, we spotted a hearse on the road. The driver slowed down alongside us. We noticed he was wearing a black mask. Appeared to be leather of some sort. Two holes were punched out around the eyes and there were pointy teeth painted over the mouth. Really quite odd."

Mrs. Flannery made the sign of the cross and shook her head. "Sounds terribly strange, sir. I've never seen the likes of it."

"Thank you. Figure I'd just check to see if you'd heard anything."

"Of course, sir."

When the housekeeper pushed a locket of grey hair behind her ear, Jade noticed her hand was shaking.

"Well, then, I best be getting back to work. I'll be down in just a few moments to make a fresh pot of tea," Mrs. Flannery said, hurrying up the stairs.

"She seemed a bit shaken up," Jade said.

Aidan nodded in agreement. "I wonder if she knows something she's not comfortable sharing?"

Jade shrugged her shoulders. The day was getting stranger by the minute. They walked toward the spiral staircase, where Mrs. Flannery disappeared. Before they hit the first step, Dougal appeared around the corner, sliding across the marble floor. He rolled over on his back with his pink tongue rolling to the side in a grin.

Aidan bent down to pet his dog while Jade laughed. Together, they headed up the stairs. The couple watched the terrier's short legs clear the steps.

"I'll meet you back in your room in a few minutes. I just need to find Dougal's leash. Would you like to take your packages?"

"Yes, please." Jade reached for the bags of candies and souvenirs. "Thanks again for spoiling me today." She stood on tiptoes and pecked Aidan's cheek. When she turned to walk away, he grasped her hand and kissed her firmly on the mouth. She closed her eyes, feeling the passion behind his kiss.

"You're welcome, darlin'."

✦

JADE WATCHED DOUGAL FOLLOW HIS MASTER BACK TO HIS ROOM, HIS stocky tail wagging all the way.

When she opened her bedroom door, she was greeted by Morrigan's eager caws.

"Poor darling. Give me just a moment, baby," she said, blowing her a kiss.

She left her packages on the desk in the corner before going to the powder room to freshen up. Jade ran her silver brush through her golden curls and refreshed her mauve-colored lipstick.

Once she'd put her coat back on, she headed over to the eager raven.

"Let's take a bit of air, sweetie." Morrigan flew from her perch and landed on her shoulder. Aidan and Dougal joined them, and they made their way downstairs. Several staff members turned their heads at the sight of Jade and her pet raven.

Aidan pulled open the set of doors in the back of the castle, which led out to the expansive outdoors. Primroses and Scottish moss carpeted the grand garden. Set throughout the fenced landscape were raised beds of herbs, vegetable plants, and various flowers. A row of ivory stones bordered a steep cliff overlooking the sparkling sea. A heavy mist cloaked the garden in a dreary light.

"My God, Aidan." Jade held her breath, taking it all in. "It's just like the dream I had about your great-grandmother and her white raven."

"My great-grandfather breathed his last breath right where we're standing." Aidan shook his head, walking toward a marble bench. "He died protecting the woman he loved. His wife, Edina, would have certainly perished if she hadn't left through the underground tunnels during the fire."

"It's amazing." Jade looked around. "Oh, look!" she said pointing to a majestic tree loaded with golden apples. "It's just how I imagined."

Aidan's brow rose. "How you imagined, darlin'?"

"Remember the strange dreams I had during your kidnapping? One of them was particularly vivid. I dreamed of a lovely garden by the sea. There was an apple tree and a white raven in its branches. A beautiful auburn-haired woman collected herbs in her basket. I believe it was your great-grandmother, Edina."

"Ah, yes. I remember now. You truly have the sight, darlin'. This is where my great-grandmother spent hours planting, and working the soil, making tinctures and cures for her people. She mentioned her garden several times in her diaries." As he said this, Morrigan flew from Jade's shoulder, landing atop a branch heavy with golden fruit.

Jade's mouth fell open as she watched her pet perch among the glistening apples.

"It's really quite strange, but I feel connected to your ancestors, Aidan."

"I feel it, too. Such a bizarre coincidence concerning your white raven. What are the odds?"

"I know. It appears we're just beginning to scratch the surface of the mystery of the MacFie clan. I wonder what else might be waiting to be discovered?" she said, gazing toward the sea.

Aidan stepped behind her, placing his hands around her waist.

"I promise, we'll get to the bottom of all of this," he said, kissing her on top of her head. Mrs.

Mrs. Flannery padded over the groundcover with her silver tray of tea and cakes.

"Well, now, this should tide you both over until supper." She glanced at Jade. "We ordered more vegan scones from our local bakery. Hope you enjoy them."

"Thank you, Mrs. Flannery. That's very thoughtful."

"You're welcome, Miss Mackenzie."

Once she'd left, Jade poured tea into the porcelain cups. They took their seats at the marble bench beneath the shade of the apple tree. Dougal pounded his tail in anticipation of a treat. Aidan pinched a piece from his cake and gave his dog a bite. Dougal took it from his master's hand and laid down next to his boots.

Jade sat back in her chair, enjoying the peacefulness of the moment. They were halfway through their tea when Aidan's cell phone rang. He answered on the second ring.

"Hello, Johnathon. Good to hear from you. Hold on just a second, the reception in the garden is spotty. I'll take the call inside."

He turned to Jade and whispered, "I'll be back in just a few moments, love."

She watched him head toward the castle. Once he was gone, she sat back in her chair and enjoyed her tea. A soft breeze blew her hair back from her face as the clouds parted. Sun rays streamed across the lush garden. Morrigan ruffled her pearly feathers, pecking at a golden apple.

Turning toward the azure sea, Jade watched dozens of billowy ships sail by. Overcome with happiness, she closed her eyes and surrendered to the moment. As she listened to the waves crash along the shore, a soft melody blended with the natural sounds of the ocean. It grew in volume, dozens of voices merging into one. Jade's eyes fluttered open, and she tried to make out the source. Standing from the table, she made her way across the vast garden, passing an ancient looking greenhouse, beds of roses, herbs, and perennials. An outcropping of stone separated the dunes below. She gazed across the sand. The melody was strangely familiar.

A hand touched her shoulder, and she turned toward Aidan in surprise.

"Everything alright, darlin'?"

"Yes, but do you hear the singing?"

He was quiet for a moment, listening. "Afraid not. Do you?"

"There was definitely music coming from the shore. I was trying to get closer to hear."

"Well, there's a door just a little farther down leading out toward the beach. Would you like to take a walk?"

"Oh, could we? I'd love to."

He took her hand and led her down a pebble-strewn path. After they reached the end of the trail, a golden framed archway allowed them access to the beach.

"Oh, Aidan. This is beautiful. They followed a dewy field for a quarter of a mile before the mossy ground gradually turned to white sand.

"So, was there any news from Johnathon?" Jade asked.

"Afraid so."

She turned toward him in alarm.

"It appears that someone tampered with the plane equipment after all."

"Oh, my God, Aidan. Do you think the Hunters are involved?"

"It wouldn't surprise me." He scratched the back of his head. "From everything my uncle said, they're capable of anything."

"And what about that hearse earlier today? The driver in the mask seemed to be following us."

"Appears so." Aidan frowned, noticing Dougal digging frantically by the shore. "I'm hoping we find out more during the meeting tonight."

"What's that pup up to now?"

As they drew closer, Jade gasped. Dougal trotted back carrying something in his mouth.

"Drop it, boy."

The terrier released the prize by his master's feet.

Aidan reached down, retrieving a periwinkle-colored cloth from the sand. It was drenched with salt water.

"That's a pretty scarf. I wonder who left it?" Jade asked.

"Probably a staff member. They have access to the grounds when they're not working. I'll bring it up and give it to Mrs. Flannery. I imagine she can find the owner."

A frigid wind blew past, while the clouds darkened over the beach. Jade rubbed her shoulders.

"Cold, darlin'?"

"Yes, the weather sure changes quickly around here!" Jade said.

"Aww, welcome to Scotland." Aidan reached for her hand. "Should we head back?"

She nodded, while he stepped closer, his lips grazing her ear. His warm breath sent a shiver down her spine.

"I bet you're chilly in that kilt," Jade said, admiring his strong legs.

"Just a wee bit, lass."

Her face flushed, wondering what he was wearing underneath, if anything.

"Ye look a bit tired. There's time for a nap before supper."

"Oh, that does sound lovely."

"I agree. Just wish I could join you." He offered his lop-sided grin.

"You do now?" Jade's brow raised in question as she gave him a flirtatious smile. "What's stopping you?"

"Believe me when I say it's killing me not staying in your room." The corner of his mouth rose. "It's important for me to have the staff respect you. As I said before, they're a traditional bunch."

"Oh, of course. Traditions are traditions." *Always the gentleman.* She should count herself lucky he just looked so damn good in his kilt and boots.

They made their way back to the garden, bracing against the icy wind. Morrigan flapped her wings in the apple tree before heading back to her mistress' shoulder. Jade noticed the tea set and silver tray were gone. She'd never get used to being waited on like royalty.

"Looks like Mrs. Flannery cleaned up after us. She's a dear woman," Jade said.

"She's definitely part of the family," Aidan said.

A rumble of thunder sounded overhead as a flash of lightning streaked across the ruddy sky.

"Speaking of family, may I show you one more thing before we head back?"

"Of course."

They followed the mossy path behind the castle. A large stable surrounded by white fences appeared in the distance.

Jade's heart raced. Once they arrived, Aidan took her hand and led her inside. The aroma of hay and horses was like coming home. She'd spent every summer during her childhood on the back of a horse. It had been almost a year since she'd last ridden and she missed the sense of freedom which came along with the equestrian life. A long row of stalls housed a variety of purebreds ranging from Thoroughbreds, Friesians, and even Clydesdales. An elderly man with a shock of white hair met them at the gated corral. Jade recognized the gentleman from the employee meet-and-greet from the previous evening.

"Hello, Rusty. Great to see you again," Aidan said.

"Good afternoon, Laird MacFie and Miss Mackenzie. We were just finishing up with grooming today. Have ye seen our latest addition?"

They headed to a stall where a teenage boy was tending to a dapple-grey gelding. The groom smiled.

"Donavon is my newest apprentice. The lad's been doing a fine job."

The boy blushed with pride. "Thank you, sir. It's been a pleasure working at the MacFie Stables."

Rusty studied the horse behind the gate. "Well, our new pony has been a bit of a devil, but Donavon has a way with horses and has him eating out of his hand now."

Jade admired the gelding standing patiently for his grooming. The horse nuzzled Donavon's sleeve, enjoying his brushing.

Aidan escorted Jade by the arm, leading her down the long line of stalls. Jade marveled at the variety of pedigree horses. When they reached the end of the stables, a palomino filly with a satin bow lifted her head over the stall door and whinnied.

Jade's eyes widened at the sight of the dainty horse.

"Oh, she's adorable, Aidan! Just look at her pretty lavender bow." Aidan and Rusty exchanged amused looks.

"Yes, she's a gentle girl. Just two years old and already a fine ride. Exceptionally good under the saddle for a filly. Do you ride, Miss Mackenzie?" Rusty asked.

"I do, but it's been a while. Been so busy this past year. I haven't had a chance to visit the stables near my home, but I just adore horses." Aidan opened the stall door.

"Here's a sugar cube if you'd like to feed her." He handed Jade the sweet treat before she approached the curious pony.

"Oh, you're a gorgeous girl."

The horse nuzzled her hand. Jade opened her hand palm up. She laughed when the soft muzzle eagerly scooped up the sugar cube. Aidan smiled. "Do you like her?"

"Oh, yes. She's a true beauty. And she's so gentle taking her treat. I could gaze into her soft brown eyes all day," she said with a sigh.

"I'm happy to hear that because she's all yours, darlin'."

Jade's mouth fell open. "Mine?"

"Aye, lass. You told me you loved horses when we first met, so I thought you might enjoy one of your very own. We'll go riding when the weather permits, and you can try out your new filly."

"Aidan!" Jade flung her arms around his neck, smothering him with kisses. He hugged her tight, happy she was pleased.

"Are you sure? She's breathtaking. I don't know what to say," Jade said.

"You don't have to say a thing, darlin'." He grinned, gazing into her sparkling eyes. "Your face says it all. I'm thrilled you like your pony."

Jade walked toward the filly and stroked her flank. The horse whinnied a greeting, eyeing her new mistress with curiosity. "I'll have to come up with a name for her."

"Good idea. Do ye have any ideas?"

"Hmm…" Jade noticed a brush hanging on a peg next to the stall door. She picked it up and moved closer to the filly. The horse dropped her head, enjoying the attention.

"That's a good girl. Let me think. You're a Scottish pony, so let's give you a bonnie name."

Aidan grinned, enjoying watching Jade with her new pet. It was obvious she had a way with horses. It didn't surprise him. He could see her love for animals the first time Dougal met her in his penthouse.

Jade moved the brush through the horse's shiny mane. "Why don't we call you Bonnie? You're such a lovely girl." She glanced up at Aidan and smiled. "What do you think?"

"Aye, it's perfect, love."

Morrigan flew from Jade's shoulder and landed on Bonnie's back. The pony snorted and dropped her head toward the ground with her eyes closed.

"Looks like Morrigan has a way with horses," Aidan said.

Jade laughed while Dougal pawed at the door.

Aidan turned toward the terrier. "Sorry, boy. You know you can't come into the stalls. Spooks the horses." He turned his attention back to Jade. "If you don't mind leaving your filly for a few minutes, I'd love for you to meet someone."

"Absolutely," Jade said. She turned to her pony before leaving, planting a kiss on her soft muzzle. "I'll be back later."

Morrigan and Bonnie watched the couple leave, seeming content with each other's company. Donavon had moved to another stall and was busy grooming a jet-black stallion inside.

"Oh, my," Jade said.

The stallion stomped the ground and snorted.

Aidan turned toward the horse. "I haven't forgotten about you. This is Blackjack."

Jade stepped closer, and the dark thoroughbred lowered his head. She stroked his shiny mane.

"Ye have a way with horses, Miss Mackenzie." Donavon's eyes sparkled. "Blackjack isn't usually keen with strangers. He's a bit unpredictable."

"That's true. He's a wild thing, but he has a pure heart." Aidan said, offering his horse a sugar cube from his sporran. The horse took it greedily, nuzzling his master for more.

Jade admired his shiny coat and bright eyes.

"He looks like Black Beauty," she said, eying the horse's face. "Blackjack has a similar white star on his forehead."

"Yes. He's one of a kind. When the weather permits, I thought we might take the horses for a ride on the beach."

"I think it will be magical," Jade sighed. "A dream come true." Before leaving, Aidan turned to the stable hand.

"You're doing a fine job, lad. The horses look great. Keep up the good work."

The teenager's face beamed with pride. "Thank you, Laird MacFie. I sure will."

Aidan and Jade walked back toward Bonnie's stall, with Dougal following close behind.

When Morrigan saw her mistress, she flew to her shoulder and cawed.

"Good girl. Did you make a new friend?" Jade asked, stroking her raven's snowy cheek.

Bonnie snorted, shaking her head up and down.

"Oh, they love each other, Aidan!" Jade laughed while her raven cawed to the pony.

"Seems like everyone's getting along famously. If you're ready to head back, we can visit the stables tomorrow morning."

"I'd love that!" Jade said, reaching up to kiss Aidan's cheek. "I still can't get over my surprise. It's truly a dream come true."

"I'm so happy you like your pony, darlin'." He took her hand and led her outside into the misty daylight. They hurried back toward the castle, bracing themselves against the powerful wind. After they entered, the couple moved through the front parlor and headed for the stairs. "Oh, before we head up, I better ask if anyone's missing their scarf," Aidan said.

"Good idea."

The couple noticed Mrs. Flannery and her daughter walking toward the great hall.

"Supper will be served in two hours, Laird MacFie."

"Perfect, Mrs. Flannery. We found someone's scarf on the beach. Figured it might belong to one of the staff," Aidan said. He handed the damp cloth to Mrs. Flannery.

The housekeeper's face grew dark when she eyed the soft material, her lips pinching together. She turned toward Marcail with knit brows. "I've told ye a thousand times not to leave your things around. Do you expect someone to clean up after you, child? Go, put this in your room and hurry back to get supper started."

The teenager's face flushed a startling shade of crimson. With her arms folded over her chest, she stared at the marble floor, blue eyes stinging with tears. Marcail grabbed the scarf from her mother's hand and ran down the hallway.

Jade glanced at Aidan. Mrs. Flannery's angry response seemed out of character for the head housekeeper. She'd been nothing but kind since they'd met.

"It's truly not a problem, Mrs. Flannery. Your daughter's welcome to head down to the beach anytime she likes," Aidan said.

"Thank you, Laird MacFie. I appreciate your kindness. It's just I wished she'd listen to me every now and again. That child has an iron will. Always has, I guess. Rushing off to the seaside, staying out until dark." She bit down on her bottom lip and shook her head. Mrs. Flannery straightened the apron over her uniform and took a deep breath.

"I'm sorry for my outburst, sir. Guess I just worry about her is all. Silly girl of mine."

She folded her hands behind her back and feigned a smile. "Well now, supper will be served at six p.m. tonight. I better oversee things in the kitchen."

"Thank you, Mrs. Flannery. We're looking forward to your meal."

Aidan touched Jade on the small of her back and led her toward the staircase. Once they were in front of her bedroom, she stifled a yawn.

"Well, darlin', I think a little catnap would do ye good. I'll be sure to wake you before supper if you oversleep." He took her hand and kissed her forehead. Dougal waited by Jade's side as her raven nuzzled against her cheek.

"Looks like the pets are staying with you."

Jade smiled down at Dougal's hopeful face. "Sounds good to me. The more the merrier." The terrier followed her inside, his stubby tail wagging. Once she'd closed the door, Morrigan flew to her perch and started preening. Dougal trotted over to the four-poster bed and jumped up onto the lacy comforter. He circled several times before snuggling down into the soft covering.

Jade put away her coat, shoes, and purse in the wardrobe, then changed into an oversized t-shirt. The wind rattled against the large window and sheets of rain streaked the glass. She climbed beneath the blankets, closing her eyes. The sound of the sea was a comforting background music as she drifted off to sleep.

⚜

JADE BLINKED, TRYING HER BEST TO FIND HER WAY IN THE DARK. CRIES OF *agony echoed in the night.*

In the distance, soft candlelight revealed elderly selkies assisting their younger counterparts. Their pregnant bellies rested on the cave floor. The upper half of the expectant mothers appeared human while their seal tails wiggled and arched in response to their labor pains. Older members of the clan sang to the younger mothers-to-be. Before long, the sound of crying infants replaced their mother's keening. Tears of joy rolled over their pale faces while they snuggled their newborn pups.

An ancient-appearing matron galumphed back and forth between the new mothers offering praise and encouragement. They received her words with reverence, some even bowing their heads as she made her way across the nursery. Once the infants were feeding, she pulled forth a kelp net toward the center of the cave. Carefully, her long fingers sorted beaded necklaces of pearl and coral. The young selkies were presented with a gift, signifying their graduation into motherhood.

Outside the cave walls seagulls cried in the night while white mist hovered over the dark shore. A shadow fell over the cave's entrance. The mothers turned toward the darkness. For a moment there was silence, the selkies clutching their babies to their breasts. And then there were screams.

Chapter Three

Jade sat upright in bed, a scream escaping her parched lips. Her heart raced while images of the nightmare flashed before her eyes.

"It wasn't real," she whispered. Dougal licked her hand and snuggled close to her chest. She hugged him against her trembling body.

Once her heart slowed to a normal pace, she left the comfort of her bed and stood by the fire. After warming her hands a few moments, she walked to her wardrobe and retrieved her evening outfit. Standing before her window, she watched the dusky sky turn a dazzling shade of scarlet. The crimson light caressed the rising tides below. Leaving Dougal resting on the bed, she wandered down the hall toward Aidan's room. She tapped softly, imagining he was still in bed. A moment later, he opened the door. He smiled sleepily, rubbing his eyes with the back of his hand.

"Did I wake you up?" Jade asked.

"Glad you did. I overslept," Aidan replied.

He held the door open while she stepped inside. His room was slightly smaller than her own, but still grand. A four-poster bed was adjacent to a roaring fireplace. An oval window on the opposite side of the room allowed a partial sea view. The aperture was modest in comparison to her bedroom's panoramic view of the ocean. Jade realized Laird MacFie had gifted her the master suite. She glanced over at his bed, imagining the sheets were still warm from where he slept.

51

Aidan studied her face, sensing something was wrong. "Everything alright, darlin'?"

She shrugged her shoulders and shook her head. "I just had another nightmare. It was really awful."

"I'm sorry, lass." He took her hand and led her to the side of his bed. Once she sat down, he gathered her onto his lap. They held each other in silence while his afternoon shadow brushed against her warm cheek. Jade closed her eyes, enjoying his protective embrace. "Do you want to talk about it?"

She shook her head, gazing into his loving eyes. "Not now, maybe later. Would you just hold me?"

"Of course." He wrapped his powerful arms around her petite body, pulling her against his brawny chest. She ran her fingers down his washboard abs, stopping at the waist of his boxers. She looked into his sleepy eyes and imagined there might be other more enjoyable things to do than talking. Raindrops pelted the window while the roar of the wind blanketed the lush countryside.

Jade felt his lips on her mouth, and she closed her eyes. Within moments, gentle kisses became urgent, and he pulled her closer, laying her down onto his satin sheets. They were still warm as she imagined, his clean scent lingering on the cloth. When he moved her beneath his body, his face grew serious, eyes filled with desire.

"God, you're a breathtaking lass," he said in a husky voice.

She smiled up into his loving eyes, stretching beneath his eager embrace. As he lifted her hips against his, she felt his manhood awaken.

Her heart pounded as his fingers grazed over her silk blouse, releasing each button with expert care.

"I want you so badly, lass. The hell with tradition! Do ye feel the same, love?"

"I do." She blushed hotly as he looked down into her hopeful grey eyes.

While his pupils darkened, his hands slowly parted her blouse, enjoying the feel of the black lace beneath. Leaning toward her supple breasts, his tongue flicked over her curves. Gently, he eased her clothes from her trembling body, freeing them from all constraints. He gazed at her nude form beneath him with reverence, overwhelmed by her flawless beauty.

Her body quivered in anticipation, aching for his hands to explore every inch of her. They locked eyes as his fingers grazed her inner thigh, inches from her aching desire.

A tapping on the door made them both jump in surprise.

Aidan closed his eyes in frustration, gently covering Jade with his blanket. The couple quickly dressed before answering the door. Jade walked toward the window, looking out toward the sea.

"I'm sorry," Aidan whispered, watching the dying twilight stream across her golden tresses, setting them aflame in the darkening room.

"It's alright, darling. I imagine it must be time for supper." Jade tried her best to smile, but her body was on fire everywhere Aidan's hands explored. The feeling was like nothing she'd ever experienced, and she ached for more.

Aidan made his way toward the door. Marcail waited outside with her hands behind her back. She smiled shyly, but her grin faded when she noticed Jade at the window. Her eyes darted toward the unmade bed and tousled sheets. The young maid's mouth pinched together while she studied the marble floor.

"Supper's ready, sir."

"Thank you, Marcail. Miss Mackenzie and I will be down shortly."

"Yes, sir." Her eyes fluttered beneath her thick eyelashes, her cheeks burning. She turned on her heel and rushed down the hallway.

Jade noticed the strange exchange and shook her head. There was no longer any doubt in her mind that Marcail had a terrible crush on the master of the house.

"I'm sorry, lass." Aidan joined her at the window and pulled her against his chest. "I promise you we'll have our time together soon. There won't be interruptions next time."

"It's alright. I'm sure this will make for some gossip for the staff. Just hope it doesn't get you in trouble."

"Trouble? I don't think so." He chuckled, pushing back his wavy hair falling over his eyes. "I own the estate after all. Sticking to the old ways has kept the staff happy over the years. Figured I'd keep to their customs. Everything will all work out in the end." He bit down on his lower lip. "I have some surprises in mind, lass. I hope you enjoy em'."

"Oh?" She ran her fingers down the side of his face, relishing the feel of his afternoon shadow. "What kind of surprises, Laird MacFie?"

"Now, then, it wouldn't be a surprise if I told you now would it, Lady Mackenzie?" He kissed the top of her head.

"Just a little hint?" Jade batted voluminous eyelashes and her lips drew down in a pout.

"You're a stubborn one, lass." He studied her in the darkening room. "You'll know soon enough. How about we go down to supper? Hungry?"

"Yes, I am actually. You always know how to distract me."

"We'll have a nice meal before leaving for our meeting tonight. Should be interesting." His arm wrapped around her slender waist, leading her out of the bedroom.

"I bet it will," Jade said. Her brow creased. It was a daunting notion trying to figure out the Hunters' plans. She listened to the wind howl outside the stone walls while they passed through the long corridor leading downstairs. Golden sconces lined both sides of the hallway, illuminating their path.

Jade noticed the groom's boy, Donavon Dunsmore, standing on a ladder in the middle of the hallway lighting candles atop an ancient looking candelabra.

"Good evening, Laird MacFie."

"Good evening, Donavan. You must have finished with the horses early. Thanks for helping out inside."

"You're welcome, sir. I'll make sure to check on the horses after supper to see how they're getting along. Blackjack gets a little wild when there's thunder. Supposed to be a terrible storm passing our way."

"Appreciate it. I was going to check on them myself. Always difficult for the animals when we get bad weather. Thanks for your diligence regarding the stables," Aidan said.

"My pleasure, sir." Donavon said, glancing down the hall. His eyes lit up when he spotted Marcail heading toward them. He grinned when she rushed past, but she barely noticed the handsome youth. "Evening, Marcail."

"Hey," she said, scarcely looking at him. "Good evening, Master MacFie and Lady Mackenzie."

Jade blinked in surprise. After she'd disappeared around the corner, Jade looked at Aidan in astonishment. "Lady Mackenzie?"

"Aye, lass. The staff already sees you as the lady of the house, as do I." He looked down at her shocked face, taking her hand. He grinned, watching her blink, the breath caught in her throat.

"Let's have our dinner," Aidan said, leading her down the hallway. A thousand thoughts raced through Jade's mind as they made their way to the great hall. Within moments, the couple was surrounded by their evening servers.

Aidan escorted Jade to her usual seat, pulled out her chair, and then walked around the long mahogany table and sat opposite. A pewter candelabra glowed as the centerpiece, surrounded by generous portions of steaming vegetables and various vegan dishes. Aidan passed her a bowl of fresh farmers' market salad.

"Wow, this is lovely," Jade said.

Mrs. Flannery hurried to the table with a bottle of fresh Italian dressing.

"Hope you enjoy your supper tonight. I made sure the kitchen ordered the freshest produce from the village. Jenny and Avery stopped by the farmers' market earlier this afternoon. Also picked some lovely lettuce and herbs from the castle's garden."

"Thank you, Mrs. Flannery. We appreciate all of your hard work," Aidan said.

Bowls of rice, steamed tofu in saffron sauce, and a pot of lentil soup were placed along the table.

"Everything looks delicious, Aidan."

"I'm glad you like it, darlin.'"

Mrs. Flannery brought a silver wheeled tray with champagne and flutes, while her daughter followed in her mother's shadow. Jade noticed the teenager seemed particularly out of spirits that evening, imagining her argument with her mother wasn't helping her mood.

"Go ahead and open the bottle, lass."

Marcail glanced at Aidan nervously. Her small hands shook as she unwrapped the golden foil. She twisted the top in vain, trying to uncork the champagne. Seeing she was struggling, Aidan stood up.

"Champagne bottles can be a challenge. Here, lass, let me help you."

Marcail glanced back to her mother. Mrs. Flannery's lips pinched together in disapproval.

Jade felt pity for the girl, imagining her mother would have words about it later that evening.

"Marcail, you shouldn't be bothering Laird MacFie when he's having his supper. Use your senses, girl. Try a hand-towel if the bottle's giving you trouble." Mrs. Flannery shook her head at her daughter, reaching for a towel on the silver cart. "I'm so sorry, sir."

"No need for apologies. We all must start somewhere," Aidan said, placing the towel around the cork.

"Are you right-handed, lass?"

The teenager nodded, avoiding eye contact.

"Very good. So, take the bottle in your left and put your right hand on top," Aidan said, placing her fingers over the cork. Her face flushed while he demonstrated. She held her breath until she heard the sharp pop. Fresh bubbles rose to the surface while she rushed to pour their drinks.

"See? Just takes a little practice. You'll have it figured out in no time. Great first try."

"Thank you, sir." The young woman smiled up in gratitude.

"Thank you, Laird MacFie." Mrs. Flannery rolled her eyes at her daughter and shook her head. "You're very kind."

"Not a problem at all," Aidan said.

Marcail set Aidan's flute in front of him, sneaking peeks at his handsome face beneath her thick lashes. Once she'd served Jade, the teenager followed her mother back into the kitchen. After they were alone, the couple ate in comfortable silence. They listened to the heavy rain strike the large window surrounding the great hall. The logs in the fireplace crackled, while the wind howled inside the towering chimney flue.

Aidan glanced toward the window, watching the sheets of rain roll down. "Be prepared for some crazy weather tonight. You should bring a heavy coat when we leave. Scotland in November can be quite chilly, especially during a storm."

"Yes, it's a shame we have to go out in it. I'd much rather curl up by the fire with you."

"Aye." Aidan smiled. "Wish we could, darlin'."

"I'll bring my peacoat." Jade sighed. "It's nice and warm. You should probably change out of your kilt. Although, I'll be sad to see it go."

"I think you're right, lass. I'll change after we feed the pets."

"Sounds good. Do you think the meeting will last long?"

"I honestly have no idea what to expect. My uncle is closing his pub early tonight, so he can host the gathering. Sounds like his members move locations quite a bit. Guess they don't want the Hunters finding out where they assemble. Safer that way."

"Makes sense. I just hope we get down to the bottom of all this. My nightmares are getting pretty bad," Jade said.

"I'm sorry. Do you want to talk about it?"

"Yes, I probably should." Jade pinned a loose curl behind her ear. "There was a lovely distraction after my nap, or I'd have mentioned it earlier."

Aidan grinned, picturing Jade beneath his covers, her soft body pressing against him. He bit his lower lip, recalling the moment. "Yes, it's a shame we were interrupted."

"I agree." Jade took a sip of her champagne and glanced over her shoulder. A kitchen server offered to fill her water glass, and she thanked her. Once they were alone, Jade leaned forward and lowered her voice. "I had a dream about...the mothers."

Aidan's brow rose. "Go on."

"It was much more detailed this time. There were dozens of female selkies gathered inside a large cave. They were obviously in labor and experiencing terrible pain. Their swollen bellies arched with each contraction. An elderly woman was tending them, soothing the young ones with her lovely voice. It was a beautiful lullaby. Couldn't quite make out the words, but the melody comforted them. Once the babies were born, the senior selkie presented each mother with a pearl necklace. I believe it was a gift to commemorate the young mothers. It was a lovely image...until the Hunters arrived."

"Hunters?"

"They flooded the cave and attacked the families." Jade put her hands to her face. "I couldn't help them, Aidan. The Hunters had weapons, harpoons, and knives. It was horrific. We need to stop this from happening. I realize it was just a dream, but it seemed real."

"Jade, your nightmare could be a glimpse of the future if we don't do something about it. Are you comfortable speaking about your visions tonight? Perhaps my uncle's friends might make sense of it."

"I'm willing. I just hope they don't think I'm some crazy American." She shook her head while her stomach tightened. The idea of discussing her premonitions was suddenly quite daunting. *What am I getting into?* She folded her napkin on her lap into a tight square and bit the inside of her lip. Staying at the castle the rest of the evening seemed like a much safer idea, but she'd promised Aidan and didn't want to disappoint him.

Aidan noticed her unease and smiled. "They won't think you're a crazy

American. Just a gorgeous one," he said with a wink. "Don't worry. I'll have your back the whole time. Just describe what you remember. If these people know about the Hunters and selkies, they've probably heard it all before."

"Thank you. I just hope the dream doesn't come true. It was horrible." Jade picked at her dinner, eventually pushing the china plate to the side. Not being able to finish, she sighed, leaning back in her chair. "I can't wait for this to be over. It would be so lovely to just relax and enjoy being in Scotland."

"Aye, lass. There's plenty of things I'd rather be doing with ye than going after the Hunters." She could feel the heat rising in her cheeks when she imagined herself in his powerful arms. Oh, what she wouldn't give to be back in her boyfriend's warm bed. He seemed to read her mind as the corners of his mouth rose.

Aidan took a sip of his champagne, keeping his gaze locked on Jade's. "So many things we could be enjoying right now, but I promise you, lass, we'll get there. We need to be patient."

Jade lifted her glass into the air. "Then I toast to patience."

He chuckled, raising his glass.

Once they'd finished their meals, the staff cleared their plates. Jade turned toward Aidan. "I'll never get used to being waited on every minute of the day. I'm getting spoiled here, Laird MacFie."

"You should be spoiled, Lady Mackenzie." He moved to her side of the table, kissing the top of her head before pulling out her chair.

Jade and Aidan walked back to their rooms to change before heading to the car. Aidan dressed in a pair of trousers, sweater, and wool coat while Jade slipped on a tailored pair of black dress pants, an ivory cardigan and navy blue peacoat.

Rain sliced sideways as the beams from the Rolls Royce lit the cobblestones. The couple was quiet, not knowing what to expect.

The Seal Cave Tavern's window sign was turned to *Closed*. With raindrops blurring her vision, Jade cupped her hands and peered through the opaque glass. The pub appeared dark, other than the neon lights strung above the bar.

Aidan tapped the front door three times as instructed. A few moments later, the couple was ushered inside by cousin Molly. They were led back toward the wine cellar in the basement of the bar. There were candelabras lit atop several round oak tables. Men and women of various ages grouped together, speaking in hushed voices. They turned and stared openly when Aidan and Jade entered the meeting hall. Jade shifted her feet, listening to the rain strike the stained-glass windows.

Uncle Brodie put his hands over Aidan's and Jade's shoulders.

"This is my nephew, Aidan MacFie, and his lady friend, Jade Mackenzie. They'll be joining us tonight. They've recently dealt first-hand with the Hunters in the States. And, as I mentioned earlier, they were present when the leader was killed. Please, don't hold anything back in conversation tonight. They're deserving of all the information we can give em'."

A tall woman sitting next to the coal fireplace stood from her chair. A curtain of pearl-white tresses trailed down her back and narrow hips. A band of gold was fastened on the top of her striking locks. The group stood from their seats as she walked forward. Jade was startled by the woman's unearthly appearance. Her striking aqua-marine eyes matched Aidan's in depth and clarity.

She smiled at the young couple, grasping their hands in her own. An electric current flowed from her cool fingers and Jade released a breath she hadn't realized she'd been holding.

Uncle Brodie cleared his throat before addressing the mysterious woman.

"Nephew, I'd like to introduce you to Lady Skye Roland," Uncle Brodie said, his eyes softening.

"Aidan MacFie. I knew your parents well. My heart broke when I heard of their passing," Lady Roland said.

"Thank you. I appreciate it, ma'am."

Jade watched the stranger's irises change color when she spoke. The vivid blue turned an alarming shade of ebony. "Laird MacFie, your life may be in peril considering you have a foot in both worlds."

Aidan held her gaze despite the unnerving change to her appearance. "So, you know then?"

Two fiery-red headed men with bushy beards stepped forward, flanking the woman. Jade glanced between their ruddy faces, realizing they were twins. They had the same aqua-marine eyes of their mother, but their irises appeared normal.

"You're not alone, brother. We are of the same blood and bone, both selkie and human."

"My husband passed away from his mortal coil a few years ago," the woman said. "He was human."

Jade and Aidan glanced at one another with wide eyes. Aidan considered the ivory-haired stranger with curiosity. "So, are you…?"

When she smiled, her dark eyes changed back to a calming blue. "I'm selkie. I chose to join this world many years ago. My dearly departed husband was the love of my life. God rest his soul. I've never regretted my decision. There is no shame in belonging to both worlds. There is honor in the choice."

Jade noticed a glistening strand of pearls hanging from her slender neck. Images from her nightmare surfaced while she studied the necklace.

Aidan pushed his right hand through his dark waves. "I have so many questions. It's unbelievable realizing there are more of us out there."

Lady Roland patted the back of his left hand and smiled. "I'm sure this comes as quite a shock," she said, glancing toward Uncle Brodie. "I'll share my story, but I suggest some drinks to go along with it."

"Yes, of course, my lady. Sorry for being a poor host." Uncle Brodie glanced at the crowd.

"What ye say, scotch all around?" Most nodded, while a few requested something non-alcoholic.

Aidan glanced at Jade, knowing she wasn't a fan of whisky. "Would ye have something a little milder, Uncle? Perhaps wine?"

"Of course. Red or white?" asked Uncle Brodie.

"White, please. Thank you," Jade said.

While father and daughter went behind the bar to prepare drinks, the crowd took their seats.

All eyes rested on Lady Skye Roland.

"Well, now, where to start? Many of you know my story, but our lovely guests are new to our ways. First, I'd want to say that the selkie folk are a private, peace-loving community. Why the Hunters have singled us out to destroy our clans has always been a mystery to my people. Perhaps it has to do with the ancient tales of sailors' wives and widows taking up with selkie men. Of course, these stories have been greatly exaggerated over the years. Although there have been some instances, I imagine the fact we can produce hybrid offspring with humans weighs heavily on their minds. Then again, we never force ourselves on mankind. This would bring dishonor to our race. If anything, the opposite has always been true. Humans possess the ability to claim our pelts and hold us captive in their world. There are many stories of female selkies being lured from the sea and forced into relationships with their human abductors. It is not uncommon for the victims to give birth to unwanted bairns. Sometimes, selkies regain their pelts and manage to escape back to the ocean never to return. Sadly, most leave behind their hybrid offspring. It may seem cruel and unimaginable, but the pull of the sea can become too powerful to resist. My people have always been in danger concerning the human world. And they are particularly vulnerable right now."

Jade glanced at Aidan with a grimace. He took her hand while they listened.

"Every sixteen years, there is a *Great Birthing*. The selkie pod leader, known as a bull, is responsible for caring for multiple wives and offspring. It's a consensual relationship, though some yearn for a more monogamous way of life. This accounts for the reason female selkies occasionally come to shore, seeking a non-traditional existence. This is my story."

Lady Roland folded her long fingers together and gazed out toward the crowd.

"When I was sixteen, I discovered a young fisherman manning a small boat near Tobermory Bay. The seas were particularly rough that day. I watched him from a distance, struggling to pull his nets inside, but they'd tangled on some outcroppings. When he leaned toward the ropes, a gust of wind blew him into the churning sea. Without thinking, I swam to his rescue. He was barely conscious when I reached him, but I was able to bring him to shore. When he finally opened his beautiful brown eyes, I knew we were destined to be together. To his bewilderment, I shed my pelt while he gasped for breath. Once he'd recovered, we went together to his small fishing cabin nearby. Since I had not an ounce of clothing, he covered me in a long shirt and started a fire in the hearth. I watched the flames in wonder, never seeing anything like it before. Afterward, he fetched a blanket and offered me a mug of coffee. I found it odd drinking from a cup. It was warm, unlike anything I'd tasted before. This new human world held many surprises. We talked until dawn, sharing our hopes and dreams, falling in love while the minutes turned to hours. I explained how it was nearing my time to join the other young selkie females, to vow ourselves to the clan leader. He begged me to stay on land and share my life with him.

I know it sounds strange, but we'd fallen in love the moment we looked into each other's eyes. Before dawn the next day, we called my people to shore. I told them my wish to join my mate on land. My family was heartbroken, but reluctantly gave their blessing. As with the rules of my people, it was understood that I would not have contact with them again."

When she recalled the memories, her dark eyes shone with tears. Lady Roland's slender fingers touched the clasp of pearls hanging from her throat.

"The next *Great Birthing* will be taking place soon and this puts my people in mortal danger."

Jade cleared her throat, trying to summon her courage. In a voice just barely above a whisper, she said, "I've dreamed about the *Great Birthing*."

All eyes turned toward her. Lady Skye Roland smiled, gesturing with her unusually long, white nails.

"Please come up and stand with me, Lady Mackenzie."

Jade's body felt heavy, unable to move. Aidan smiled down, releasing her hand. "It's alright. Tell them what you can. I'm right here."

Jade nodded, her heart thrumming. She stood from her chair and faced the crowd. Her mind raced, unsure of where to begin.

"Brodie MacFie mentioned you have the gift of sight. Would you share your visions with the group?"

The members listened quietly while Jade told her story, beginning with the Hunters in Pacific Grove. She explained discovering the seal pelt on her porch, the mysterious portrait, the kidnapping, and the killing of the Hunters' leader. When she described her dreams of the *Great Birthing* and the river of blood, audible gasps arose from the crowd.

"My dreams may be glimpses of the future, but it's not set in stone. I'm only just beginning to understand my strange gift."

Lady Roland placed a cool hand on Jade's shoulder. When she gazed into the selkie's aqua-marine eyes, a feeling of peace radiated over her body.

Jade released her pent-up breath. "How did you do that?"

"We all have our own unique gifts, Lady Mackenzie." The selkie smiled. "I felt yours the minute I touched your hand. Our group has needed a seer for some time. We would be honored for you to join our cause." Lady Roland turned to the crowd with her arms raised. "What say you?"

Jade's heart raced when the men and women raised from their seats and begin pounding the tables and chairs. They chanted in unison: *Gabh sinn! Gabh sinn! Gabh sinn! Gabh sinn!*

Jade glanced around the room in confusion.

Lady Roland grinned, taking Jade's hand in hers, raising it toward the ceiling. "The members are asking you to be the group's seer. This is a great honor. If you agree, say, Bidh mi còmhla ribh. "

Jade looked out at the crowd and noticed Aidan smiling proudly.

She took a deep breath before raising her voice in answer. "Bidh mi còmhla ribh."

The crowd cheered, pounding their fists on their tables. Lady Roland took Jade's hand. "Our new seer will be a useful member for our secret community. There is no doubt she possesses second sight. Lady Mackenzie accurately described the ancient birthing traditions of my people." She turned toward Jade, long fingers grazing across her strand of pearls. "I explained how I was not allowed to see my selkie family when I joined my husband on land." Jade nodded.

"Well, I did, in fact, have one more opportunity. A year after we said our goodbyes, I gave birth to my twin boys, Caelan and Duncan. It was the most joyful time in my life, but I missed my mother terribly. On a cold autumn evening, I carried my newborn twins to Kilvickeon Beach.

"The pull of the sea was strong that night. If I listened carefully, I could hear the song of my people within the rising tides. The sound beckoned my very soul. I yearned to jump into its dark depths, back to the life I once knew. If it weren't for the bairns in my arms, I may have given in to its power. In anguish, I watched the rising shore, torn between two worlds. And then, beneath the light of the harvest moon, my mother rose from the waves.

"Her silver hair floating around her angelic face. I could barely believe what I was seeing. She'd left the safety of the pod to present me with my strand of pearls. How she knew I'd be waiting for her, I'll never know. She risked everything by disobeying the clan's rules, leaving the protection of the pod alone in shark-infested waters. But a mother's love is strong. She was willing to take the chance." While recalling the memory, the selkie's dark eyes shone with tears. She touched the strand of pearls around her neck and closed her eyes, recalling her mother's face.

"Lady Mackenzie, you dreamed of the sacred ritual of my people. Our birthing traditions are ancient ones passed down from the beginning of time. Young mothers are honored with the gift of the *Neamhnaid* by way of the old ones."

"I'm so sorry you were forbidden to see your family." Jade's eyes glistened with tears. "What a terrible choice to have to make."

Jade watched Lady Roland's eyes turn from blue to ebony once more.

"Life often requires sacrifices. Once a selkie chooses to leave the pod, family ties are forever broken. It is the same for the mothers who go back to the ocean after finding their stolen pelts. They are the ones forced into the human world. Once they break free, they must make a terrible choice. Stay with their captor, or escape, leaving their children behind. Sometimes, the pull of the sea is too great. And sometimes, like myself, the love of a human is too strong." She smiled sadly, searching Jade's face. "But something tells me you know of loss, little one."

Jade swallowed, feeling the cool touch of Lady Roland's hands on her own. An electric current flowed between the women, connecting them in mind and spirit.

"You're only beginning to realize your powers, Lady Mackenzie. In time, you will master your gift."

"Thank you for saying so. I only hope I can figure out everything before the Hunters make their next move. We can't let what happened in my nightmare become a reality." Her steel-grey eyes blurred with tears as the horrible images came to mind. While Jade tried her best to hide her emotions, a dark-haired woman came forward from the shadows, her hand resting on the curve of her shapely hip.

"I think I can help."

Everyone turned, watching in silence. The stranger's mahogany hair was cropped in a pageboy, flattering her high cheekbones and cupid bow lips. A black cocktail dress revealed an hourglass figure and long, shapely legs. Red-bottomed heels clicked over the wooden floorboards, flattering her graceful calves. Jade's mouth fell open, realizing she was the same woman she noticed at the bank earlier in the afternoon. She appeared even more beautiful in the soft candlelight.

The attractive lady flashed a smile to the gentleman she'd left behind at the table. He folded his hands over his tweed jacket and leaned back in his chair. His dark hair and eyes complimented his fair complexion. He watched with interest as his partner faced the crowd. Her ebony eyes appraised the situation, resting on Aidan a little longer than the rest. She flashed a suggestive smile, pursing her scarlet lips together. Two triangular-shaped jewels hung from her earlobes. Jade studied the jewelry with curiosity. They were nearly two inches long and sharp enough to cut flesh.

Uncle Brodie came forward. "This is Detective Fiona Glass and her partner Detective Malcolm Boyd. They work for the Tobermory police department. They've been investigating the Hunters closely these past months. In fact, Detective Glass has important information to share with us tonight."

Jade smiled at Lady Roland before taking her seat next to Aidan. He took her hand while they listened to the detective.

"Yes, there's some powerful events about to take place in the Hunters' community. I've learned plenty about their customs and beliefs while attending their meetings this past year," Fiona said.

Uncle Brodie glanced at Aidan and Jade. "She's the mole I mentioned earlier."

"With time and patience, I've earned their trust and worked my way up in their twisted society. There's nothing I won't do to bring this group to their knees." Her dark eyes narrowed while she studied the crowd. Her scarlet nails pushed a strand of chestnut locks behind her ear.

"The Hunters hurt someone very special to me and I intend to pay them back."

"I'm sorry to hear of your loss, Detective Glass. May I ask how you managed to get inside their community?" Aidan asked.

"Oh, I have my ways." She fluttered her long lashes and pursed her lips.

Jade studied her hour-glass figure, imagining she could be quite persuasive. Her partner, Detective Malcolm Boyd, shot Aidan a steely glance. Jade sensed there was more than business happening between the two detectives. Her partner watched her with a soft smile while Lady Roland's eyes darkened. Jade sensed the selkie's agitation.

Detective Glass glanced toward Jade. "You mentioned you dreamed of the *Great Birthing* and the Hunters' attack on them. Your vision mirrors the truth, Lady Mackenzie. A date has yet to be set, but I have it on good authority they're planning a *Great Reaping*. Every day, I'm getting closer to their inner circle. It's just a matter of time before I uncover the details of their sinister plans. Since the pod could give birth anytime, we need to be prepared. The Hunters have weapons, manpower, and financial backing. It's unfortunate, but their society is funded by many wealthy patrons around the world."

"Why?" Jade shook her head. "I don't understand how anyone can support their cruel practices."

"Some consider the selkie community a great threat to humanity. They do not want mankind's bloodlines to be 'spoiled'." The detective made air quotes with her manicured nails.

"Although their leader was killed in the States, high-ranking members have already picked his successor. Believe me when I say she's just as cruel and ruthless. Perhaps, more so."

Jade glanced at Aidan in surprise. "She?" Jade whispered, recalling the Hunters' leader. Meeting him in Pacific Grove, he proved nothing short of evil. She cringed, remembering Aidan's face while he was dragged toward their bonfire. If Deputy Rheinstein hadn't shot him, their leader would have burned her boyfriend alive.

After the detective finished her briefing, the members mingled. Aidan and Jade met many interesting characters that evening. They agreed to gather again in three days after Fiona's next meeting with the Hunters. For now, they were on high alert.

Chapter Four

Hooded figures chanted in Latin while they followed their leader to the raging shore. Each member held a flaming torch. The wind howled as they made their way over the dunes. Once they'd reached the tides, the Hunters faced their Mistress. One by one, they pushed back their black hoods, revealing leather masks with crooked smiles. After the followers unveiled themselves, their leader removed her own dark covering. A curtain of scarlet tresses cascaded around her black cloak. In awe of her beauty, the minions fell to their knees.

Within the swirling waters, a figure struggled to free himself from a tangled fishing net. The Mistress gestured her gloved hand toward the commotion. Immediately, three Hunters rushed toward the waves. A few moments later, they'd managed to pull their prey to the sandy shore. Bound and helpless, the male selkie struggled against the ropes. His seal-like tail thumped the ground in vain, trying to release himself from the trap. His startling blue eyes widened before turning a shade of ebony. The Hunters' queen moved forward, her blood-red tresses swirling in the darkness. Managing to pull himself upright, the selkie clawed toward the sandy shore, gazing between his captors in abject terror.

"Why are you doing this? I've done nothing wrong. Please, just let me go. I won't come back or tell anyone. I give ye my word."

The Mistress smiled sweetly and lowered herself next to the frightened selkie.

"What's your name?"

He studied her emerald eyes with a glimmer of hope.

"Jadawa."

"That's a charming name. What are you searching for so close to shore? Perhaps a lonely human female?" She stretched down beside him. Her fingers worked the buttons of her cloak, letting it fall from her side. She wore a black leather dress beneath, accenting her curves. "Well, I'm lonely." Her crimson lips pouted while she held his face to her chest. With one finger, she touched his trembling lower lip.

He stared in wonder, unable to look away from her flawless face. The Huntress encircled long, slender arms around his shoulders, cradling his head on her lap.

"Close your eyes."

Trembling, he obeyed. He released his breath as her fingers ran through his dark curls.

"There, there." She bent over his muscular body, pressing her mouth against his cold lips.

With bated breath, manicured nails traced over his abs, then dropped lower. "I'll let you go now." His eyes darted open. A glimmer of hope in his vivid eyes.

"You will?"

"Of course." Without making a sound, she reached her hand beneath her dress. The corners of her mouth rose when she unveiled the jagged knife resting against her shapely thigh. In a blink of an eye, the blade tore into the youth's neck, releasing a spray of blood across the white sands.

When the selkie's death throes mercifully ceased, his limp body was dragged across the beach. Two burly guards lifted him by his tail and chest. He was tossed unceremoniously onto the bonfire. The aroma of burnt hair and flesh mingled with the ocean air.

The Mistress wrinkled her nose in response to a gamey odor. Within the boundless sea, a thousand voices cried their lament. Beneath the stars, the leader raised her long arms toward the misty sky.

"Let us pray."

Chapter Five

Jade woke to the sound of light tapping on her bedroom door. She blinked her eyes open, wincing at the first light of dawn. Rubbing her temples, she groaned and sat upright. Flickers of light clouded her vision. Her pounding head suggested one of her dreaded migraines. She'd stayed up late talking with the group, trying to work out a solid plan to defeat the Hunters. In the end, they unanimously decided to wait for Detective Glass' next report. Hopefully, Fiona Glass could find something useful tonight.

The combination of lack of sleep, troubling nightmares, and cheap Chardonnay was the recipe for a painful headache. Pulling on her robe, she found her slippers and headed to the door. Aidan was outside dressed in a pair of grey sweatpants and matching t-shirt.

"Good morning, lass. Thought you might like to go for a run this morning. There's a break in the weather and figured we might take advantage of it." He grinned, waiting for her answer.

"Oh, Aidan, I'd love to, but I have a terrible headache this morning."

Worry filled him, and he stepped inside. "Poor, darlin'. Is there anything I can do?" When he reached for her hand, he noticed it was icy cold.

"Thank you, but I just need to stay away from the bright light for now. Some coffee might help."

He squeezed her fingers. "I'll go downstairs and fix you some."

"Thank you. I'd appreciate that. I hate these stupid migraines. They pop up at the most annoying times."

"I'll let the staff know you're not feeling well." He gave her a peck on the cheek and was startled by the coolness of her skin. "I'll set you up with some strong coffee and fetch you something for breakfast."

"Thank you." He took her hand and led her to the bed. "I think you should just take it easy today. You need some rest, love. Don't worry about anything. I'll be back in a few."

Aidan found the kitchen empty because it was still early. He discovered an espresso machine beneath a cupboard and worked on making a strong pot. As he finished placing a porcelain teapot on the tray, light footsteps sounded behind him. He turned to see his housekeeper standing behind him.

"Laird MacFie, you shouldn't trouble yourself with that." Mrs. Flannery rested her plump hands on her hips and shook her head.

"Thank you, but it's really not a problem. Lady Mackenzie has a migraine this morning. She's pretty much shooed me away, but I thought I'd bring her some coffee before my morning run."

"Aww, the poor darlin'. Well, coffee is good for a start, but I have a lovely tea blend that will fix her right up. I'll get started on it right away. Since she's not feeling well, I'll prepare her pet's meal as well."

"Thank you." Aidan smiled, setting the tray on the steel cart. "She'll really appreciate it. I'll be back in my room after my run doing some work, so neither one of us will be down for breakfast this morning."

"Very good, sir. I'll make sure to get your meals brought up to you when you're ready."

"Thank you. Oh, one more thing, Mrs. Flannery…"

The housekeeper turned toward Aidan and smiled. "Yes, sir?"

"I have a surprise for Lady Mackenzie when she feels better. Would it be possible to prepare the room behind the library? I know it hasn't been used in quite some time."

Mrs. Flannery's eyes filled with curiosity. She lowered her voice, placing her hands together on the marble countertop. "Of course, sir. If I might ask, would there be any news you'd like to share?"

Aidan smiled. "Hopefully soon, Mrs. Flannery. Once we figure out our business in Scotland, I'm hoping to surprise Lady Mackenzie with something very special. Do you mind keeping this our little secret for now?"

"Oh, of course, sir. I'll get to work on it right away."

"Thank you. I can always count on your loyalty and discretion. Truly means the world to me.

I promise to share more details when the time comes. Hopefully, everything works out."

"It's always been an honor and a privilege for my family to serve this house. We've kept our duty close to our hearts for many generations. I hope we'll have the opportunity for years to come."

"I know they have, and it warms my heart. You've always been family." Aidan patted her hand before turning to leave.

Mrs. Flannery watched him push the cart down the hall. Her mind raced, while she prepared a special pot of tea. She had the feeling things were about to change for the good of the MacFie Legacy.

৩৬৩

WHEN AIDAN MADE HIS WAY BACK TO THE MASTER BEDROOM, HE NOTICED the drawn curtains. Jade's hand rested on her head.

"My poor, darlin'," he said, wheeling the cart next to her bed. Dougal leaned against her pillow with his fuzzy paw balanced on her shoulder. Aidan poured her a cup of steaming coffee with almond milk and sugar.

Jade squinted in the darkened room, listening to the sound of a metal spoon striking porcelain.

"I want you to go for your run this morning. I'll be fine—I just need a bit of rest and coffee."

Aidan pushed back the curls from her cool forehead. "I don't want to abandon you here in pain."

"Honestly, I'll probably just sleep until the migraine goes away. And this feels like it might stay awhile. I'm afraid I won't be of much help today."

"Don't worry about anything, darlin'. I want you to rest and feel better. Are you sure you'll be alright?

"I'll be fine."

Aidan bit down on his bottom lip and shook his head. "I hate to leave you when you're not feeling well. I won't be gone long. I need to figure some things out in the fresh air. A run always helps. I'm going to bring my phone, so call if ye need anything. When I get back, I'm planning on reading Edina's diaries. So, I'll be just down the hall after my run. Oh, and Mrs.

71

Flannery told me she's working on a special tea blend that will fix you right up." Jade gave him a weak smile.

After several minutes of uncertainty, Aidan reluctantly agreed to give Jade her space. With a heavy heart, he closed the door to her bedroom and headed out for a run.

❧

JADE MOVED TOWARD THE CUP OF COFFEE WITH A TREMBLING HAND. FLECKS of light covered her field of vision. It was a relief to finally be alone. Feeling nauseous was the next stage in her migraine journey. The last thing she wanted was her boyfriend holding her hair back when it was time to pray to the porcelain goddess. No, thank you. Dougal cuddled on her lap as she prepared for the painful day ahead.

❧

THERE WAS SO MUCH ON AIDAN'S MIND CONCERNING THE PREVIOUS NIGHT'S meeting. He figured fresh air and exercise might help put things into perspective. After he left Jade's room, he noticed Mrs. Flannery was already outside with her silver cart.

"Thank you for preparing the tea. I'm not sure if the coffee I gave her will help. I'll have my phone on me if she needs me," Aidan said.

"Don't worry about anything. She'll feel better in no time."

"Thank you. I appreciate your help."

"Very good, sir."

Feeling better about leaving, Aidan made his way down the stairs and headed toward the parlor. Once outside, he breathed the heady scent of honeysuckle and the salty ocean air. The torrential rains receded, so he followed the path leading down to the shoreline. Emerald ground cover eventually tapered off to reveal white sandy beaches. Aidan jogged along the shore, listening to the frosty waves crest and the seagulls cry out their morning greetings.

The frigid Atlantic was covered by a thick blanket of fog. After about a mile, the soft morning light was replaced by a hazy gloom, making it difficult to see more than a few feet in either direction. Despite the murky scenery, Aidan eventually found a comfortable pace. While he ran across the damp sand, he considered the words of Lady Skye Roland. He still couldn't believe he'd been given the opportunity to meet one of his kind.

Realizing he wasn't alone opened endless possibilities. It was humbling to understand he belonged to a clan of ancient beings. With the knowledge came great responsibility. He'd do everything in his power to stop the massacre. And once things were settled in Tobermory, he could finally take the steps to start a new life with Jade. The thought made his heart race. His mind drifted, following the curve of the shore.

Auburn curls flashed within the murky haze. From the corner of his eye, he realized he wasn't alone. In the distance, a teenage girl waded in the churning waters. Aidan slowed his pace and squinted his eyes in disbelief.

A sliver of light broke through the cloud barrier, dancing across the woman's cinnamon-colored hair.

"Marcail?"

The teenager looked over her shoulder and smiled. "Oh, Laird MacFie. I'm sorry to disturb you."

"You're not disturbing me, just didn't realize anyone was out here." Aidan stopped at the water's edge and smiled.

"Aye, the fog is like pea soup this morning." Marcail lifted her skirt above her knees and moved back to the sandy shore. Blotches of red covered her pale legs, and she quickly covered up.

"Isn't it a bit cold to be in the tides today?" Aidan asked.

The young woman shook her head and laughed. "Aye, it's nice, Laird MacFie. Doesn't bother me a bit. I love coming out to the beach before my shift starts to clear my head."

"The sea is always a lovely place to gather one's thoughts."

Marcail cocked her head to the side, studying Aidan beneath thick lashes. "May I ask you a question, sir?"

"Of course," said Aidan.

"Do you suppose the tales of the selkie folk to be true?"

He tried to hide any reaction. "Hmm. That's an interesting question. Why do you ask?"

"I wonder sometimes." She folded her freckled arms over her chest and gazed at the churning tides. "There's been stories for as long as I can remember. And many mention the MacFie Clan. I figured if anyone knew the truth, it would be you, sir. I hope I'm not overstepping, Laird MacFie. Just wondering."

Aidan flashed a disarming smile, trying to put the girl at ease. "It's perfectly fine to ask questions. Well, the world is full of mysteries. Anything's possible. I do want to mention one thing before you investigate this further."

Marcail's brow furrowed. "Yes, sir?"

"I'd be very careful looking into this right now."

"Oh?"

"I don't want to frighten you, but there are some people that not only believe in selkies but want to harm them. It might be safer to explore this subject at a different time."

"It's funny you say that. Ma tells me the same thing. Gets mad at me anytime I ask about the selkie folk. Says it's all a bunch of nonsense. It's just curious."

"I'm sure Mrs. Flannery only wants to keep you safe." Aidan smiled. "You shouldn't be worried about these things anyway."

"I guess so." A hint of a smile flickered as she watched a horse and rider appear from the mist.

The stable apprentice, Donavon, rode toward them on a dapple-grey gelding.

"Oh, hello, Laird MacFie." He turned toward Marcail and tipped his tweed cap, his brown eyes lingering on her pretty face.

"Decided to bring Kelpie out for a short ride this morning. He's healing nicely from his injury last summer."

Aidan patted the horse on the shoulder, admiring his shiny coat and vivid eyes.

"He looks fine, lad. You're doing a great job with the horses. Keep up the good work. Before you know it, you'll be managing the stables."

He grinned at Aidan in surprise. "Thank you, sir."

"Are you enjoying your time apprenticing, so far?"

"Yes, Laird MacFie. It's been a great experience."

"Very good, lad. I hope to see you stay with it. It's a relief knowing the horses are well cared for when I'm back in the States." Aidan noticed the way Donavon's eyes lingered on Marcail. He smiled, turning back toward the shore. "Well, I better get back to my run. Hope you two have a great day."

Aidan disappeared into the mist, leaving the young people alone.

"Mrs. Flannery sent for ye, lass. Guess it's time to start the morning service," Donavon said.

Marcail groaned. "Thanks for reminding me. I better head back before I get another lecture from my ma."

She gathered her mauve sweater around her shoulders and headed toward the castle. The teenage boy watched her turn to leave and dismounted his horse. "May I give you a ride back, Marcail?"

She looked over her shoulder and considered his hopeful brown eyes. "Sure. I'd appreciate it."

"Great. Let me help you up." The young man cupped his hands and smiled. Marcail stepped up, and then swung her pale leg over the saddle. Once she was comfortable, Donavan climbed behind her. He grinned and took the reins. Together, they moved across the sandy shore.

"I could barely see ye in the fog. Glad I found you."

"Thanks for letting me know my ma's been looking for me. Guess I spaced out on the time," said Marcail. "She's been in a mood all week. The last thing I need is to show up late for my morning shift."

Donavan took a deep breath, letting it out slowly. His heart pounded, and he tried to summon his courage.

"I was wondering if you're not busy this evening, maybe...you'd like to go to the movies with me. There's a new horror film out tonight. Oh, uh, unless you'd like to see something else. I'm up for whatever."

Marcail glanced over her shoulder and smiled. Donavon watched her push a locket of cinnamon-colored curls out of her eyes.

"I love horror films. I think that sounds fun. What time?"

Donavon hesitated, trying to contain his excitement. He'd figured she'd say no, so her response was a pleasant surprise. "There's one at seven if you can make it."

"Sure. Sounds good."

When they arrived at the stables, the boy dismounted, offering his hand to Marcail. He helped her down, gazing into her soft blue eyes.

"Do you want to meet in the parlor? We can take my jeep," Donavon said.

"Sure, that works for me."

Donavon grinned while he watched Marcail walk toward the castle.

WHILE THE TEENAGERS TALKED, AIDAN JOGGED ACROSS THE WHITE SANDS. The sun had finally managed to penetrate the thick cloud covering. He admired the sparkling sea, making sure to keep a distance from the rising tide. His mind was overwhelmed by everything he'd discovered the previous evening. Meeting Lady Roland exceeded all his expectations. Being in the presence of another selkie connected him to both his past and present. He'd transformed, what he called the *metamorphosis*, several times. Yet he had never met either a hybrid or a full-blood member of the selkie clan. He had so many questions. Aidan breathed in the crisp sea air, remembering his eighteenth birthday. The day had been painful, just a few months since his parents were killed in the plane crash. Trying to escape the memories, he made his way down to Lover's Point in Pacific Grove. He wanted desperately to be alone, just leave the world for a while and its terrible suffering. Beneath the full moon, he undressed and sprinted toward the raging waters.

After swimming out several yards, a searing pain ripped through his abdomen and lower body. Within minutes, his legs melded together, forming a torpedo-like tail. In his confusion, Aidan believed himself to be dying. His agony eventually subsided, replaced by an overwhelming sense of peace. After the transformation was complete, he was able to speed through the water with ease. All his confusion melted away and his body and soul became one with the ocean. It felt like an eternity passed before his thoughts turned toward his life on land and his newly adopted family.

He realized Sheriff Carpenter and his wife would be devastated if he failed to return. They'd been nothing but kind and generous since his parents' passing. Reluctantly, he turned to shore. As soon as his body touched the earth, his flesh transformed once again. Although painful, the sensation was not nearly as shocking as before. Over time, he would learn to control his metamorphosis, always making sure to change in the darkness of night. He managed his urges.

That changed, however, the day he discovered Jade drowning at sea. When he saw her limp form bobbing in the waves, he was unable to stop his body from transforming, and was able to rescue her just in time. Unfortunately, the Hunters were waiting to take advantage of the situation. Aidan shook his head, trying to think of cheerier topics.

There were so many questions concerning his past and future. He hoped the answers waited within the pages of his great-grandmother's diaries. His thoughts turned back to Jade. Worried about her migraine getting worse, he cut his run short and headed back to the castle.

After he climbed the spiral staircase, he quietly made his way down the hall toward the master bedroom. He let himself inside, walking slowly to her bed. Dougal wagged his tail but refused to leave her side. Mrs. Flannery's tea worked its magic and helped Jade drift into a deep slumber. Happy she was resting soundly, Aidan headed for his bedroom for a hot shower and to change.

He stood inside the clawfoot tub, enjoying the aftermath of his run. His endorphins gave him a natural high. Water ran down his firm muscles. Once he dressed in a pair of jeans and a pullover, he went to his desk and sorted through the leather satchel. Before he sat down to read, he removed the small jewelry case inside. Clicking it open, he studied the sapphire and diamond ring. The dazzling jewels shone in the soft morning light. He walked back to his closet and pushed the door open, a safe was secured in the back. After clicking the correct numbers, he set the ring inside.

For the next several hours, he read Edina MacFie's diaries. They told a story of love, loss, and new beginnings. Halfway through, Mrs. Flannery stopped by with a tray of hot coffee and blueberry scones. He thanked her before getting back to work.

According to the diaries, the MacFie family ancestors settled in Virginia in the late eighteenth century and stayed until the mid-nineteenth century. His great-grandmother, Edina, lived to be one hundred years old. After she passed, the diaries' handwriting changed. Her granddaughter started the next entry.

April 12th, 1870, The Year of our Lord.

"As I write these words, my tears flow over the page. Many years after my grandmother's passing, our family was forced to leave our Virginia estate and travel west. The Hunters discovered our secret. Our journey was long and difficult, but we arrived in Monterey with significant savings to start anew. Happily, we've met a kind family, the Mackenzies', who have helped my parents secure a new property. It turns out our clans were acquaintances back in the old country. Things seemed peaceful until just the other evening.

My pa discovered a seal carcass by the stables. Along with the gruesome discovery, there's been strange chanting sounds outside our home.

July 4th, 1870, The Year of our Lord.

Dear Diary,

It's been a while since I last visited. Things have been horrible, but we finally have a glimmer of hope. Sadly, there was an attack on our homestead last week. The Hunters appeared in the dead of night, wearing monstrous masks made of sharkskin. They arrived at our property at midnight with torches and harpoons. They threatened our lives, shouting obscene names, and calling us the Unclean Ones. We would have surely perished if not for the help of the Mackenzies'. They arrived with the Sheriff just before the Hunters broke down our door. The masked men were taken into custody. The Sheriff assured us they would not come back. I pray this is true. We will never know how the Hunters found us, but mother believes they know about my condition. I'm afraid it's difficult to admit even to you, diary. I have been gifted with the ability to turn. I hope and pray my secret will remain hidden and we will be left alone in peace.

Although the granddaughter did not mention the Hunters again in the diaries, her great-grandchildren continued their own personal accounts in a collection of leather-bound journals. According to their writings, a generational pattern suggested the hybrid gene surfaced every fifty years or so. Aidan was alarmed by the mention of the shark masks. It sounded like the driver of the hearse they'd spotted earlier in the week. The room darkened by the time he finished his family's passages. He stood and stretched, eager to share the new information with Jade.

WHILE AIDAN WAS FINISHING READING HIS FAMILY'S JOURNALS, JADE WAS tossing and turning beneath her covers.

In the distance, Marcail stood at the edge of the sea. Her cinnamon curls shone in the amber light of twilight. She stripped off her clothes and dove into the scarlet waves. When she was several yards away, her lower body transformed. Soon she was paddling across the raging waters with her newly formed lower half. Nearly an hour passed before she came back to shore. Her body writhed, her selkie flesh reshaping back to human. Gathering her clothes, she quickly dressed. When turning back to the castle, she was surrounded by Hunters.

JADE STIRRED FROM HER DREAM WITH THE SOUND OF THE DOOR CREAKING open. Aidan peeked into Jade's room and smiled.

"Feeling better, love?"

"Yes, I think the tea really helped. I just wish I could find something to stop my dreams." Mrs. Flannery poked her head around the door. "Oh. lovely to see you up, Lady Mackenzie. Supper will be ready in about fifteen minutes."

"Thank you, Mrs. Flannery. Your brew worked miracles. I'm feeling so much better. I'd love to get your recipe. I'm usually down for a couple of days when my migraines flare."

"Aye, that's wonderful news, lass." The housekeeper walked toward the side of her bed to retrieve the tea cart. "I'm so happy you're feeling better. You looked white as a ghost this morning. Your color's back. I'd be happy to share my recipe. Let me know whenever you're ready and we'll make some in the kitchen."

"Oh, I'd love to, Mrs. Flannery. That's kind."

Aidan looked down and smiled. "Why don't you get dressed? I'll meet you downstairs."

"Sounds good." Jade tried not to think of the dream as she took a quick shower and dried off. After she changed into a pair of jeans and sweater, she brushed her hair and put on a light application of lipstick. She prayed this was just a nightmare caused by her headache.

Aidan was waiting for her in the great hall. He pulled her seat out, then went to his side of the table.

Mrs. Flannery carried a pitcher of water with lemon, but she seemed preoccupied. Her cheery disposition was gone. Jade noticed Marcail's absence, and her stomach tightened.

While the matronly housekeeper poured their drinks, her hands trembled.

"Mrs. Flannery, is your daughter working?" Jade asked.

"Well, yes. Marcail should have been down by now. Her shift's usually not over until after 7:00 p.m. She asked to leave early tonight, and I gave her the time off. Silly girl." Aidan glanced at Jade sensing something was wrong.

A second serving girl brought a tray of fresh sourdough bread to the table.

"Ma'am, I believe your daughter was at the beach a little while ago. She enjoys watching the sunset."

Mrs. Flannery shook her head. "She's always at the beach, my daughter, but it's dark outside," she said, looking toward the window. "Marcail should have been back by now. I'll go look in her room if you don't mind, Laird MacFie."

"Of course."

Jade picked at her bowl of rice and vegetables, trying not to panic.

"What's wrong, lass?"

"I hope it's nothing, but I had a terrible dream about Marcail." She quickly filled Aidan in on the details while his brow furrowed.

"Hmm, that's a bit troubling."

"I know. I just hope it was a nightmare and nothing more."

While they dined, Mrs. Flannery went to check on Marcail. Seeing she wasn't in her bedroom, she came down the stairs, heading back to the great hall. Aidan and Jade watched her asking various staff members if they'd seen her daughter. Frustrated, she headed back to the dining table and began clearing dishes.

"Any word on Marcail?' Aidan asked.

"No, sir. She's not in her room. One of the kitchen staff mentioned she was at the beach earlier. But it is not like my daughter to miss an entire shift. Can't help but to be a bit worried."

Jade and Aidan exchanged glances. They heard footsteps behind them. Donavon approached with hat in hand.

"Sorry to interrupt, I was just wondering if anyone's seen Marcail? We were supposed to meet by the parlor tonight and see a movie in town."

Mrs. Flannery's face paled and tears sprang in her soft blue eyes.

The boy searched her face, seeing she was visibly upset. "I'm sorry, Mrs. Flannery. Did I say something wrong?"

"No, lad." Aidan stood from his chair and approached them. "We can't seem to find Marcail. The last we heard she was taking in the sunset by the beach."

"Well, that sounds like her." Donavon pushed his dark curls from his eyes. "She loves to watch the tides at sunset. Funny, though, it's not like her to miss her shift. I'd be happy to go down to check to see if she's outside."

"Good idea, lad," said Aidan. "I'll join you."

When he turned his attention back to the women, he noticed Marcail's mother wringing her hands. "Jade, why don't you stay with Mrs. Flannery in the great room? We'll head out and look for Marcail."

Jade nodded, slipping her arm around the housekeeper's shoulder. "Let's go sit by the fire. We'll figure this all out."

When they turned to leave, a serving maid walked past them on her way to the dining room table.

Aidan turned toward her. "Janet, would you mind bringing a pot of tea to the great room for Mrs. Flannery and Lady Mackenzie?"

The young woman looked at Mrs. Flannery in confusion, but did as she was asked. "Yes, sir." Jade led her to the sofa by the fireplace.

⚜

WHEN THEY WERE OUT OF EARSHOT OF THE WOMEN, DONAVON TURNED toward Aidan and spoke in a hushed voice.

"I have kerosene lamps and flashlights in the barn. Maybe we could take the horses down to the beach. It might speed things up. There's a pretty bad storm coming tonight."

"Good idea, lad." They rushed to the stables and gathered supplies. Donavon saddled up Kelpie while Aidan readied Blackjack.

Armed with flashlights, they headed outside. The wind was fierce as they rode along the shore. A sliver of moonlight illuminated the powerful breakers.

"Marcail's favorite spot is over here by a patch of willows. It's the same place she was this morning," Donavon said, pointing toward the shore.

"Alright, let's head over. Has she ever disappeared like this before?" Aidan asked.

"I don't believe so, sir." The young groomsman shook his head. "Marcail loves to hang out at the beach, but she always comes in before dark. This is odd for her. I hope everything's all right."

81

When they approached the shore, Aidan aimed his flashlight across the white sand. The soft glow illuminated a strand of pearls.

"There's something on the beach," Aidan said, dismounting his horse.

Donavon jumped down, eying the necklace with wide eyes. He reached for the strand then held it up to the light.

"Those are Marcail's. She always wears 'em."

Being a seasoned fireman, Aidan was used to emergencies. He ignored the fear rising in his mind and focused on a plan of action. Finding her necklace was not a good sign, but they couldn't afford to panic. "Let's keep looking for her. If we don't find Marcail in the next hour, I'll call the police."

Donavon looked up in surprise, sensing Laird MacFie was holding something back. Together, they rode up and down the beach for over an hour. They were just about to head back when Aidan noticed a black object lying in the sand. His stomach tightened, reaching for the leather-looking material. Donavon pointed his light on the black mask and his mouth dropped open.

"What is that?"

Aidan closed his eyes, passages from the family diaries fresh in his mind.

"It's a mask," Aidan whispered between clenched teeth. "We need to head back. I'm calling the sheriff."

Chapter Six

ONCE THEY ARRIVED AT THE STABLES, THE MEN DISMOUNTED. "DONAVON, can you finish taking care of the horses? I need to call the authorities."

"Yes, sir." The groomsman took the reins and led their mounts toward the stalls. Before opening the paddock door, he turned back. "I can't stand the thought of her missing, Laird MacFie." His dark brown eyes shone with purpose. "I'd like to come back to the castle tonight once the horses are settled in. I can help with the search."

"Of course, lad. Why don't you meet us back in the great room when you're finished here?"

"Thank you, sir."

Aidan called the Tobermory Police Station when he was back inside the castle. The receptionist told him that officers would arrive within half an hour. After he clicked off his phone, he discovered Jade and Mrs. Flannery waiting by the fire in the great hall.

Mrs. Flannery jumped from her seat when she saw Aidan approach. When she noticed the strand of pearls in his hand, her face paled. Jade stood from her chair, studying him with a grimace.

Mrs. Flannery's mouth trembled, and her blue eyes filled with fresh tears. "Sweet Jesus, where did you find those?"

"Try not to panic, Mrs. Flannery." Aidan placed his hand over her icy

83

fingers. "We found the pearls by the shore, close to where Marcail enjoys watching the sunset according to Donavon."

The older woman put her hands over her face and began weeping. Between sobs, she spoke. "The pearls belong to my daughter. She never takes them off. Someone must have taken her. I had a terrible feeling all afternoon. I knew something was wrong when she missed her shift. We have to find her!"

"We don't know for certain, Mrs. Flannery." Jade put her arm around the distraught mother's shoulders.

Shaking her head, the housekeeper rushed toward Aidan. "May I have the necklace?"

"Of course." Aidan placed the strand in her trembling hands.

"Look!" she said, holding the pearls up to the fire. "The clasp is torn. Something terrible has happened!" She put the back of her hand against her mouth, choking back a sob. "The pearls were given to Marcail by her birth mother."

"Her birth mother?" Jade asked, glancing toward Aidan.

"I've called the police station. The detectives can take a closer look. They will be here shortly, and we can get to the bottom of this. Please try not to panic, Mrs. Flannery. I promise we'll figure this out." Aidan said.

Jade took Mrs. Flannery's hand and led her to a chair by the fire. "Let's sit down and talk this through. I remember my teenage years. It's an emotional time and your daughter may have simply gone somewhere to blow off steam."

"Yes, it's true Marcail's been in a mood the last few weeks, but it's just not like her to go off and hide. And I have a feeling something is terribly wrong. It's difficult to explain, but a mother's intuition is not to be taken lightly."

"I believe you, Mrs. Flannery. We'll figure this out."

The distraught mother reluctantly took her seat on a velvet chair. Aidan and Jade sat next to her on each side.

"Mrs. Flannery, you mentioned her mother giving her pearls. Do you think the disappearance could have something to do with her birth mother?"

She shook her head. "Ye won't believe me if I told you."

Aidan moved his chair closer and leaned forward. "I know you've heard the stories of the MacFie Dynasty. Our family tree is rich with tales of magic and unbelievable fables. Your family has held an honorable place in our castle for over two centuries. You've earned our trust and I promise anything you tell us will be said in private."

"It's true, Mrs. Flannery," Jade added. "Aidan and I have been through some unbelievable things in the past few months. Nothing you say will shock us. And it will be kept in strict confidence."

Mrs. Flannery searched their faces and took a deep breath before responding. "You're both kind and generous. I'll tell you my story because of the history between our families." Mrs. Flannery took a sip of her tea before beginning her tale.

⚜

"MY HUSBAND AND I WERE QUIET ABOUT THE DETAILS OF MARCAIL'S adoption. We tried for years to have our own children, but the Good Lord had other plans. We'd just about given up hope of raising a family of our own." She looked down at her arthritic hands and folded them gingerly onto her lap.

"One morning, I was collecting oysters near the shore." She glanced at Aidan with a sad smile. "You must have been about ten. I remember you were visiting MacFie Castle during the summer with your parents."

"Aye, I remember, Mrs. Flannery. It was a wonderful vacation."

"Aye. Well, it was a lovely morning. I'd nearly collected a bucket's worth and was planning to head back. And that's when I saw 'em."

"What did you see, Mrs. Flannery?" Aidan leaned closer, taking her cold hand in his.

She gazed at the fireplace, reflective light dancing over her salt and pepper hair. "At first I couldn't believe what I was seeing. There was a young woman carrying what appeared to be an animal pelt. It was obvious she was having trouble making her way toward me. I ran over to help, and she blinked, a small glimmer of hope in her bright blue eyes. I asked her if she was hurt. But she kept saying repeatedly, 'I must return to the sea'.

"She was emaciated, her skin nearly translucent in the bright summer haze. The poor girl could barely walk. She dragged the bundle over toward the shore, seeming to look for shelter. My eyes widened when I realized what was inside the pelt she carried. A wee bairn was wrapped in the bundle.

"Fearing for them both, I said, 'Why don't' ye sit down by the cove,

85

where there's protection from the wind'. The young woman nodded, following close behind.

"Once she sat down, her sky-blue eyes filled with tears. The girl stared at the waves for several moments without speaking. I was thinking she wasn't going to say another word when she reached for my hand, clutching it fiercely. Her eyes were full of purpose, and she asked me to sit with her so she could tell her story. So, I took off my coat and put it over her shoulders.

"She said, 'I beg ye to listen to my tale. You may think I'm mad afterward, but I can prove everything I say.'

"The young woman desperately needed someone to listen. Of course, I told her. She clutched the babe to her breast and gave me a soft smile, over what I imagine, was once a lovely face, now gaunt with sunken eyes.

"When she began speaking, I imagined she must be out of her mind. For nothing she said made any sense. It seemed to belong to fairy tales. She told a tale of the Old Ones. The stories I grew up with and knew well. She spoke of the selkie folk. I know Laird MacFie knows of 'em." He nodded.

"Yes, she said she was a selkie. When she was but a teenager, a man discovered her alone by the beach. She had changed into her human form and was sunning herself by the shore. The young woman believed the stranger to be quite handsome. When he asked her to come with him, she obeyed. Without a word, he wrapped his coat around her nude body. His car was parked close by, and he helped her inside. She'd never seen anything like it before. Little did she realize; her world was about to change in unimaginable ways. Because this fairy tale did not have a happy ending. He wrapped her pelt in a canvas bag and placed it in the trunk. She would not see it again until the day of her escape.

"Riding in his car, she was mercifully unaware of her fate. For this young man, though handsome, possessed a dark heart. He was familiar with selkie legends and had been watching her for some time." Mrs. Flannery folded her arms across her chest and her lips pinched together. "I'll never forget the way her soft blue eyes turned ebony when she spoke. It was alarming, but nothing compared to the rest of her story. You see, once the man brought her home to his cabin, he immediately revealed his true nature. He imprisoned her in a small room, forcing her to cohabitate with him. She begged to leave and cried for mercy, but he only laughed and mocked her attempts of escape.

"Her life became one of darkness. Locked up away from the sun and sea.

The stranger had his way with the poor girl whenever the mood struck and beat her when she refused. He seemed to take joy in tormenting the lass.

"He withheld food and water from his victim until she became weak and docile. Somewhere along the way, she became pregnant with his bairn. I don't know how she managed to give birth to a healthy child in her condition. Once the baby was born, she begged her kidnapper for supplies for her daughter. He refused, but she was persistent, fearing for her daughter's life. Her constant requests angered him. In a drunken rage, he beat her bloody and stormed off into the night. After waking from the attack, she tested the lock and found it open. The young mother searched the home, eventually found her pelt wrapped in a tarp in the cellar, but that was not the only thing she discovered.

"Along with harpoons and knives, there were leather masks stored inside a locker beneath a pile of blankets. Some of these masks were painted with shark teeth across the mouths." Aidan glanced at Jade, and her face paled.

"And if that wasn't strange enough, the young mother discovered books containing vivid pictures of her kind, some dismembered. She told me how her people feared a group called *The Hunters*. They'd stalked and threatened her folk for centuries. And now it appeared she had been kidnapped by one of its members. Realizing she was kept as a kind of plaything made her sick to her stomach. After her gruesome discovery, she managed to escape from the cabin. She walked for hours, trying to get as far away from the property as possible. She was shivering by the time she finished her sad story, so I wrapped my coat tighter over her frail shoulders. I tried to convince her to leave with me. I'd hoped to get help from your parents, possibly report her kidnapper, and find her a safe place to stay. She refused; her eyes locked on the pounding shore.

"The young mother kept repeating, 'I love her, but I must return to the sea. There's nothing here for me now.' Her dark eyes slowly turned back to soft blue. She said, 'You're a good human. Will you take care of my bairn?'

"I was astounded. As much as my husband and I yearned for a child of our own, I didn't want to take a baby from a desperate woman. Surely, we can get you help, I told her. And then I mentioned the MacFie family and suggested they might be able to assist. Perhaps they could speak to the sheriff and arrest her abuser.

"But the young mother simply shook her head. She said, 'I'm afraid no one can help me.' With trembling hands, she removed her pearl necklace from her bruised throat and said, 'My mother passed this down to me before she died. Selkie women are given pearls to commemorate their graduation to motherhood. It's an honored tradition.' She looked down at the infant in her arms, her mouth trembling. 'My bairn's name is Marcail. It means pearl. Promise me you'll give her the necklace when she's older?'

"I nodded, unsure of what else to say. After the mother kissed the baby's forehead, she handed her to me, along with her quilt and pearls. I looked down at the sleeping infant, my mind reeling. As much as I desired a child of my own, I pleaded with the selkie to stay. 'Please, we can go to the MacFie Castle. They'll help you, I told her.'

"The young mother shook her head and smiled. 'You're a good woman. I can feel these things. You'll take good care of my bairn,' Without another word, she lifted the grey pelt by her bare feet and dragged it toward the raging sea. I followed her to the shore, clutching the child against my chest. I feared she might try to hurt herself, but what she did next is forever burned into my mind. When the young woman reached the tides, she laid the pelt across the sand and undressed.

Her torn nightgown fell around her ankles. I gasped at the sight of her emaciated body. Almost every inch was covered in cuts and bruises. I felt outrage, for whoever did this was an absolute monster. I remember the wind whipping through her cinnamon curls, her soft blue eyes gazing toward the heavens. She kneeled on top of the skin, put her hands together and prayed. After several moments, she laid down on her back with her face to the cloudless sky. At first it appeared she was sleeping. Without warning, her body seized, and the pelt wrapped itself around her. A soft keening escaped her lips."

"I was mesmerized watching her body transform. Her legs dissolved into the pelt, and the skin melded around her lower body. Once she'd fully transformed into a selkie, she moved toward the rising tides, diving headfirst and she never looked back.

"I was astounded, gazing toward the shore with the wee bairn in my arms. I loved my little girl the moment I looked into her beautiful blue eyes. My precious Marcail."

"Of course, my husband was astounded when I told him the story. It took him several days to process everything, but his love for our new daughter was evident from the beginning. Laird MacFie's family welcomed our baby with open arms. They respected our privacy and did not pry into the details of our adoption." She turned toward Aidan and smiled. "I always sensed your mother suspected something, but she never asked. I was always grateful for her discretion. We provided a loving home, but it soon became apparent Marcail wasn't like other children."

Mrs. Flannery turned toward the fireplace, shaking her head. "Our little girl loved the sea. I remember she had terrible temper tantrums whenever we tried to bring her home after a day at the beach. She'd dive right into the ocean as a toddler without a second thought. Being older parents, it was quite the challenge keeping up with her.

"And of course, we knew the stories relating to the selkie folk. Living and working at the MacFie Castle provided all the best folklore in town. Not everyone believes the tales. I was skeptical myself until I met a selkie in person. Seeing my daughter was showing selkie characteristics, I needed to learn more. Every night after work, I researched everything I could find on the subject. This eventually led me to learning about the Hunters. It was all quite shocking. After reading up on their centuries-old vendetta, I feared for my daughter's safety. I worried these people might somehow discover Marcail's true nature. What if they tried to harm her like her poor mother?"

Jade now understood. This was why Mrs. Flannery was so strict with her daughter. It all made sense. Marcail's mother was simply trying to protect her.

Mrs. Flannery sat upright in her chair. "And then there was the issue of her natural father. My husband and I never learned who he was or where he lived. If we had, we would have reported him to the authorities. So, you see, I've lived in fear all these years. I worry about my precious daughter. I know she thinks I'm overbearing at times. It's just I can't stand the thought of something happening to her. She's my life."

Jade reached for Mrs. Flannery's hand. "Is that why you were so upset with her for leaving her scarf at the beach?"

"Yes, dear," the housekeeper said. "She's forever wandering over to the shore, losing time staring out at the waves. The more I told her to stay away from the sea, the more she yearned for it. I didn't want to lose her. I know I've been strict with her this past year. It seems every time I turn my back, the girl's wandering away. I've been afraid she might leave, like her mother." Her eyes filled with tears. "I hope and pray we find her before something terrible happens." The housekeeper covered her eyes with her hands and wept.

"Please don't cry, Mrs. Flannery." Aidan leaned forward and placed his hand on her shoulder.

"We'll find your daughter. Ye have my word."

She looked up, tears rolling down her pale cheeks. "Thank you, sir."

The sound of knocking echoed throughout the castle. Mrs. Flannery jumped from her chair and raced to the door. Aidan and Jade followed close behind. Two detectives waited outside, bracing themselves against the fierce wind.

Chapter Seven

Detective Glass was dressed in a grey pencil skirt and matching jacket. Her partner wore a navy suit. They flashed their badges and were escorted inside.

Aidan and Jade exchanged glances.

Fiona Glass focused on Aidan, ignoring the rest. "Laird MacFie, we received news of a missing servant from your estate."

"Yes. This is Mrs. Flannery, her mother. Her daughter, Marcail, went missing several hours ago. She didn't show up for her shift this afternoon."

Detective Glass smirked. "Well, good help is hard to find these days."

Jade's face showed her shock.

Aidan's mouth drew down in a grimace. "Marcail is a well-respected member of our household. I'd appreciate it if you'd show more consideration."

Glass noticed Mrs. Flannery shooting daggers toward her. The detective's face softened while she considered Aidan's words.

"Of course, Laird MacFie. I'm just trying to get to the bottom of all of this. I'm sure it's not the first time a staff member has missed a shift. Just trying to make a point before we call this a missing person's case." She smiled, batting her long lashes. "Perhaps we could start from the beginning?"

Jade glanced at Detective Malcolm Boyd, who quietly listened.

"Mrs. Flannery's sixteen-year-old daughter, Marcail, went missing earlier today," said Aidan.

"As I said before, I consider her and her mother part of the family. I should also add, Mrs. Flannery is familiar with our cause."

"Is that so?" The detective's ebony eyes widened in surprise. "Then we can discuss things openly, I assume?"

"Of course." Aidan gestured for everyone to follow him. "Let's talk in the study."

He led them out of the parlor, across the castle, toward the smoking room. Opening a large mahogany door, he ushered them inside. There were several leather chairs set around mahogany tables.

Jade placed her arm around Mrs. Flannery's shoulder as they walked.

Once they were seated, Aidan turned toward the worried mother. "Would you mind telling the detectives what you told us? They know about the Hunters and are trying to stop them."

The housekeeper's eyes glistened with tears. "I pray you can find my daughter."

Detective Malcolm Boyd took a chair across from the grieving mother and smiled. "Ma'am, please take your time and tell us everything you can remember. We will include the 'normal parts' in our official reports."

The detectives listened closely while Mrs. Flannery repeated her story concerning her daughter's disappearance.

Detective Glass exchanged glances with her partner before she crossed her shapely legs and tilted her head to the side.

"We can file a missing person report for now. I'll call in some officers to comb the beach. If you think the Hunters are involved, we need to take this seriously," Detective Malcolm said.

"Yes, I will be meeting with a group of Hunters tomorrow. Let me try to find out if there's any information concerning your daughter. I'm working undercover, so they won't suspect anything," Detective Glass said.

"Oh, dear. Will you be safe, young lady? I hear the Hunters are dangerous," Mrs. Flannery said, reaching a trembling hand to her throat.

"That's very kind, but I've been involved with the group a while now." The corner of the detective's mouth lifted when she regarded the housekeeper. "If there's any news on your daughter, I may be able to find out tomorrow."

"Do you think they will hurt her?" Mrs. Flannery asked, her eyes brimming with tears.

Although the detective smiled, it didn't reach her ebony eyes. Glass combed back a brunette lock behind her ear with scarlet nails.

"Probably not right away. If they kidnapped Marcail, I'm sure they have something unpleasant planned for her. So, we'll do our best to get to her before something happens to the girl," Detective Glass said, studying the housekeeper with interest, noticing the way her body trembled beneath Lady Mackenzie's hand.

"You mentioned a strand of pearls were found at the beach. Do you have them with you?"

Glass noticed Mrs. Flannery's lips narrow into a thin line. She sensed the mother's reluctance as she pulled out the necklace from her apron pocket.

The detective watched Aidan and Jade exchange concerned looks regarding the housekeeper.

Tears rolled down Mrs. Flannery's pale cheeks. With a trembling hand, she held the pearls up to Glass.

"They are special to Marcail. Her birth mother left them with her..." she trailed off.

"Yes, you already mentioned that fact, Mrs. Flannery." Fiona stood from her chair, looking down with apathy. "If you don't mind, we'll take them to the lab to dust for prints, see if we find any matches in our database."

A hush fell over the room while she reluctantly handed the strand to the detective. Fiona smiled coldly, and then dropped the pearls inside a plastic bag.

Detective Boyd studied Mrs. Flannery's pale face, watching her daughter's jewelry disappear into the briefcase.

"Perhaps you might feel better if you rested, Mrs. Flannery." He reached into his coat pocket and retrieved a business card. "Please call day or night. Your daughter's welfare is important to us." He patted the back of her hand and smiled. "I promise you we'll reach out the minute we hear something."

Fiona Glass smiled dismissively while her partner consoled the housekeeper. She regarded Detective Boyd's handsome face with indifference, watching him coddle the servant with words of encouragement.

"Thank you, Detective. I do feel a bit worn out," Mrs. Flannery said.

"You look a bit overcome," Jade agreed. "It might be best to lie down. I'll walk you back to your room."

"All right, but please let me know the minute you hear anything."

The group stood from their chairs while Jade led Mrs. Flannery outside.

After they left, the detectives turned their attention to Aidan. They asked him a series of questions concerning his staff. When Jade returned, she took her seat. Detective Boyd smiled in her direction, while Fiona studied Aidan.

Detective Glass folded her hands beneath her chin. "As I mentioned at the meeting last night, a new leader has been chosen. Believe me when I say she's as ruthless as she's beautiful." Jade's mouth fell open in surprise.

The detective turned toward her with a smirk, while her ebony eyes narrowed. "You seem shocked. Why wouldn't the leader be female? Mistress Baines is a powerful and brilliant woman. She's quite capable of leading her people." Jade glanced at Aidan.

"I'm just surprised. It's not that a woman isn't capable. I remember the Hunters' last leader was a monster," Jade said.

"Well, I guess it all depends on your point of view. Mistress Baines was groomed for the position from the time she could walk. In fact, she was the predecessor's 'special project.'"

჻

JADE FLINCHED, RECALLING HIS LECHEROUS GAZE. THE THOUGHT OF HIM mentoring a young girl was incomprehensible.

"We really need to find Marcail." Aidan stood from his chair. "I trust our talk tonight will help aid the investigation, but I need to actively help with the search. I can't just stay here all night while Mrs. Flannery's daughter's missing. I've known the girl since we were children. She's family."

He pushed his fingers through his dark hair. Jade noticed the muscles twitching in his sturdy jaw. Aidan was doing everything in his power to stay in control, but his patience was ebbing.

"I appreciate your offer, Laird MacFie." Detective Glass stood from her chair, fluttering her long lashes toward Aidan. The woman's dark eyes wandered over his muscular body with an appraising air. "I'm sure you could be of service, no doubt."

Jade's hands tightened into fists by her sides. Fiona's shapely hips swayed seductively when she crossed the room. Detective Glass gazed out the window, studying the gas lamps illuminating the sea. With her back to the group, she said, "I do appreciate your dedication to your staff." She turned her head slightly, eyeing Aidan with dark eyes. "Your willingness to involve yourself in our investigation is ill-advised. Your family is well-known in Tobermory. If Mistress Baine discovers you're planning on hunting her down, she could harm the girl to hide the evidence. The Mistress appreciates her captives. Enjoys toying with them before ending their lives. So, it's more than likely she'll keep the girl for a while. Please allow the detectives to do their jobs without interference."

"That's horrible," Jade said, her eyes narrowing. "How do you know what she enjoys doing with her captives? Are there others being held against their will?"

Detective Boyd stood at the accusation. "I assure you; Detective Glass has put her life and reputation on the line infiltrating the Hunters' community. She's not able to discuss the specifics of the case currently. Revealing what she has already done puts her life at risk."

Detective Glass tilted her head toward Boyd, offering him a polite smile before turning back to the window.

Jade walked over to Fiona and stood by her side. "I understand you've shared more than you're probably comfortable with, Detective Glass. We do appreciate it. However, we need to take every opportunity to save Marcail. Every minute she's gone, the girl's safety is at risk. What if you're wrong?"

A small smile flickered, and she turned toward Jade. Detective Glass was nearly a foot taller, and by her expression, she wasn't pleased by the questioning. Despite the detective's directness, Jade refused to back down.

"If I'm wrong, the girl dies. Plain and simple. But I don't think so. I know their leader well. There's a chance I can even have an opportunity to see Marcail tomorrow if she's a prisoner of the Mistress. What else do you want? Perhaps you'd like to have a try yourself, Lady Mackenzie?" Before Jade could answer, the detective crossed her arms over her chest and shook her head. "No, I think not. The last thing we need is an emotional tourist rushing the scene and ruining our sting operation. You should stay home where you belong." Jade glared at the detective with her arms crossed.

"Lady Mackenzie is more than able to hold her own." Sensing her anger, Aidan moved closer. "I've seen it firsthand when we battled the Hunters in the States. She deserves your respect."

Fiona laughed, turning toward Aidan with an insouciant smile. With half closed eyes, she curtsied low. "Laird MacFie, I beg your pardon." She flashed pearly-white teeth in his direction.

"My apologies, sir. I take my job very seriously and don't want anything to ruin our investigation. I respectfully request you both remain at the castle tonight. If we need your help, we'll contact you tomorrow." With that, the two detectives gathered their items and walked toward the door.

"Tonight, we'll do a sweep of the grounds of the castle, inside and out. Of course, the girl could still show up. Teenagers are notorious for drama, but we'll treat this as a missing persons case all the same." While she spoke, Detective Boyd used his cell phone and called in for backup.

Before she left the room, Detective Glass glanced over her shoulder. Jade wanted to punch her when she realized that the detective had sensed her flirtations were not working, tried a different approach.

"Oh, and one more thing. If the Mistress is indeed aware of the girl's hybrid status, then she's likely aware of you, Aidan MacFie. In fact, the Hunters may already be cognizant of your visit to Tobermory. After all, you're responsible for their previous leader's death."

"It's a shame, really." Her brow raised as she studied Aidan. "You might be the one the Mistress really wants. The girl may simply be a pawn in her game."

Aidan's mouth drew down at the corners, her words penetrating with cruel precision. Jade bet the thought of him being responsible for Marcail's disappearance made his stomach clench.

Jade studied Detective Glass, sensing she knew more than she revealed.

"You seem to be an expert concerning Mistress Baine. Have you spent a lot of time with her?" Jade's grey eyes narrowed, awaiting her answer.

"Let's just say she's not someone to take lightly." Detective Glass pushed back a lock of mahogany hair from her forehead, biting the inside of her lip. "The Mistress is ruthless and has no qualms about killing anyone in her path. If the girl's been taken, I'll find out tomorrow evening. She's requested the Hunters gather for a special occasion."

"Isn't there any way to check earlier without arousing suspicion?" Jade moved to the door.

"You've been to their hideout. Couldn't you just take some officers along with you tonight?"

"Afraid not. You see, there are multiple hideouts. It's too risky. We need to bide our time and be patient," Detective Glass said, pursing her ruby lips. "Americans are not fond of patience, I've heard. Sounds like you've watched too many westerns, Lady Mackenzie. You can't just call in the Calvary to save the day." Fiona chuckled and shook her head. "We'll be in touch." Jade narrowed her eyes at the officer.

Detective Glass ignored her and focused her attention on Aidan. "Just teasing."

Detective Boyd turned off his phone. "The officers have arrived and are ready to search the beach. Do you mind giving us a layout of your grounds?"

Aidan nodded his head, glancing out the window. The glass was covered in light mist. "I'll give you a quick rundown, but I'd like to show you a couple areas myself." He turned to Jade and smiled. "Do you mind keeping an eye on everyone inside?"

"Of course."

Before leaving, Aidan leaned close to his girlfriend's ear and whispered, "Donavon and I discovered a mask down by the shore earlier. Didn't want to bring it up in front of Mrs. Flannery. I'll give it to the detectives outside."

Jade's brow raised in response to the news. "Good idea, darling. Please be careful." He kissed her cheek while Detective Glass smirked.

Jade caught her expression and her dislike for the woman grew. She couldn't shake the feeling Fiona knew more than she admitted to. It angered her how she barely acknowledged her while cozying up to Aidan. Once they left, a group of officers came inside to interview the staff members. Jade spent the next couple of hours overseeing the interviews.

It felt like an eternity passed before the police left and Aidan returned from outside. His wavy hair was drenched, along with his sweater and trousers.

"Oh, you're going to get chilled. Let's get you changed and warmed up." Jade said.

Lightning flashed outside the bay windows. Together, they moved toward the stairwell.

"Thank you for taking care of everything inside. We searched the beach but didn't uncover anything unusual. I just hope Marcail's safe tonight."

"Me too. I'm worried about poor Mrs. Flannery. She must be terrified for her daughter."

"Imagine so, lass."

Jade's mouth pinched together. "Did you learn anything else from the detectives?"

Aidan turned toward Jade with his brows raised. "I have the feeling you're not a fan of Detective Glass."

"You're right. I'm not. There's something off about her."

"Interesting."

Jade frowned and placed her arms across her chest. *Detective Glass dismissed me the moment we met. It was infuriating. If we weren't in such need of her intel, I'd like never to see the woman again. It's difficult expressing my feelings without sounding jealous. The entire meeting had been nothing but frustrating.*

Aidan studied Jade's pained expression. "Are you all right? Is your migraine coming back?"

"No, I'm fine." She shook her head and tried her best to smile. "Just worrying about everything that's happened today. Poor Mrs. Flannery must be beside herself."

"I'm sure she's in a terrible state. If you're feeling better, I wondered if I might share something with you. I discovered some interesting diary passages earlier. Thought you might have some ideas about 'em." He grazed his hand on the small of her back and led Jade toward the spiral staircase. Once inside Aidan's bedroom, she shivered and moved toward the fireplace.

A cool draft sneaked beneath the door.

"Let me change into some dry clothes and I'll be right back." While Jade waited, Aidan went to his wardrobe and sorted through the drawers before retrieving a change of clothes.

"Make yourself comfortable, love."

Jade walked toward the curtained window, pushing aside the velvet covering. Flashes of lightning streaked across the inky sky.

A few minutes later, Aidan came out of the bathroom.

"You must be freezing," Jade said.

"A bit. The castle is drafty. Let me add some wood to the fireplace. The diaries are over on the bed if ye want to read through 'em. I bookmarked a couple of passages of note."

Jade slipped off her boots and climbed onto Aidan's four-poster bed. She cuddled up against the satin pillows, reaching for the nearest diary. The light scent of aftershave lingered on the bedding. Breathing in his clean aroma, she glanced toward the hand-written journals with interest. She opened the leather-bond cover of the one closest to her and eyed the yellowed pages.

"Oh, Aidan. These are so old. I can't imagine the history we're about to uncover. I felt the same way when I read my great-grandmother's diary. I could see the great frontier through her eyes."

"Yes. It's fascinating going back in time. I'm eager to hear your thoughts." After preparing the fire, Aidan took a seat next to Jade on the bed. He'd changed into a white t-shirt and a pair of grey shorts. Jade eyed his toned legs while he stretched out on top of the quilts. He moved his arm around her shoulders as she leaned against him.

The warmth of the fireplace was soothing, while the sound of the rain against the windowpanes eased her tired mind. They were both lost inside the pages of the MacFie diaries when a light tapping on the door brought them back to reality.

Aidan slipped on a terry cloth robe before opening the door. His eyes widened when he saw his housekeeper waiting outside with a silver cart.

"Mrs. Flannery, you shouldn't trouble yourself tonight. Ye should be in bed resting."

She shook her head while pushing the tea cart into the bedroom. "Aye, it's better this way. I'll simply go crazy worrying about my daughter, Laird MacFie. I brought some tea for you both. And Lady Mackenzie, I figured I'd bring you a pot of my special blend. Don't want your migraine coming back tonight." Without looking back up, she poured the fragrant brew into a rose-colored porcelain cup.

When she was finished, Jade walked over to the matronly woman and took her hand. It was cold to the touch. She studied her soft blue eyes, which were red rimmed from crying.

"Your tea was a godsend, Mrs. Flannery. My migraine was terrible today. One of the worst ones I've had in a while. Figured I'd be in bed the rest of the day, but your special brew took the pain away."

"I'm glad, child. You just let me know if ye be needing anything else." She lifted a cover off a silver plate. The housekeeper offered a small smile, which didn't reach her eyes. "Here's some fresh cherry tortes to go with your tea. Hope you enjoy it." Jade's heart ached for the poor woman.

"Mrs. Flannery, we're going to be reading my great-grandmother's diaries, seeing if we can piece together information on the Hunters. I'd rather be out with the officers right now, but they seemed to think it might do more harm than good," Aidan said.

"I appreciate all you're doing, Laird MacFie. I imagine the detectives know what's best. Just wish we would get word about Marcail tonight. Don't know how I'll sleep wondering where my daughter is and if she's safe." She wrung her hands together, glancing toward the window. "Well, I best be letting you two do your research. I'll be in my room if ye hear anything."

"Is there anything we can get you, Mrs. Flannery?" Jade asked.

"No dear." She shook her head. "Just please let me know if you hear anything about my daughter. I'm saying my Rosary tonight. I'm putting her in the Lord's hands."

"That's a good idea. I'll say my prayers as well."

"Thank you, dear. You're a kind soul. Could see it the moment we met." She patted Jade's hand and turned to leave.

After she left the bedroom, Jade and Aidan took their tea before sitting down on the edge of the bed.

"Poor woman," Aidan said. "I'm hoping one of these diary passages might provide clues for the whereabouts of Mrs. Flannery's daughter."

"I hope so," Jade said, pressing close to Aidan.

He smiled down, trying to focus. "I spent the entire day reading. Apparently, my great-grandfather hired his own spies to infiltrate the Hunters' organization. He was getting close to finding their meeting house right before the attack on the castle. My great-grandmother, Edina, mentioned the *Great Birthing* at the end of the second diary. According to the passage, the Hunters made sacrifices right before the event."

Jade shook her head. "Wow. It's crazy how history may be repeating itself. Hopefully, if we keep reading, we'll find something to speed up the investigation."

"I agree. At least we're doing something," Aidan said.

For the next hour, the couple quietly studied the various diary passages. After a particularly loud thunder strike, Jade put her hand on Aidan's arm and whispered, "I found something here," she said, pointing to a yellowed journal page.

"The Hunters cover their faces in dried shark skin, hiding their identities behind their masks. Only their eyes are exposed. Jagged teeth appear painted over the mouth covering. The image is both terrifying and deadly. For my people fear the sharks of the ocean as much as the Hunters on land.

If their intention is to instill terror in the hearts of the selkie folk, they've accomplished their aims."

"Yes, that's one of the pages I marked earlier." Aidan bit down on his lower lip. "The driver of the hearse wore one similar. If the Hunters are following us, they could have members watching the castle. Poor Marcail may have been simply down at the beach at the wrong time."

"It does seem to fit the description in the diary." Jade shuddered, recalling the masked driver.

"The driver's mask resembled a shark. And he noticed us."

"I think you're right. They're probably spying. If they've heard of our involvement in their leader's death, we're targets for sure," Aidan said.

"I'm also concerned about Marcail's safety for another reason," Jade said.

"Oh?"

"I didn't want to mention it when Mrs. Flannery was in the room, but remember my strange dream about Marcail?"

"God, if the girl's part selkie, she would be a definite target. I wonder if she turned this afternoon. And if she did, was it her first time? If so, she must be incredibly confused. If there's Hunters keeping an eye on the castle, they very well could have taken her." Aidan shook his head. "I mentioned earlier Donavon, and I discovered a leather mask down by the shore this evening. It's troubling. Makes me believe the Hunters are most likely involved in her disappearance. The poor girl must be terrified. I know the detectives want us to stay away from the investigation, but this is driving me crazy."

"I know." Jade placed her hand over Aidan's clenched fist. "Let's see what else we can find in the diaries. Maybe we can go down to the police station tomorrow and see how their investigation is going."

Aidan sat back against his pillow. He thumbed through the journal, trying to piece together clues. They continued reading until three in the morning. When the pages began to blur together, Jade closed the last diary. Aidan moved his arm around her shoulder.

"I think we've done all we can tonight, darlin'. I re-read the journal from 1870. Edina's great-granddaughter ended her passage with a strange warning. It read, *'Beware of the Hunter in plain sight.'*"

"That's a bit troubling." Jade wrinkled her nose. "I wonder what it means?"

"I imagine she's warning us to keep an eye out for Hunters blending in with the rest of society. Perhaps they're like wolves in sheep's clothing."

Jade shuddered at the thought. "That's seriously creepy."

Sensing her discomfort, Aidan took Jade in his arms and pulled her close to his chest. "I promise to keep you safe, love."

She closed her eyes, listening to Aidan's heartbeat while the logs crackled in the stone hearth. Outside, the storm raged on.

Chapter Eight

Marcail awoke in darkness, her body shivering uncontrollably. She rubbed the knot on the back of her head, trying to make sense of her surroundings. She remembered gazing toward the sea, feeling its familiar pull. Its soothing melody called her forth. Somewhere in the back of her mind, she realized she should be getting ready for work and her movie date with Donavon.

Ignoring the demands of her earthly life, she stripped down to her bra and panties and dove into the frigid water. The sun was setting, casting amber light along the waves. She didn't feel the cold, her only thought was becoming one with the sea. There were other times she'd heard the calling. She'd never fully given into it, always returning to shore before losing control. Yet, this time was different, her need was too great. The yearning is irresistible. Her body tingled from her head to her toes, an electrical current awakening every cell, and then there was the pain. It was alive and hot. Her feet and legs trembled, as if pierced by a thousand knives. When her human skin sloughed off, she opened her mouth to scream, and the salty water filled the void. Her legs fused together, forming the lower half of her selkie body. In her metamorphosis, she realized she was not alone. She'd never truly been alone. A feeling of sublime peace embraced her soul. The faces in the water felt familiar; almost like a memory she couldn't grasp. For the first time in her young life, she was a part of something important. Dozens of selkies raised their faces to the setting sun and their voices rang out in perfect harmony. Marcail rolled on her back, closed her eyes, and drifted with their lullaby.

Floating on the edges of night, her fingers splayed out while moonbeams caressed her face.

She felt a warm breath against her cheek and heard a voice, "It's time to go back, little pearl."

When she opened her eyes, she was on shore. Her seal-body transformed back to its human form, and a deep sense of loss overwhelmed her. Reluctantly, she dressed beneath the inky sky. Trembling, she turned to the castle, realizing she wasn't alone. Slivers of moonlight illuminated strangers in black cloaks. Ebony masks covered their faces. Marcail raced toward the castle, but the group cut her off before she could reach the moss-covered path. One man placed a leather glove over her face. As she struggled, his fingers tightened around her neck, pulling her pearl necklace tight against her slender throat. Blackness followed.

Marcail squinted, trying to make sense of her surroundings. As her eyes adjusted to the dim light, she could make out the bars of her prison door. A scurrying noise came from the right, sending chills down her spine. She listened to the sound of water dripping above her head, landing just inches from her shivering body. While ominous shadows lingered in the corners of the room, a golden sconce flickered above the damp corridor adjacent to her cell. She tried to stand but was prevented by thick chains around her ankles and calves. Her hand slipped down toward the cold manacles, and she wept. After several hours, the cell door opened. A hooded figure moved forward. Marcail blinked up at the kerosene light, trying to see the face of her captor.

The stranger pushed back her hood and scarlet tresses flowed down her black cloak. "Aww, the pup is awake. Very good."

Marcail's mind raced in confusion. *Who was this woman, what did she want, and why did she call me a pup?*

"Who are you? I don't understand." Her voice sounded like a stranger's, desperately in need of water. The woman in black signaled to a guard behind her. The hooded figure was well over six feet tall with broad shoulders. He set down what appeared to be a dog bowl on the floor by her feet.

"Drink, child. You've been through an ordeal."

She looked at the water greedily, desperate to quench her thirst. With trembling hands, she lifted the bowl to her mouth and drank.

"Better?"

Marcail shook her head, tears in her eyes. "Please, I don't understand why I'm here. I've done nothing wrong. If you let me go, I promise not to tell."

When the woman moved closer, candlelight fell over her auburn waves. Despite the situation, Marcail couldn't help but marvel at her face. Her porcelain skin and green eyes appeared flawless, but then she flashed a smile. Marcail pulled back instinctively against the cold wall of her cell. The stranger's teeth were pointed at the ends. Sensing her horror, the woman in black stepped closer and whispered, "Now, now. No need to get in a frenzy. You're our guest. You must stay a little while longer. We have plans for you, young one."

"I don't understand what you want of me. Please let me go."

"All in good time, pup. Did you know you're very special? Was that your first metamorphism?"

The woman in black studied the teenager's face, sensing her confusion. Her emerald eyes glistened in the shadows. She smiled again, this time with her mouth closed, much to Marcail's relief.

"Oh, I see. This was your first time. You must have so many questions, but first, you must eat and rest, and then we can discuss everything."

"No, please let me go home. I want to see momma."

The woman in black knelt on her haunches, tilting her head to her side. "You want to see your momma? Which one?"

Marcail's blue eyes filled with confusion. "What do you mean?"

"Didn't your momma tell you, little one? You belong to two worlds, but we'll talk about that tomorrow."

A second guard came forward and set a bowl by her legs. When he stood back up, his hood fell backward, revealing a black mask with painted teeth. Marcail let out a scream, pushing her back hard against the concrete wall.

"Don't worry, pup. He won't bite if you're good." A third guard moved a tray with stale bread and moldy potatoes by the teenager's bare feet.

"We'll talk in the morning. Pleasant dreams." The scarlet-haired woman motioned for her guards to follow. The teenager listened to the cell door shut, and the bolt clicked into place. Marcail watched the strangers behind the iron bars in disbelief. *Surely, this is a terrible nightmare. It can't be real.*

The woman looked over her shoulder, flashing another toothy smile. "If you promise to behave, you can have a little light for the evening," she said, gesturing to her lantern. "Rats tend to get bold when it's dark and there's food around. There's just enough kerosene to last for about an hour or so. You better hurry up and eat."

The woman moved the light on the floor and pushed it through the bars. Before leaving, the scarlet-haired stranger reached a lantern pole toward the corridor torch and extinguished the flame. Her guards held their own lanterns and escorted their mistress away from the gloomy cell.

Marcail listened to the strangers' footsteps echo down the dark passageway. Once it was quiet, she stretched her right hand toward the light. At first, it seemed she was not going to be able to reach it with her constraints. It took several attempts before she moved the end of the lantern with her fingertips. Once secured in her right hand, she dragged it toward her. The cold metal scraped the ground with an unpleasant ring. Her hand trembled while moving the beacon in an arch, illuminating her surroundings. Twenty-feet high stone walls rose on each side of the cell. A small widow's peak on the opposite side suggested they were near the sea. A high-pitched squeaking made her cringe. When she aimed the lantern in the direction of the noise, several red eyes stared back. Marcail shuddered and recoiled toward the stone wall. The rodents were obviously interested in her supper, but then again, wouldn't the rats target her once the food was gone? The thought made her stomach clench.

She was reluctant to eat but loathed the idea of the rats getting closer. She listened to the scurrying sounds across the floor. Then, the unthinkable happened. The lantern flickered twice before going out altogether. Marcail's heart pounded in her ears. With trembling lips, she hugged her knees against her chest, wrapping herself into a tight ball. The sound of squeaking coincided with the sensation of warm fur against her bare foot. The reverberation of the teenager's screams blended with the storm raging outside the castle walls.

Chapter Nine

JADE AWOKE TO A BEAM OF SUNLIGHT STREAMING ACROSS HER SATIN pillowcase. Strong arms enfolded her. She sighed as Aidan snuggled against her back beneath the covers.

"Good morning, Lady Mackenzie."

"Good morning, Laird MacFie."

She turned and gazed into vivid blue eyes. His dimples deepened when he smiled, and she leaned back against the mattress.

"I guess we fell asleep researching, love."

"Looks that way." Jade sat up in bed, pushing away her golden tresses from her eyes.

"Funny, I've imagined many times waking up to ye, lass. Didn't think you would be fully clothed, however." He chuckled, kissing her on the forehead.

"Being dressed wasn't in my daydreams either," Jade said.

"Oh, so you've imagined, too?"

"Maybe." She blushed while his cerulean-colored eyes glimmered in the morning light. His fingers grazed over her hips, pulling her closer. She let out her breath as she felt his awakened manhood pressing against her body.

A soft tap on the door made them both sit up. Dougal padded over, wagging his tail.

Jade left the bed and moved across the room. Aidan sighed and walked to the door. Mrs. Flannery wheeled in the tea cart.

"Laird MacFie, Lady Mackenzie wasn't in her room...oh, dear," she trailed off, noticing Jade by the window.

"Yes, we were up until the wee hours of the night reading the MacFie diaries."

"Oh my, you two are a blessing to me." Mrs. Flannery's soft blue eyes filled with tears.

"Lady Mackenzie, I went ahead and fed your raven. She was cawing when I checked your room. I had the coffee and your pet's mash on my tray already."

"Oh, thank you! I almost forgot poor Morrigan. We were up so late..."

"No need to explain. You're doing me a kindness trying to get to the bottom of all this."

Jade noticed the dark circles beneath her eyes and frowned. "Did you get any sleep last night, Mrs. Flannery?"

"Not much, I'm afraid. I just want to see my daughter. It was so cold. I wondered if she was warm and dry during the storm?" Her voice cracked and fresh tears welled in her eyes.

"We're going to do everything we can to find Marcail." Jade hurried over to comfort her, putting her arm around the housekeeper's shoulder. "Hopefully, more information will be revealed tonight. Detective Glass is attending a meeting with the Hunters."

"That's right. She may find something useful. Lady Mackenzie and I will check in at the police station after breakfast. We're also planning to visit my uncle later today," Aidan said.

"Thank you. It's a relief knowing everyone's working on the case. I should let you have your coffee in peace. Would you like me to take Dougal down to the kitchen for his breakfast?"

"That would be great, Mrs. Flannery, but please take it easy today. You really don't have to work. Try to get some sleep."

"Thank you, but I need to keep busy." She turned toward the terrier and smiled. "Come on, boy. Let's get you some kibble."

Dougal trotted over, wagging his stubby tail.

Once they'd left, Jade shook her head. "That poor woman. I can't imagine what she's going through. We need to find her daughter, Aidan."

"I know. We will."

Jade poured their coffee, and they took their seats on the sofa by the window.

After the caffeine worked its magic, Jade stood up and stretched. When she looked out the window, she gasped.

Ivory feathers flashed toward the cascading waves.

"Oh, my God! I think that's Morrigan!"

"What do you mean?"

"There's a white raven flying by the beach. How did she get outside?"

"Are you sure it's Morrigan?"

Jade shrugged her shoulders, slipped on her boots, and headed out the door with Aidan close behind. With her heart pounding, she ran back to her bedroom and swung the door open. She felt her stomach tighten at the sight of the empty perch.

"Oh, no!"

Aidan wrapped his arms around her waist and whispered in her ear. "Love, try not to panic. I'm going to go back to my room for my shoes and jacket. You should get your coat. I'll meet you in the hallway and we'll go down to the beach together."

She barely heard his words. "Look, Aidan. The windows ajar. Why is it open?"

"I'm not sure, but we'll find her. I'll be right back. Just wait for me."

"All right." Trying her best to remain calm, Jade grabbed a heavy jacket from the wardrobe.

Once they were outside, Jade ran toward the beach, calling Morrigan's name. Aidan followed, scanning the shore for signs of the lost raven. After several minutes searching in vain, a cawing sounded from a grove of heather plants.

Morrigan left the protection of her hiding place and flew toward Jade's shoulder.

"Oh, thank goodness you came back."

Aidan's brows raised. "There's something in her beak."

"Appears to be jewelry of some sort." The bird dropped the earring in Jade's hand, and she frowned.

"I've seen this before, Aidan. Detective Glass was wearing a pair at your uncle's pub."

"Well, she was combing the beach last night. Maybe she dropped it during her investigation," Aidan said.

"But she wasn't wearing them last night. I noticed because her earrings were so unusual. She had simple gold studs when she stopped by."

"Wow, I didn't even notice."

"I just remember how unusual they were." Jade shrugged. "Lady Roland mentioned the detective's earrings during the meeting. She didn't like them because they reminded her of shark teeth."

"You're right." Aidan grimaced, studying the earring. "It does appear to be a shark's tooth.

An odd choice for a fashion piece. Maybe this has something to do with her undercover work? A way to fit in with the Hunters? It might have fallen out of her purse or coat."

"I guess so. It's odd. Funny that Morrigan found it." Jade scratched the back of her pet's pearly head. "You're a good girl, but you can't be flying outside by yourself. Scared me to death." The raven nuzzled her owner's cheek with her pale beak.

"Maybe we should have a quick breakfast and head into town. I'm hoping Uncle Brodie might have some ideas concerning Marcail's disappearance. If not, we can check into the police station and speak to the detectives," Aidan said.

"Sounds good."

Together, they went back to the castle to shower and change.

After returning to her bedroom, Jade assisted Morrigan to her perch and prepared for the day. Once breakfast was finished, they met their driver in front of the castle. Dark clouds suggested another storm front was on its way. Their first stop of the day was the Seal Cave Tavern. Uncle Brodie was engaged in a deep conversation with Lady Roland behind the bar. They looked up in surprise when they heard footsteps behind them.

"Ah, pleasure to see you again so soon," Lady Roland said. Her vivid blue eyes were a startling contrast against her fair skin. The color appeared unearthly in the soft morning light.

"Good to see you. I'm glad you're here, Lady Roland. We have some upsetting news to share, and we hope you can help us. We brought along my great-grandmother's diaries. I imagine you could have some insight."

Uncle Brodie and Lady Roland exchanged glances. "Let's take a seat at the table." Uncle Brodie led the group toward the bay window in the back of the tavern.

Aidan placed the stack of diaries on the cherrywood table and thumbed through one.

"What's going on, nephew?"

Aidan's mouth pinched together, trying to gather his thoughts. "Mrs. Flannery's daughter went missing last night. She didn't show up for her afternoon shift. She also failed to go to a movie date with our groom's boy, Donavon. She was spotted at dusk near the beach by the castle. During our search last night, we discovered a leather mask close to where she was last seen before her disappearance."

Jade watched Lady Roland's eyes turn ebony.

"This is terrible news." Uncle Brodie shook his head. "Mrs. Flannery must be beside herself."

Jade turned to Aidan before speaking. "Mrs. Flannery confided with us about her daughter. This may come as a shock but…"

"She's part selkie," Lady Roland finished her sentence.

"How did you know?" Aidan asked.

"I knew her biological mother. Her name is Arabel. She was only sixteen when she was abducted by a Hunter. My people were outraged when they heard of her kidnapping. She was abused for years. The man kept the young selkie for his own personal plaything. Apparently, he'd hidden her pelt and held the teenager prisoner within his home. I can only imagine what she must have endured. After giving birth to his daughter, Arabel was desperate to escape. In fear of her life, she gave her child to Mrs. Flannery for safekeeping. I spoke to Marcail's biological mother after she returned to the sea."

"How is that possible?" Jade asked.

Lady Roland pushed a locket of pearl-white hair from her shoulder. "You see, our society can send messages to one another through song. I heard the mother's voice one evening. Being selkie, I enjoy watching the sunset by the shore. This is the time our people are most vocal. Arabel made contact at Kilvickeon Beach. She was desperate to hear of her daughter. It was through Brodie, I was able to find her answers."

"Yes, our families have been friends for many years," Uncle Brodie said. "So, I was happy to bring Lady Roland to the castle to see for herself."

"It was obvious the child is well-loved." Skye Roland smiled. "The Flannerys' are devoted parents. I visited the beach the next day to report the good news. This was the last we spoke, but the update brought her peace."

"Interesting, but may I ask, how did you know to reach out to my uncle?"

"My husband was friends with Brodie MacFie." She turned to Brodie and smiled. "We contacted him, and he reported back to us."

"Uncle, you knew about Marcail's story?" Aidan's brow raised in question. "Why didn't you mention it before?"

"It didn't seem relevant at the time. Also, I promised Lady Roland to keep the secret. The less the Hunters know about selkie folk, the better."

"I'm just sorry to hear of her disappearance. Are you thinking the Hunters are involved?" Lady Roland asked.

"We do. I called the station last night when the girl went missing. Poor Mrs. Flannery is devastated," Aidan said.

"She's a dear woman," Lady Roland said. "I can only imagine her pain."

"Detective Glass and her partner arrived with several officers. We offered to assist in the investigation, but Fiona said our presence could only interfere. So, we decided to see if we might find some information in the diaries. We were up late last night reading them," Aidan said.

"Did you find anything of note, Laird MacFie?"

"Well, my great-grandmother, Edina, mentioned something related to the case. I marked the passage. Let me find it." Aidan turned toward the back of the book. Once he found the page, he read aloud. "The Hunters cover their faces in shark skin, hiding their identities behind the mask. Only their eyes are seen, while pointy teeth cover the mouthpiece. For my people, the image is both terrifying and deadly. We fear the sharks of the ocean as much as the Hunters. So, it seems fitting that they've chosen to represent themselves on land this way."

"She speaks of our natural enemy." Lady Roland's eyes darkened. "Many a selkie has lost their life to sharks. It was our only threat until the Hunters came along."

"Makes sense," Aidan said. "We came across a similar mask the day we visited my uncle's tavern."

"What are you talking about, nephew?"

"After we left the bank, a hearse followed us for a couple of blocks. The driver wore a mask like the one described in the diary."

"I believe you were being followed by a Hunter." Lady Roland folded her hands together. "They've worn these kinds of disguises for centuries.

The image is meant to strike terror in the hearts of my kind. It's just one more of their endless cruelties."

Jade turned toward the selkie. "Yes, I remember you mentioning sharks during our meeting, Lady Roland. We were discussing Detective Glass's earrings."

Her eyes darkened when she recalled the memory. "Yes, it was in very bad taste considering her audience."

"It's strange. We found her earring on the beach this morning. My pet raven, Morrigan, picked it up in her beak. She must have escaped through my window and flew to the shore. When Marcail went missing, Aidan called the police station. Detective Glass and her partner arrived last night. Once they were done interviewing us, they searched the beach. It's odd her earring showed up near the castle. She wasn't wearing them last night," Jade said.

"That is quite odd." Lady Roland's brow creased. "Something about Detective Glass troubles me. I just can't put my finger on it."

"I don't know if this will make sense, but figured I'd add it to our discussion. Edina's granddaughter ended her final diary passage with a warning." Aidan reached for another diary and turned the gold leaf pages of a second diary to the passage he was talking about. "'Beware of the Hunter in plain sight.'"

"Hmm, she may be referring to what happened at the MacFie Castle shortly before her grandmother, Edina, left for America." Uncle Brodie shifted in his seat. "Apparently, there was a spy working for the MacFie clan. I don't know his name, but he was responsible for letting the Hunters infiltrate the castle the night my great-grandfather was murdered. She may have been referring to the fire as well."

"That's a scary thought. Imagine having someone in your home plotting against you," Jade said.

"The Hunters have always found ways of infiltrating into important roles of society," Lady Roland said. "In the eighteenth century, members of the clergy were bribed by the cult to do their dirty work. They've invariably possessed power and money. It's a mystery to when and why they began their vendetta against the selkie folk, but their ties to wealthy families is noteworthy. You never know who might be involved. It's frightening."

Aidan stacked the diaries and placed them back in his satchel.

"Detective Glass mentioned the meeting with the Hunters tonight. I think we should stop by the station to see if there's any news concerning Marcail."

"I guess we can give the detective her earring back." Jade lifted the pointy object from her coat pocket.

Lady Roland recoiled instinctively.

"Aye, it's indeed a shark tooth. Detective Glass understands their significance."

"I can't understand why she was wearing them in the first place," Jade said.

Aidan shrugged his shoulders. "I didn't even notice her earrings until Jade pointed them out."

"Not surprised, lad. I don't think many men would be paying attention, especially with her shapely figure and pretty face."

"Um, hum." Jade's brows raised in question.

"I really didn't notice." Aidan put his hands up in innocence.

Lady Roland considered the young couple with interest.

"There's something about Detective Glass I find troubling. On one hand, she's risking her life spying on the Hunters. Don't get me wrong, I'm grateful for her commitment to the cause, but her reports and observations concerning the cult are always vague. For the past few months, she's refused to give us detailed information concerning their day-to-day operations. The detective keeps us in the dark, only giving us crumbs of truth. My patience is running out." Lady Roland turned toward Uncle Brodie. "Do you agree, Laird MacFie?"

"I do. We've been more than patient with the detective. It's time she opens up about the investigation."

Jade watched the selkie's eyes soften when she regarded Uncle Brodie. She sensed there might be more than a friendship between the two.

"That's the same feeling we had last night." Aidan leaned forward in his chair. "I asked for the Hunters' location. Of course, she refused to divulge it. It's incredibly frustrating. We need to find Marcail. Every minute wasted puts the girl in more danger. Detective Glass suggested Marcail may still show up on her own, but I wasn't satisfied with that explanation and tried my best to get her to reveal the Hunters' hideout. She gave us a flimsy excuse that the group moves around quite a bit. Glass believes showing up at their meeting place would only ruin her investigation. I agreed to wait until morning. Jade and I spent the evening looking through the diaries, trying to find clues which might lead us to the Hunters. We can't wait any longer. I'm planning to press them at the station. If Fiona Glass has information which could lead us to Marcail, she needs to tell us."

"Yes, I agree." Jade said, nodding her head. "We've waited long enough. I had hoped Marcail would show up last night. Sadly, that wasn't the case. And the fact Aidan and Donavon discovered a mysterious mask near the castle really makes me worry that the Hunters are involved. Hopefully, there's news at the police station. I'll make sure to give the detective's earring back when I see her. I'm curious to see her reaction," Jade said, considering the gleaming shark's tooth.

Lady Roland grimaced.

"I'm sorry. Let me put the earring back in my pocket," Jade said.

"Thank you."

"Oh, I should mention one more thing before we go. We came across another passage which caught our attention last night. Edina spoke of the *Great Birthing*. According to the diary, the Hunters made sacrifices right before the event," Aidan said.

Lady Roland folded her hands together and glanced at Uncle Brodie. He smiled, an unspoken understanding between them.

"I think it's time to summon the pod. *The Great Birthing* may be any day now, and the disappearance of Marcail must be addressed. Her biological mother will want to know."

Jade's mouth fell open in surprise. "You can summon the pod?"

"I can, but it's rare for selkies to make themselves public. It would be best to call them in a sheltered area. I'm thinking about stopping by Kilvickeon Beach tonight at sunset."

Jade's eyes widened. "That's the beach I dreamed about. The private one with the white sandy shores?"

"Yes, child. It's secluded and most likely will be the place of the *Great Birthing*. It's a protected area."

"Would it be alright to join you tonight?" Aidan bit down on his lower lip. "I'd love the opportunity to meet the pod."

"It could be arranged. Our people are a private society, but for the most part, can sense good and evil. It's a gift we all share. Which is why it was surprising Marcail's biological mother was lured from the sea by a stranger. She must have ignored her instincts, overwhelmed by her desire for the human. I guess we'll never know. You may also bring Mrs. Flannery. She can be trusted, and I know she's desperate for answers."

"Thank you. I think she'd appreciate it. Also, our groom's boy, Donavon, is genuinely concerned for Marcail's safety. He's been eager to offer his help. I can vouch for him."

"I trust your judgement, Laird MacFie. Just remind the boy our community's secrets must never be shared with anyone outside our tight circle. It's imperative our society remains in hiding."

"Understood," Aidan said. "We'll meet at sunset as discussed."

Uncle Brodie turned toward his nephew. "Sounds good, lad. Give yourself plenty of time. It's nearly an hour and a half drive from the castle and that's in good weather. When you head over tonight, instruct your driver to turn off Craignure toward Fionnphort Road. It's just before Bunessan. There's a signpost to Scoor. You'll drive down a gravely road leading to a parking area. It's directly opposite the Kilvickeon Old Parish Church and Cemetery. Afterward, take a right to turn on the track. It's about a ten-minute hike down to Kilvickeon Beach. Just be careful where you walk. There's plenty of sheep and lots of manure."

Lady Roland turned toward the couple and smiled. "When we meet tonight, you'll want to dress warmly. And be prepared for anything."

"Thank you. We'll be there. I think Jade and I will stop by the police department before we head back home." Aidan looked out the bay window, noticing the darkening skies. "I'll make sure to call if we learn anything. We better get going before the storm hits. Looks like one's on its way."

"Oh, yes," Lady Roland said. Pushing back her curtain of pearl-white tresses from her shoulders, she glanced outside the window. "A storm is most definitely coming. Be prepared for battle, young ones."

"We're in for one hell of a fight," Uncle Brodie agreed.

He walked Aidan and Jade to the door. After saying their goodbyes, the couple braced themselves against the icy wind.

"God, it's freezing." Jade rubbed her arms and shivered.

Aidan moved his arm around her shoulders and hugged her close. Together, they rushed to their car. "Thanks for waiting, Collins. We are going to the police station next, and then home."

The driver smiled. "Very good, Laird MacFie."

Aidan reached for Jade's hand in the back seat. He smiled down at her flushed face. A light mist formed on the windows, blurring their surroundings. The driver switched on the heat and turned right on Erray Road. Once they'd parked, Aidan opened an umbrella to shelter Jade from the rain. They jumped across a puddle on their walk through the half-empty parking lot. A small line had formed in front of the reception desk. Eager to talk to the detectives, the couple waited nervously behind a middle-aged man and his teenage daughter. A few minutes later, a red-headed secretary waved them over. Aidan asked to see Detective Glass and her partner. The receptionist made a call, and then requested them to wait in the lobby. A few minutes later, they were greeted by Detective Malcom Boyd.

"Thanks for stopping by. Why don't ye come back to my office and we can discuss the case?"

He smiled and led the way. Jade considered the detective's polite demeanor and wondered if he enjoyed being partnered with Glass. When they reached the end of the corridor, Boyd held the door open for them.

"Please, take a seat. Would you like something to drink? Coffee or pop?"

"No, thank you," Jade said.

Aidan shook his head. "As you can imagine, we're quite eager to hear if there's been any news about Marcail."

Detective Boyd took his seat across from them, folding his hands on top of his cherrywood desk.

"I'm afraid there hasn't been any news to report. We do have several officers tied to the case. There's been patrol units searching the area, looking for leads. Mrs. Flannery was kind enough to send in a photo of her daughter early this morning with her cell phone. We'll use the image, show it around town. Hopefully, someone's seen her. Sometimes the smallest clue can crack a case wide open. A visual aid is quite helpful."

Jade dropped her hand in her pocket, touching the shark-tooth earring.

"Is Detective Glass in today?"

"Fiona normally arrives around ten, but I haven't seen her this morning. It's odd, since she's punctual and rarely calls in sick. I'm hoping there could be a lead in the case which might have caused her tardiness."

Jade turned to Aidan, locking gazes with him. Did he find it odd the detective had missed her shift that morning? Her instincts suggested something was off, but what exactly, she wasn't sure.

Detective Boyd leaned forward over his desk. "I'm going to make some phone calls and organize another sweep of the area. I'll let you know the minute we hear anything. I can assure you; we're taking this investigation quite seriously. It really hits close to home. I have a baby sister around Marcail's age. It's quite troubling knowing a young woman's missing in our small town. Every minute counts." The detective shook his head and stood from his chair. "I've made this case my top priority. We'll do everything in our power to bring Marcail home."

"I appreciate all of your help. Hopefully, Detective Glass discovers something tonight during her meeting if she hasn't already. We'll be in touch," Aidan said. The men shook hands before the detective ushered them back to the lobby.

Chapter Ten

WHEN JADE AND AIDAN LEFT THE TOBERMORY POLICE STATION, THE STREETS were empty. Hail pounded the cobblestone roads and walkways. Aidan opened his umbrella and guided Jade back to the car.

Once on the road, their driver reduced his speed, windshield wipers slicing through the sheets of rain. Tobermory appeared like a ghost town, empty of cars and pedestrians. The sky darkened, casting eerie shadows. Jade took a deep breath, overwhelmed by a feeling of dread.

It was a relief when they arrived home. Once inside the castle, the staff took Jade and Aidan's coats and suggested they warm themselves by the fire in the great hall.

Not long after, Mrs. Flannery wheeled a serving tray filled with mugs of hot chocolate and cinnamon teacakes. "Good afternoon. How was your visit in town today?"

"It was interesting. We stopped by the Seal Cave Tavern and met with Uncle Brodie and Lady Roland. We discovered selkie folk can be summoned," Aidan said.

Mrs. Flannery's eyes widened. "How is that possible, Laird MacFie?"

"Lady Roland explained how she can call the pod forth. It's uncommon, but possible. And she suggested you may want to join us tonight. We're meeting at sunset down at Kilvickeon Beach. This may come as a bit of a

119

shock, but Marcail's biological mother could be among the pod this evening."

"Oh, my." Mrs. Flannery folded her hands together. "Yes, I'll be there, of course. I pray we can find Marcail soon. I just want to hug my sweet girl."

Dougal trotted over, plopping down in front of the fire. His stubby tail pounded the stone floors while he rolled on his side.

"I'm glad you're coming with us. I'm also going to invite Donavon. I know he's terribly worried about Marcail. So, we can go together. Not much we can do until this evening." Mrs. Flannery walked to the floor to ceiling windows, studying the darkening sky.

"My poor daughter. I hope she's somewhere safe and dry. There's a terrible storm on its way."

DESPITE THE WARM FIRE, A DAMP MOOD BLANKETED JADE'S PEACE OF MIND. She sipped her cocoa, trying to focus on the flames, concentrating on her breathing. She closed her eyes, feeling the room closing in around her. It had been a year since she experienced her first panic attack. Her mother's cancer diagnosis sent Jade into a downward spiral. Jade prayed every night before bed, pleading for a cure, but the disease ravaged her mother in a few short months. At the end, the forty-five-year-old was a husk of a woman, lying in a hospital bed, hooked up to machines and tubes.

Jade held it together the best she could, but when her mother took her final breath, her world came crashing down. She couldn't remember driving home from the hospital, letting herself into her childhood home. In a trance, she sorted through clothes in the walk-in closet, searching for a dress for the burial. When she spotted her mother's favorite winter coat hanging in the closet, the cruel reality pierced her like a knife. Her mom would never wear her coat again. Mother and daughter would never spend another evening at home, watching old movies, snacking on popcorn. Jade's body appeared to fold in on itself, from an unbearable pressure. Her heart thrummed against her ribs, and then a cold sweat, followed by hyperventilation. It seemed to last an eternity before she came back to the real world. By the time the panic attack ended, she was curled into a fetal position inside the closet, tears running down her face.

Jade experienced many moments of anxiety since, but nothing like the day her entire world came crashing down around her. Once again, the sharp edges of panic threatened to surface.

Keep it together. One day, one hour, one minute at a time. She told herself, remembering the words of her grief counselor.

Outside, the wind howled, and the flames flickered in the fireplace.

When they were called to an early dinner, Jade followed Aidan to the great hall. After taking her seat, she stared down at her plate. The sound of cutlery on china lulled her into a meditative state, while poking absently at a chunk of roasted potato. Her stomach clenched as she tried to mentally prepare herself for their trip to the beach. Something appeared terribly wrong, but she could not place it. After the staff cleared their dishes from the table, Donavon approached the couple with hat in hand.

"Sorry if I'm disturbing your meal."

"Not at all, lad. I was just about to give you a call."

"You were?"

"Yes, we are heading over a bit to Kilvickeon Beach and wanted to see if you'd like to join us. We are hoping to find some clues in Marcail's disappearance."

"Yes, I'd like that very much. What are you looking for exactly?" Donavon asked. Aidan glanced at Jade, and she nodded.

"This may come as a surprise, but Marcail's absence could be linked to something paranormal in nature," he said. "I don't want to alarm you, but if you decide to attend, it can change your perspective on reality."

Donavon shook his head, appearing unphased. "Does this happen to relate to selkies by any chance?"

Jade's brow furrowed. "Why do you ask?"

The groom's boy bit down on his lower lip, seeming to wrestle something over in his mind.

"Well, I've been following Tobermory's urban legends since I was a child. Always thought it to be quite fascinating, especially with the connection to MacFie Castle. My ma's a believer, and I've talked to Marcail about selkies on several occasions. She's always been obsessed with the ocean. After we started to get to know each other, I did more research. Figured I might catch her interest by talking about a subject she loved." His face flushed, and he looked down at the floor.

"I'm glad you've taken an interest in the subject, but what if we told you selkies are more than only myths? Would you be willing to see for yourself?" Aidan asked.

The teenager glanced up, his eyes shining with interest. "I'll do anything to find Marcail. Even if it means chasing down mythical creatures." Donavon's brow raised. "'*There are more things in heaven and earth, Horatio, than are dreamt of in your philosophy.*' I guess Shakespeare pretty much summed up my outlook on life."

"My favorite line from Hamlet." Jade smiled. "It's come to mind quite a bit this past year."

"I'm going to ask you to keep anything unusual we see tonight in confidence," said Aidan. "It is of the utmost importance. Lives are at stake, lad. May I have your word?"

"Yes, sir." Donavon's demeanor changed. He stood taller. "You can count on me."

"Very good. Do you mind driving Mrs. Flannery to Kilvickeon Beach tonight? If she's comfortable, she could share some interesting facts about Marcail with you."

"Of course, sir. It would be my pleasure," Donavon said.

"Good, we'll meet you outside shortly." Aidan took Jade's hand and led her to the kitchen. Together, they prepared Morrigan and Dougal's meals. Once the pets were fed, they gathered their heaviest sweaters and coats and made their way to the front parlor.

Mrs. Flannery was bundled up in a wool coat and rain boots. Her salt and pepper hair covered in a lavender-colored scarf. Donavon pulled his jeep behind the Rolls and parked.

Aidan and Donavon offered the women protection beneath their umbrellas before escorting them toward the cars. Jade's eyes teared in the biting wind. Once she was inside, Aidan shook off the umbrella by the roundabout and climbed inside next to her. With a drizzle of rain hitting the windshield, the couple headed toward Kilvickeon Beach.

❦

DONAVON SMILED AT MRS. FLANNERY, MAKING SURE SHE WAS COMFORTABLE before closing her door.

The housekeeper sighed in relief when he turned on the heater. Her arthritis reared its ugly head. She reached for her bottle of ibuprofen inside her purse and washed down the pills with a few sips from a bottle of water. Once they were on the road, she turned to the teenager. He smiled at her, hoping she would be willing to talk about her daughter. A few minutes into the drive, Mrs. Flannery told the story of Marcail's birth mother and her discovery of the selkie folk.

He was quiet while she spoke, trying to take it all in.

"Do ye think I'm crazy, lad? I would not blame you for thinking so."

"I believe you, Mrs. Flannery." He glanced at the housekeeper with brown eyes full of compassion before focusing on the road and the car in front of him once again. "You have always been a trustworthy person and I can't imagine you making this up, especially when Marcail's gone missing. Your daughter is special to me. I promise to do everything in my power to bring her home."

"I appreciate it," Mrs. Flannery said. "Hopefully, tonight, we will get some answers." They studied the road, comfortable with their talk.

༶༄

WHILE MRS. FLANNERY AND DONAVON FOLLOWED CLOSE BEHIND, AIDAN and Jade quietly watched the hazy sky from the back of the Rolls Royce. Over an hour and a half later, trickles of sunlight broke through the cloud barrier, spilling amber ribbons of radiance across the emerald-green hillside. They passed an ancient cemetery along the way. Celtic Crosses stood soberly over rolling meadows. Hundreds of Scottish Blackface sheep grazed in the fields, enjoying their final feeding before the heavens released another storm. Collins waited inside the car while the group made their walk toward Kilvickeon Beach.

Ten minutes later, they crossed the final stretch. Lady Skye Roland stood at the edge of the sea, studying the glassy waves. A protected cove peeked through a curtain of grey mist. Turning toward the garnet sky, Skye held a rosy conch in her long fingers. She nodded to the group as they approached.

"Take one another's hand." She instructed, gesturing to her friends. As they gathered beneath the scarlet sky, the setting sun caressed the selkie's pearly tresses, turning them crimson in the fading light. "Let us begin."

Her lips encircled the conch, and she blew deeply, calling forth the pod. The haunting sound swept across the sea and sky. Several minutes of silence followed, and then the selkies answered the summons.

123

Chapter Eleven

MARCAIL SLEPT LITTLE THE NIGHT BEFORE; TERRIFIED RATS DISCOVERED HER in the night. She pulled at her restraints until her skin became chaffed and bloody. It was a relief when the first light of dawn flickered through the tiny window atop her cell.

Although most of the rodents returned to the shadows, an occasional squeaking broke through the silence. The piercing sound made her veins feel like they were filled with ice water. An overwhelming sense of doom gripped her heart and soul. She had never felt such terror in her sixteen years of life. Yesterday seemed like an eternity.

Was it possible I was agonizing over which dress to wear for my movie date with Donavon? It was so silly now. What I wouldn't give to go back in time. If I had only stayed away from the ocean like my mother warned. I want to be back at the castle, to see my family again. Did my momma know all along? Was she trying to protect me from some unseen danger? We argued plenty the past few months. Now it all seems trivial. I'll apologize to my mother when I see her again. If I ever see her again. The thought made her throat tighten. *And then there was Donavon. Did he think I stood him up on our date? Surely, they must be looking for me now. Why was this happening?*

Marcail tried to push the images of her metamorphosis out of her mind. Part of her believed it to be nothing but a strange dream. Deep down, however, she knew what had taken place. The reality of it threatened to send her into a full-blown panic attack. *Think about it later*, she told herself.

Her mind turned to the strange conversation with her kidnapper with the scarlet hair and pointy teeth. She shuddered, remembering the woman's smile. The thought made her cringe. There was something terrible about her teeth. It reminded her of a dreadful memory barely out of reach. Something she didn't want to think about.

What was her captor implying about another mother? It was all nonsense. She shook her head, trying to understand. Her stomach rumbled, making it difficult to concentrate. Every now and again, floaters would cloud her vision and the room spun. She closed her eyes, trying to focus. Marcail anticipated the door opening any moment and tried to prepare herself. Despite her fear of her kidnappers, she was in terrible need of breakfast. However, the door remained locked as the minutes turned to hours. With uncertainty, she watched the morning light shift through the small window above. Her tongue felt swollen and parched, like a dried-out sponge in her mouth. It seemed like an eternity since she had any water. A sensation of raw panic threatened to close in around her, then an unspeakable idea surfaced, teasing her loose grip with reality.

What if they never came back? Would anyone realize I'm locked away? How long can a person last without food and water? And then there was the problem of the rats. Surely, they were hungry, too. I can only stay awake for so long before exhaustion wins. Then, they will come for me. Yes, they will. Perhaps a bit tentative at first but growing stronger as I weaken. At some point, their hesitation would disappear altogether.

Marcail shook her head, trying to banish the thought from her mind. Her abductors took her for some reason. They must come back. She tried to will the idea into being, but the light continued to shift in the tiny widow's peak above her cell. Eventually, an amber glow filled the opening, and she dozed. It was almost sunset when the sharp rattle from the cell door woke her from a dreamless sleep.

Marcail sat up, heart racing. What she saw was nothing more than a nightmare. Four figures in black cloaks surrounded her. She looked up in horror, noticing leather masks covering their faces. There were openings for the eyes, but the mouths were sewn shut, painted over with jagged white markings. In the back of her mind, she knew what they symbolized. They were shark teeth. In silence, the figures lifted her up by her elbows and released her from her painful restraints.

With a hard poke in the back, they led her forward from the cell. She blinked in confusion, trying to make sense of her surroundings. From the look of the stone walls and floors, she guessed they were inside a castle. She noted the candelabra sconces surrounding the long corridor. She listened to the sound of chanting. It appeared to be coming from above. The deep guttural voices filled her with terror, and she screamed. Overcome with panic, Marcail bit down on the arm of one of her captors and he howled in pain. Another figure lunged forward, gripping her throat in his meaty fingers, and whispered, "Don't fight anymore, creature, or I'll take a blade to your pretty face."

Marcail stopped struggling, realizing she lost her one chance of escape. Instead, she tried to focus on the dark room, hoping to be able to describe her surroundings if she made it out alive. The idea seemed unlikely, but she needed to hold on to hope. With her hands pinned painfully behind her back, they led her up a spiraling staircase. With each step upward, the chanting became louder and more distinct. It was a familiar sound.

The images of holy candles filled her mind. By the entrance of the cathedral was a marble statue of the Virgin Mary. Her lovely face reminded her of hope and compassion. In her daydream, she gazed into the eyes of the family's priest while he prayed over the Communion banquet, offering up prayers in Latin.

The image in her mind faded, and she realized these words in Latin were not meant for her ears. Her captors were not celebrating hope and forgiveness.

Something quite the opposite was about to take place.

Once they reached the top floor, her guards moved Marcail to the front of a large gathering of more cloaked figures. Barely able to stand, a blanket of grey light swam across her vision. The metamorphosis took a toll on her body, along with her lack of water and food. She was barely aware of the men pushing her down on her hands and knees before the assembly. The masked figures continued their chanting, apparently unaware of the exhausted teenager. While she tried her best to keep her eyes open, the strangers gathered around a large cauldron billowing with smoke. Wax dripped from numerous candles encircling its base.

The assembly ceased their chanting when they noticed Mistress Baines entering the space.

They bowed low to the ground. By her side was a tall woman with an hour-glass figure. Detective Glass slipped her hood away from her face. Standing before the congregation, the women embraced. A moment later, the detective lowered herself to the ground and smiled up into Baine's adoring eyes. A solitary figure moved from the crowd and presented the scarlet-haired leader with a crown covered with sharks' teeth.

Marcail grimaced at the sight. She instinctively recoiled but was stopped by the guard behind her. She watched the leader set the crown on top of the detective's dark hair.

"Today, you receive the official title of my First in Command. If anyone has any quarrel with this, come forward or forever hold thy tongue." The room's silence was her answer.

The Mistress nodded.

"Very good. Bring the pup to me," she said, fixing her emerald eyes on Marcail.

The teenager's heart raced, while she was dragged forward.

"To her knees," she addressed her bodyguards. Once they forced the girl down, the leader stood over her. "Creature, you will be useful in today's ceremony. Being a half-breed, you have the power to move between two worlds, human and selkie. Although your very existence is an abomination in the eyes of the Lord, you do have your uses. Today, your blood will help reveal the *Great Birthing's* location." Baines turned to Detective Glass and smiled. "Let your initial duty as my First in Command be the drawing of her blood. Show us your hand, young one."

Detective Glass rose from the ground and made her way toward Marcail. She pressed her manicured nails down onto the girl's shoulders and smiled. "Better do as she commands. Our Mistress will not ask twice."

Marcail looked up into her ebony eyes. There was not a hint of softness in their depths.

"Please, I just want to go home. I promise not to tell."

"I won't ask again. Show me your hand."

Marcail shook her head, not understanding.

Fiona closed her fingers around her wrist and turned Marcail's right palm toward the ceiling.

Baines moved forward and smiled. From behind her back, she lifted a ruby encrusted dagger and raised it over the girl's trembling fingers. Flickers of candlelight reflected off the jeweled surface, painting the floor.

Seeing the polished edge of the steely blade, the teenager screamed and tried to escape the detective's vice-like grip. Before she could back away, the scarlet-haired woman dragged the blade across her palm in one sharp motion.

The pain was hot and alive. Bile rose in her throat and grey blanketed her vision. While the blood flowed from the wound, the leader collected it inside a golden cup.

After noticing Marcail had slipped into unconsciousness, the detective faced the Mistress in reverence. Baines turned to her audience, raising the golden chalice in the air. "Let us pray."

The chanting resumed while the Mistress poured the warm blood into the cauldron. Blue light formed from the heady liquid. Soon, the image of a cave emerged from the smoke.

Baines smiled in surprise. "The *Great Birthing* takes place today. We must hurry."

By the time Marcail awoke, the Hunters were well on their way to Kilvickeon Beach. The teenager struggled against her restraints, trying to sit up in the back of an unfamiliar vehicle.

Chapter Twelve

AIDAN AND DONAVON ASSISTED MRS. FLANNERY DOWN TOWARD THE SANDY shore. Jade followed close behind. The crisp wind stung their eyes, but the rain held off, which was helpful.

Uncle Brodie stood by Lady Skye Roland and her twin boys. Once the group arrived, the selkie lifted the rosy conch to her lips and blew. Amber and crimson light washed over the churning sea.

For a moment, there was nothing but the sound of the water pounding against jagged rocks. Then a song emanated from the crashing waves. Jade recognized the familiar melody from her dreams.

Hundreds of grey seals surfaced from the sea. As they moved toward the shore, the metamorphosis began. Jade watched in awe while their seal skins sloughed off, revealing human faces beneath. Their bottom halves remained intact, flippers and tail. She expected a full transformation.

When Lady Roland ceased blowing into the conch, Aidan turned toward the matriarch in confusion. "Why are their bodies only partially transforming?"

Her startling blue eyes glimmered beneath the setting sun. "Aye, it's a good question. The pod must take precautions when gathering on land. A partial metamorphosis allows them the opportunity to return to the water quickly if danger arises."

"Makes sense," Aidan said.

Their seal faces rolled back down their slippery backs like bathrobe hoods. Jade watched in shock. From a distance, they appeared to be wearing costumes.

A large bull led the pod to the edge of the shore. With powerful arms, he pulled his massive form onto the dunes.

"Why have you called us to shore, Lady Skye Roland? I know you well enough. You wouldn't sound the conch unless there was a dire emergency."

Lady Roland bowed low to the pod leader. "Forgive me, Laird Brummel, for this unexpected meeting. We have much to discuss this evening. Our people are in great danger."

The leader's blue eyes turned a startling shade of ebony and his jaw tightened. "You have my full attention, Lady Roland."

"Thank you, my laird. Before I begin, I would like to introduce the humans in my company. To my left, Laird Aidan MacFie, Brodie MacFie, Lady Mackenzie, Mrs. Flannery, and Donavon Dunsmore, and of course, my sons. I vouch for their good standing." A middle-aged selkie approached the pod's leader's right side.

She absently pushed the pearly locks from her pale face while studying the group on shore.

"I know you, human," she said, swimming closer. "You helped save my daughter many years ago. I will forever be in your debt. How is my darling Marcail?"

Mrs. Flannery's eyes filled with tears, and she stepped closer to the waves. "We came today for your help. Marcail went missing last night. We believe she was taken by the Hunters. I am desperately trying to find her."

The selkie's soft blue eyes turned jet black. The mother tore at her hair and rolled her head back, keening toward the garnet sky. The females in the pod answered in turn, crying out their lament. Jade put her hands to her ears, trying to block out the sound. It was a combination of despair and loss, something which would haunt her for the rest of her life. An eternity seemed to pass before the pod grew silent.

Lady Roland took Jade's hand and guided her to the shore. "I'm afraid there's more. Our friend, Lady Mackenzie, is a gifted seer. She has dreamed of the *Great Birthing*, but sadly, it was one of blood and bone."

Another cry rose from the tides.

Their leader raised his arms toward the pod, and there was silence once again. He turned his attention to Jade, his vivid blue eyes seemed to read her soul. His voice was both commanding and gentle as he spoke. "Lady Mackenzie, will you tell us of your vision?"

She looked toward the pod. While Jade described her dream of the *Great Birthing,* cries of agony swept through the crowd of female selkies, while some headed toward the beach.

Jade turned to Lady Roland. "I'm so sorry. I don't want to cause your people sorrow and pain."

"It's not your fault." The selkie's blue eyes turned ebony. "They must be aware of the danger.

And it appears we did not have a minute to spare regarding the news. Their time is upon us."

As she said this, several pregnant selkies swam toward the shore. Their long tresses floated on the waves. Once they made it to the sand, they moved across the land, heading toward the protection of the cove. Scarlet rays settled upon their swollen bodies writhing beneath the setting sun.

Laird Brummel's face turned stony cold.

"I am prepared to do battle." He looked toward the sky, rising his trident into the misty air, a silver glint against the crimson light.

Aidan turned to Uncle Brodie and Lady Roland. "We will help you to defend your family."

"It is appreciated, Laird MacFie. And make no mistake, they are your family, too. The MacFie Clan have been part of our community for over three centuries. Your great-grandfather gave his life protecting Edina. Our blood flows through you. We are bound together by blood and sea," the leader said. "I will keep vigil from the ocean for now. The female's place is with the mothers' to be. This is our tradition, and it remains so."

Jade and Aidan held hands while they watched Laird Brummel's wives swim forward. Their time was upon them.

Chapter Thirteen

DETECTIVE MALCOLM BOYD LEFT THE POLICE STATION WITH A HEAVY HEART. Working closely with his partner over the past year created turmoil in his life. During their time together, he'd developed romantic feelings for the pretty agent. A gnawing sensation arose whenever Detective Glass mentioned her undercover work. Fiona was secretive about her mission, insisting he stay away for his own protection. The detective kept his promise until the morning she failed to show up for work. After leaving multiple messages on Fiona's cell, Malcolm decided to stop by one of the Hunters' hideouts.

There were four separate meeting places for the bizarre cult, but the most popular was a dilapidated castle on the outskirts of town. The owners of the estate failed to keep the property in good standing, eventually abandoning it altogether. While rumors swirled around possible Hunter sightings, the local townspeople kept their distance. The building was left to rot for fifty years, a forgotten estate on the outskirts of town.

Malcolm parked outside the gates, making sure his car was hidden within the overgrown landscape. A rotting chain-link fence separated the property from the private road. In the cover of darkness, he hoisted himself over the rusty steel bars. Once he reached the top, he gingerly lowered himself over the pointed metal spikes, holding his breath while he cleared the jagged edges and dropped to the ground. The detective moved toward the back of the estate, hiding behind a thicket of European Aspens. In the stillness of the evening, Malcolm listened to the sound of chanting. The corners of his mouth lifted in relief. He'd picked the correct meeting house for the evening. Hopefully, he'd be able to find out whether Marcail was being held inside. Before he could decide his next move, the sound of footsteps echoed across the sidewalk leading to the abandoned garden.

He squinted in the darkness, holding his breath when Detective Glass appeared beneath the full moon, along with a mysterious scarlet-haired woman. In confusion, Malcolm followed the pair, making sure to stay within the cover of darkness. The melody of Fiona's soft laughter made his heart ache. In the protection of a grove, he watched the women disappear into the shadows. The sound of nightingales echoed from the branches above. Believing they were alone, the lovers embraced beneath the silvery moonlight.

Malcolm's mind raced with confusion. *Was the detective playing a part, trying to infiltrate the leader of the Hunters? Or did she really have feelings for the scarlet-haired woman?*

To his horror, his question was answered. Detective Glass gazed into her mistress's eyes.

"It will be a pleasure to finally be able to start our lives together, my love. I can't wait to shut the door on my life as a detective. All this time forced to work with those horrid selkie lovers. I've barely been able to stomach being in the same room with them."

The Mistress leaned close, taking the detective's hands in her own. "And to be so close to Lady Skye Roland and not be able to put her in her place. I don't know how you withstood being undercover so long, darling. If it were me, I'd have burned their building to the ground the first night with them."

"After tonight, we can leave this forsaken village behind us," responded Fiona. "Once the selkies and their friends are put to death, we can start our lives anew."

Malcom watched the women embrace, their whispers turning to passionate kisses.

He closed his eyes, realizing his partner was not pretending to be a Hunter. She was one. *Had she known when she took the job her life would turn out this way? Did she simply fall in love with the wrong person? Or was she involved with the Hunters from the beginning?* Either way, he was crushed. *How could she have fooled me? I allowed my heart to get in the way of my work.*

It was something I promised myself never to do.

Detective Boyd shook his head. He strained to hear their conversation despite his racing thoughts. Every word felt like a dagger in his heart.

"The guards will bring out the girl and secure her in the car, but we need to leave now. The *Great Birthing* takes place tonight." The Mistress stood from the stone bench. "Let us prepare for the *Final Reaping*, my love."

Detective Boyd moved away from his hiding place, making sure to stay close to the shadows. With a heavy heart, he observed the leader's henchmen lead a blindfolded young woman outside. Once they secured her, the group took separate cars. He watched their lights disappear down the road before racing toward the gate. After he scaled the fence, Malcolm ran to his car. Tailing the group from a safe distance, he called for backup, noticing their headlights disappear down the dark road.

Chapter Fourteen

JADE WATCHED THE SCENE UNFOLD BEFORE HER UNBELIEVING EYES. DOZENS of selkie women pulled themselves to shore, their swollen bellies dragging over the damp sand. The sunset bathed the travelers in crimson light. They headed toward the cave in silence. While the women watched the progression, the men gathered around Aidan to discuss their next move. After a few minutes, the group separated, heading to different corners of the beach.

Aidan walked toward Jade, wrapping her in his arms before kissing her forehead.

She looked up into his aqua-marine eyes in question.

"Darlin', the men are planning to spread out. We will be guarding the area, searching for Hunters. I promise to keep you safe."

"Thank you." Jade bit her lower lip. "I know you will. I have the strangest feeling about tonight."

"What do you mean?" Aidan asked.

Jade's brow raised. "I was alone in my dream about the *Great Birthing*. This is not how I envisioned it at all. I'm not sure how this will play out."

Aidan took her hand. "That's probably a good thing, considering how your dream ended."

The couple turned, noticing Mrs. Flannery and Lady Roland

approaching. Marcail's biological mother, Arabel, who was addressing the group.

"We would be honored if the female humans would join us inside the cave. You may follow." Jade noticed the selkie's startling resemblance to Marcail. Their soft blue-eyes and pixie faces were nearly identical. She was strangely youthful in appearance, considering her age. If not for the pearly tresses, mother and daughter could pass for sisters.

Lady Roland smiled. "It's a great honor, Arabel." She turned to Jade and Mrs. Flannery. "Ladies, would you like to be part of today's birthing ceremony? It's a communal event. The pregnant mothers will need all the help they can get tonight." Mrs. Flannery smiled, glancing at Jade.

"We would be honored," Jade said.

"I would love to help," Mrs. Flannery added.

Aidan kissed Jade on the cheek. "I'll be nearby if you need anything, darlin'."

"Please, be careful." Jade said.

"Always, love." He squeezed her hand before turning to walk away.

As she watched Aidan join the other men, she whispered a silent prayer for his safety.

Lady Roland took Mrs. Flannery and Jade's hands in hers, her startling blue eyes glowing with purpose. "What you are about to witness is a secret ceremony known only to the selkie race. Our communal ties bond us to one another for life. Remember this as you go forward. What happens to one, happens to all."

She released their hands and placed a canvas bag on the sand.

Jade blinked in the dimming light.

"I brought three candelabras to help light our way," said Lady Roland. "You may each take one. There's bottles of water and clean towels and blankets for the expectant mothers."

"Good idea," Mrs. Flannery said.

Jade's eyes widened in surprise. "Lady Roland, how did you know it was going to be time for the *Great Birthing*?"

"Aye, it is an excellent question, child. My people are perpetually connected to one another. Even if a selkie leaves her pod, the family bond is never truly severed. I felt a change coming from the tides this afternoon. It was a distant call I couldn't ignore. We are eternally linked."

Mrs. Flannery glanced at Jade in wonder. They sensed tonight was going to be a life-changing experience. The women turned and followed the pod of selkies galumphing toward the cave. Once they reached the entrance, the three women lit their candles. Within the darkness, a sense of eternal sisterhood embraced the newcomers. For Jade, she imagined entering an ancient womb. Stepping inside, they held up their candelabras to illuminate the darkness.

Mrs. Flannery took her light to the far end of the cave and sat it down on top of a raised area against the wall. Lady Roland and Jade followed suit, setting their candelabras at opposite ends, creating a triangle of light. Outside, the sun set, darkness shrouded the entrance.

Cries of pain echoed in the dampness. The pregnant selkies lay on their sides, flapping their tails as contractions wracked their swollen bodies.

"How can we help?" Jade asked, feeling useless.

Lady Roland smiled and touched her arm. "Many of these selkies are first time mothers. They're afraid and uncertain."

Jade watched while several grey-haired selkies assisted the younger members of the pod.

"Our matrons are helping their children and grandchildren. If you notice someone alone, you may offer your support." The selkie reached inside her tote, retrieving a stack of towels and blankets. She handed them to the women. "You may dry off the bairns once the birthing is complete."

When their keening became louder and more urgent, the selkies assisting began to sing. By the time darkness settled in, the cave was filled with over a hundred pregnant pod members. Jade noticed a red-haired youth by herself in the corner. While Lady Roland and Mrs. Flannery chose the individuals they intended to help, Jade made her way toward the lone female. She kneeled next to her and smiled. The wide-eyed mother-to-be glanced up in confusion and pain.

"I'm Jade Mackenzie. What's your name?"

The young selkie shuddered, biting down on her lower lip as her contractions wracked her petite frame. Once the pain subsided, she pushed herself up with her arms and leaned back against the wall of the cave.

"My name is Caitriona." Her soft blue eyes swam with tears.

"That's a lovely name." Jade studied her with curiosity. She wore no covering over her firm breasts and seemed unbothered by her state of undress. Her seal-like lower half rippled with contractions. Although she had witnessed Aidan transform into a selkie while she was drowning, the memory was vague considering her brush with death. Trying not to stare, she noted the selkie's grey pelt was covered in a light covering of fur. Her human-like waist blended seamlessly with her lower half. It appeared as if she was wearing a hood, but the upper body and head of a seal hung down her back which formed the top half of her pelt. A dozen questions filled her mind. The image was both beautiful and other-worldly.

Caitriona shuddered with a low moan, clawing, and gritting her teeth against the pain.

When the contraction passed, Jade gently touched the back of her hand and smiled. "May I help you? I've never delivered a baby before, but I'd like to offer my assistance if you're comfortable."

"Yes, please," she said. "It's kind of you."

"Do you have family here?" Jade asked, searching the cave for her mother or grandmother.

Caitriona shook her head, her blue eyes filling with tears.

"No, my parents were killed by a school of sharks. It is only myself and my king, and of course, my sister wives. Laird Brummel took me as his wife after my parents' passing." Caitriona rubbed her swollen belly, indicating their relationship.

"I'm so sorry for your loss. My parents passed, too. My mother just last year."

"You know the pain; I see it in your eyes, Lady Mackenzie." Caitriona squeezed her hand.

"Thank you for sitting with me. This is my first pup. I really don't know what to expect."

Jade's brow raised in surprise. She smiled, trying to hide her astonishment at hearing the young mother refer to her baby as a pup. Everything was so new and surprising regarding the selkie lifestyle. Jade wanted to learn everything she could about their traditions. She hoped their discussion might distract the young-mother-to-be from the pain of labor.

"That is exciting. I can't imagine giving birth at such a young age. May I ask how old you are?"

"I'll be seventeen next month. I was married last year, along with several other young wives. The ceremony was beautiful. There's always a grand wedding for the younger members of the pod before *The Great Birthing*."

Jade's eyes widened. "So, you know when there will be a Great Birthing?"

"Yes, every sixteen years. Not that we don't have pups between times. It is just the largest cycles that take place in sixteen-year intervals. The younger wives become pregnant at the same time. That way, we're able to help each other with the newborns." Jade bit down on her lower lip. "May I ask you a personal question?"

"I suppose so," Caitriona said.

"I noticed a few young male children in the waters, but no men other than Laird Brummel.

Are all the females betrothed to one man in your pod?"

"Why, yes of course. It's our tradition. We're his wives."

"Do you have a choice in the matter?"

"Haven't really considered anything else. Once a bull turns sixteen, he leaves the community to start his own pod. There are some who stay bachelors for life, and there are those who enjoy the company of other males. It just depends. Of course, there are rare occasions when a bull chooses a mate from his pod before leaving, but this happens only if given permission. The selkie must present their case before the laird in charge."

"What if they are not granted permission?" Jade asked.

"Well, it really depends. There are times when a younger pod member challenges the laird, but it is not common. Then again, females and males have fallen in love with humans in the past."

"Yes, I know. My boyfriend's a hybrid. His great-grandmother was selkie and his great-grandfather was human."

"Laird MacFie is your betrothed?"

"Well, not exactly. We're not engaged."

She stared blankly, not comprehending.

"In our community, we often have a courtship before getting married," Jade said.

"Oh? That does sound interesting. I've never heard of the tradition before."

"Yes, I guess it would seem different." The teenager bent forward, grimacing.

"You poor thing," Jade said. "Are the contractions getting stronger?"

"Yes."

"It appears they're about five minutes apart. For human females, it would mean your time is getting close," Jade said.

She frowned, squeezing her hand. "It feels like something is about to happen."

Caitriona's cries were joined by several others in the cave. When the pregnant selkies moaned, their helpers answered by singing. Soon, the entire cave filled with song.

"Our time is near," Caitriona said, managing to sit up. Jade rubbed her back and then wiped her brow with a cool cloth soaked in bottled water.

"Our time?" Jade asked.

"Yes, the births will take place simultaneously," Caitriona said.

"Really?" Jade watched as the young mother grimaced and another contraction gripped her petite frame.

"It hurts so bad. I don't know if I can do this," she whimpered.

"You can," Jade said. Her thoughts raced, trying to remember something she'd read in the yellowed pages of her great-grandmother's diary. Cathy Mackenzie was a natural healer. She assisted in a birth which took place along the Oregon Trail. Jade tried to concentrate, focusing on words from so long ago. Her ancestor had forged the way. Jade opened a bottle of water and offered it to the young woman.

"Take a sip. It's important you keep hydrated." Caitriona's hands shook while she held the water bottle, gulping greedily with her eyes closed.

Jade studied the teenager, trying to decide what to do. In the diary, her great-grandmother suggested her pregnant friend sit upright during the birth. It made it easier for the mother to deliver. She studied the selkie's body. Her anatomy prevented the position, considering Caitriona's seal-like abdomen and tail.

Just as she was trying to figure out the best possible birthing position, the girl flopped onto her stomach. With her fingernails digging into the sand, she screamed into the night. Her pod mates groaned in unison. Before long, their keening was answered by the song of their birth coaches. They soothed the expectant mothers with their soft lullaby. The older members sang in a foreign tongue. Jade held her breath, listening to the unearthly melody. Although their words were unfamiliar, the harmonious chorus soothed her soul. It was both sad and sweet, a story told over many generations, celebrating the power of the female spirit.

Before she realized it, Jade added her own voice to the mix. Caitriona closed her eyes, enjoying a moment of peace and clarity.

The young mother-to-be was quiet for nearly three minutes before her next contraction.

When it hit, she struck the ground with her tail and moaned. Tears streamed over her pale face.

Seeing she was struggling, Jade continued to sing to Caitriona. Her sweet voice blended with the pod's communal psyche, losing herself within space and time.

Jade watched the pregnant selkies stretching themselves out onto the sandy floor and sensed their time was near. She continued to sing, feeling the power of their matriarchal bond. Jade placed towels toward the back of Caitriona's tail. Astonished, she watched a pair of flippers emerge. Three pushes later and the seal kit was dropped into her outstretched arms.

Jade instinctively reached for the newborn, laying a soft beach towel beneath its warm body, but she hesitated when she realized the cord was still attached. An older selkie knelt by Jade's side, wrapping her long fingers around the cord and bit down, detaching the baby from the young mother's body.

Once mother and child separated, Jade cleaned the infant off with towels and gently handed the baby to her overjoyed mother.

"Oh, she's beautiful," Caitriona said.

Jade grinned, watching the pair closely. Once the child was dry, she noticed a layer of silky white fur covering the baby. There was no trace of humanity. The infant resembled a newborn grey seal.

The older selkie, who assisted with the umbilical cord, smiled. "You look astonished, Lady Mackenzie."

"I guess I expected there would be more human characteristics. It's amazing."

"Don't worry. The infant will develop them in time. Her white fur turns grey in a few weeks. Once the pup turns one, her human face will have fully formed beneath the seal skin. By three, there are traces of human flesh attached to the blubber. You see, we are seals in the ocean. Only human when we shed our pelts onshore.

"But why are you both seal and human on land? I noticed your human face and chest, but the rest of your body resembles a seal."

"The birthing process demands us to embrace our duality. When we leave today, the pod will change back fully to their seal forms."

Jade was astounded. She imagined selkies were more like mermaids in the sea, embracing their human and seal selves equally. She turned in wonder, watching the pup suckle her mother's breast.

The matron selkie reached into her seaweed-knitted sack and pulled out a strand of pearls.

"Congratulations, it's a girl."

The cave filled with song once again. This time, it was one of celebration.

Chapter Fifteen

THE MEN KEPT WATCH OUTSIDE THE CAVE. LAIRD BRUMMEL REMAINED NEAR the shore, holding his trident in his large hands. Aidan walked over to him and bowed. He had so many questions but didn't know where to start. The leader smiled kindly, sensing his hesitation.

"Laird MacFie, your family has been held in high esteem in our community for centuries. I'm happy to finally meet you. I just wish it were under better circumstances."

"Thank you. It is an honor to meet you, Laird Brummel. Truthfully, I was not aware there were others like me until a few weeks ago. If the Hunters had not kidnapped me in Pacific Grove, I may have never learned the truth."

"Yes, news travels fast. We celebrated the death of their leader. He was a vicious man, responsible for many deaths. Without your help, he would no doubt be causing great harm to our community."

"Thank you. Police officers attempted to capture him after he was shot by my friend, Deputy Rheinstein, but it was a pod of seals which finished him off."

Laird Brummel's vivid blue eyes widened. "Seals, you say?"

"Yes, there were dozens of 'em. They were different species, but the creatures emerged on land like one great pod. They crushed him when he tried to flee from the police. Left nothing but broken bones and pieces of his flesh on the sand."

"Our people are obviously connected to seals. We share many of the same qualities, including bloodlines. Therefore, we can transform completely. Being you are a hybrid, your body will never fully turn."

"I've wondered about this for some time," Aidan said. "I have been able to turn while swimming in the ocean. I'm normally in control, but a few weeks ago, the Hunters forced my transformation by luring my girlfriend out to sea. When I realized she was drowning, my body metamorphosed?"

"Yes, it's different with hybrids. In some way, you're quite lucky, having the best of both worlds. You can stay on land without the threat of humans stealing your pelt," Laird Brummel said.

"Yes, all evidence of my selkie self dissolves after the change," Aidan said. He studied the pod leader with curiosity. "May I ask you a personal question?"

Laird Brummel smiled, sensing what the question might be. "You may ask."

"Isn't it difficult caring for so many lasses at once? You must have over a hundred wives? How do you divide your attention between them?"

Laird Brummel chuckled. "I might ask you the same. How do you manage having only one mate?"

Surprise filled him. "Well, Lady Mackenzie is everything I need in a woman. I don't desire anyone else. She'd have my head if I even suggested it."

Laird Brummel smiled. "Yes, human females tend to be possessive of their mates."

Lady Roland appeared at the shore, bowing before the men. "Laird Brummel, your wives have delivered the next generation."

Without another word, the pod leader left the protection of the sea and began galumphing toward the cave. Once inside, he beamed at his wives. The new mothers held their suckling pups to their breasts.

"My lasses have done well," he said, smiling proudly.

Aidan noticed Jade in the corner, assisting a young mother. She pushed a locket of scarlet tresses out of Caitriona's eyes as she tended to her newborn. During that moment, he imagined Jade holding their own child. Human in appearance, but possibly carrying the hybrid gene.

Would she be willing to take the chance one day? he wondered.

The group enjoyed their final moments of joy and celebration before chaos ensued. Seconds later, Uncle Brodie rushed inside the cave, his face red and perspiring.

"There's a group heading our way. They're wearing black capes and carrying torches."

Laird Brummel bellowed in rage, his body trembling from head to toe. After several painful minutes, his seal-like lower half transformed. He pulled himself upright on his newly formed legs and faced the group. Jade's brow raised at the sight of his well-endowed form. *No wonder he was able to keep his women satisfied*, she thought, trying her best not to stare. The pod leader rushed toward the cave entrance, and his new friends followed.

Chapter Sixteen

DETECTIVE FIONA GLASS SAT IN THE PASSENGER SIDE OF THE BLACK HEARSE. Marcail was out cold inside the carriage compartment. She figured the lack of food and shock of their ritual was too much for the exhausted young woman. It was just as well. The last thing she needed right now was a hysterical teenager and her annoying cries for help.

Fiona turned and smiled at her mistress, admiring her attractive profile. Her skin was alabaster, perfectly formed like a Victorian doll. She loved kissing her cool face, feeling soft lips on her own. Her lover tasted like peaches on a warm summer evening. She did not intend to fall in love with the scarlet-haired beauty. Her job was to infiltrate the Hunters and put several high-profile arrests under her belt. The ancient cult had been an elusive mystery, becoming more of folklore than reality.

She knew officers in her department who made it their life's work to take down the organization. Of course, rumors have been circulating around Hunters working in the Scotland police department for years. The syndicate had money to grease many hands, and sometimes it was too much temptation for the average deputy. A few officers disappeared after becoming involved with the wealthy members. They were relocated, never to be seen again. That was what she understood anyway.

The Hunters' leader was beautiful and powerful, two things which attracted her from the start, but it was more than her physical appearance which captivated her heart. Her spirit and strength made her fall in love with her soul. Her mistress risked everything for the cause, suffering greatly under the hands of their previous ruler. She endured and worked hard until she rose to the top of their secret community.

Fiona understood what it was like to struggle in a male-dominated culture. Many of her colleagues focused on her figure before ever realizing her skills as a detective. Even her partner, Malcolm Boyd, ended up falling for her in the end. She saw his feelings as weakness, and soon used them to her advantage. It was easy keeping her partner in the dark concerning her undercover work. Fiona would begrudgingly provide only the smallest crumbs when it came to her investigation.

By doing so, she was able to keep the detective at bay and aid her people. Being accepted into the Hunters' family filled a void in her life. It was unexpected, but her mission brought her meaning and love. Once the *Great Reaping* was over, she looked forward to lying in her mistress's arms. Tonight would be a sweet release from an unpleasant chore, but when it was over, they could finally be at peace.

Chapter Seventeen

WHILE AIDAN AND LAIRD BRUMMEL SPENT TIME WITH THE MOTHERS AND their newborn pups, the Hunters crossed the trail leading to Kilvickeon Beach. Once the hearse stopped, Fiona dragged the sleeping teenager from the back of the vehicle. Marcail blinked in the darkness, disoriented from lack of food and water. The Mistress came around the side, placing a rope around the young woman's neck. Too exhausted to resist, Marcail was led down the mossy path toward the shore.

The soft lulling of sheep sounded from the field.

Uncle Brodie, Caelan, and Duncan were busy keeping guard outside the cave when they noticed the light of the torches. Aidan's uncle turned to the twins.

"Guard the entrance. I will be right back." He rushed inside, startled by the sight of the breastfeeding mothers and newborn pups. Aidan turned in surprise.

"There's Hunters coming from the coastline. They'll be here any minute."

"Stay inside, wives." Laird Brummel's blue eyes turned ebony. "We have company." Jade locked her gaze with Aidan's.

"We'll keep you safe," he told her. "Don't come out until we've cleared the beach."

148

"Let us know when it's safe." She looked down at Catriona and her pup. The mother's blue eyes were wide with terror.

Once outside, the men spotted the Hunters' torches illuminating the shore. Marcail was out in front, bound wrists and a heavy rope around her neck. A scarlet-haired woman pushed her forward like an animal to slaughter.

⁂

WHEN THEY REACHED THE CAVE, THE HUNTERS GATHERED INTO TWO LINES approaching from each side. With their knives and harpoons ready, the mothers and newborns would be helpless to defend themselves. Detective Glass did not relish the idea of the gory bloodshed, but she knew her lover demanded the sacrifice. *The Unclean Ones* would be slaughtered as soon as they made it inside the cave. Seeing their enemies' small numbers guaranteed their success.

Marcail blinked in astonishment, noticing Laird MacFie and his men waiting outside. A glimmer of hope surfaced in her hazy mind. As the teenager was pushed forward, the Mistress handed the rope to Detective Glass before holding her arms to the sky.

"Aidan MacFie and the selkies belong to us, gentlemen. Anyone not part of the MacFie family may leave. If you choose to stay, you will be slaughtered along with the *Unclean Ones.*"

Marcail listened to the roar of the sea, trying to make sense of her surroundings. Her headache made it difficult to concentrate. She watched Brodie MacFie glance at his friends and wondered why they nodded.

"We're not leaving, so you'll have to get past us if you intend on harming anyone inside," shouted Aidan.

"Very well. You have made your choice, and we will make ours." Without hesitation, the Mistress shouted her command. "Kill them all."

Dozens of cloaked figures raced toward the cave with their harpoons raised. Simultaneously, a roar of thunder echoed, and the inky skies released torrents of hail. Laird Brummel met the Hunters with his trident, knocking several down with a single swing of his weapon. One of the masked invaders tossed his harpoon, just missing the pod king by inches.

Laird Brummel stabbed the man in the heart, killing him instantly. Meanwhile, the twins tried their best to avoid the sharp blades headed their way. They dodged the attackers, disarming several men in the process. Together, they stopped over a dozen Hunters from entering.

Without a weapon of his own, Aidan managed to fight bare-knuckle with his opponents. He was determined to keep the Hunters away from the mothers at all costs. He ducked out of the way from a harpoon, just grazing the side of his face. Once he managed to grab the spear from his attacker, Aidan proceeded to pummel the man with his fists. While Laird Brummel and his men struggled against the cult members, the shore filled with dark figures. Dozens of grey seals moved across the beach, galumphing toward their common enemy.

Two bull seals plowed into a group of men in black, tossing them backwards into the icy depths of the sea. Their screams turned silent when the dark waters filled their mouths. While chaos ensued, one of the cult members managed to sneak inside the cave.

⚅

JADE WAS HORRIFIED WHEN SHE SPOTTED THE MASKED INTRUDER RACING toward Caitriona with a raised harpoon. Relying on only instinct, she shielded the mother and baby with her own body. The Hunter grabbed her painfully by the arm, before shoving her back against the wall of the cave. She fell to her knees with the wind knocked out of her. Trying to catch her breath, she watched the stranger drag Catriona outside. Her newborn pup lay on the cold floor. Jade crawled toward the infant, reaching for her with trembling hands. The pup appeared unharmed, so she lifted the fuzzy baby in her arms and tried to stand. Once the room stopped spinning, Jade called Caitriona's name while racing toward the cave entrance.

Jade was greeted by chaos outside. Grey seals chased the Hunters, while others tried their best to reach the cave. Jade noticed several police and special constables arriving. It was unclear how they found them, but she was relieved they'd turned up. A few officers made arrests while others subdued the masked men and women.

Jade raised her hand to her throat, watching Aidan punch a Hunter in the face just moments before nearly impaling a selkie mother with his harpoon. He dropped his weapon and fell toward the sand while the mother gathered her pup in her arms and headed toward the ocean. Jade called his name while pointing to a Hunter dragging a selkie down the beach.

150

"Aidan, help Catriona," she shouted, motioning toward the young mother and her assailant. "I have her child!"

Aidan ran toward the masked figure, taking him down with a powerful punch to the jaw. When he reached for his harpoon, Donavon rushed forward from the crowd, giving him a quick kick to the ribs, stopping him in his tracks. While the Hunter crawled into a fetal position, begging for mercy, Jade ran to Caitriona.

"Your baby is safe," she said, handing her the fuzzy newborn.

The teenager held out her arms, taking her baby in gratitude. The pup's blue eyes were a startling contrast against its white coat. Caitriona cooed to the baby and kissed the back of her downy head.

"Thank you, Lady Mackenzie. I will forever remember your kindness."

"I'm honored to have been part of your sacred event. I'll never forget you, Caitriona."

The selkie smiled. Beneath the light of the moon, the young mother lifted her pelt to the back of her head. Once the hide touched her human flesh, the two skins morphed together. Jade was perplexed while she watched her face and chest change back into seal flesh. Within moments, Caitriona no longer held any trace of humanity. Taking her pup by the scruff, mother and child returned to the sea, disappearing beneath the frothy waves.

Aidan ran to Jade, wrapping her tightly in his protective embrace.

"Are you all right, lass?"

"Yes, I just can't believe what's happening. Have all the Hunters been accounted for?" Jade asked.

Aidan turned toward the sound of a woman screaming. The couple watched Marcail run toward the protection of the open cave. In the chaos of the fight, she managed to break free from the kidnappers. Panicking, she failed to notice her friends nearby.

"Marcail!" Aidan yelled, watching her disappear into the darkness. One of the masked Hunters was close behind. Mrs. Flannery wrapped a newborn in a soft towel when she spotted her daughter.

"Momma!"

She looked up in astonishment. "Marcail!"

Before she could reach her mother, the masked Hunter grabbed the teenager by her waist and dragged her outside, kicking and screaming, into the night.

"Marcail!" Mrs. Flannery ran toward her beloved child, shouting her name. She was only a few feet behind when her feet tangled in a clump of seaweed. She fell to the ground, unable to move.

While Marcail clawed at her assailant's face, she managed to pull off his mask. Enraged, he grabbed her wrists and pinned them above her head. She gazed into familiar blue eyes.

From the cave, Arabel headed toward them.

"Let her go, Thomas!"

Marcail stared at the selkie, recognizing her face. Except for her white locks, it was like looking into a mirror.

The man in black pulled the youth to her feet. He held her in his left arm, while he clutched a knife in his right. "So, you came back after all these years, Arabel? You left without even saying goodbye, and you took our half-breed daughter with you. You must think yourself quite clever, creature."

"I had no choice, Thomas. You are a monster. I would rather die than allow my bairn to be raised by a Hunter."

"Well, it looks like you will get your wish." A smile spread over his handsome face. With one swift movement, he flung his knife toward the selkie, hitting her fully in the chest. A rose-shaped pattern formed around the edge of the blade. Arabel fell backward into the sand, blood dripping from her parted lips. Marcail screamed, trying to release herself from her father's grip. Laird Brummel, having witnessed the scene from across the beach, ran toward them with a trident in hand. He grabbed Thomas by his throat, lifting him off the ground.

"You will pay with your life, human!" He swung his trident down into his abdomen, tearing through flesh and bone. A bubble of blood escaped Thomas' lips, and he breathed his last. Dropping him onto the sand, Laird Brummel ran toward Arabel, gathering up her limp body against his chest.

Marcail raced toward the couple, falling to her knees.

"Is it true? Are you my birth mother?" she asked.

"Yes, my darling girl." Arabel's ebony eyes turned a dazzling shade of blue, tears streaming down her pale face. "I was held against my will by your biological father. When you were born, I vowed he would never harm you. After escaping his home, I yearned to join my people. I thought it best to find you a new home. I chose Mrs. Flannery. I sensed she would be a good mother to you. Every day since, I have yearned to see your sweet face. Have you had a good life, baby?"

Tears ran down Marcail's face, and she clutched her mother's hand.

"Yes, my mom and dad were the best I could ever hope for, but I never knew I was adopted. I have so many questions. How can it be I am only finding you now?" She looked down at the blood pooling around her mother's body and grimaced. "I don't want to say goodbye."

Arabel tried to smile. "We will meet again one day, little pearl. Please understand, I did what I believed was best. I wanted to protect you from Thomas. He was a cruel man. He kidnapped me when I was about your age, stole my innocence, and locked me away from my people. When you were born, I knew I must escape. You should know I've thought of you every single day since we parted."

Mrs. Flannery limped over toward Arabel and Marcail.

The selkie smiled. "There now, your mother is here to take care of you, child. I picked well that day, for I can see she loves you."

"You gave me the greatest joy of my life the morning we met sixteen years ago." Mrs. Flannery gazed into the eyes of the dying mother and took her hand. It was icy to the touch. "Marcail is my heart and soul. I promise to always love and protect her. Your memory will be kept close to our hearts."

Arabel smiled as the lights dimmed around her. "Your words are a gift from God. I am grateful, Mrs. Flannery—"

The dying mother turned back to Marcail, squeezing her hand with the last of her strength. "My clan will always look after you and protect you from the sea. You are now of age to explore your selkie side. Do not be afraid, daughter. You will be watched over when you turn, and Mrs. Flannery will care for you on land. You are safe, child. Go forward and have a blessed life."

Arabel's vivid blue eyes glazed over. When she breathed her last, Laird Brummel tossed his head back and uttered a blood-curdling bellow.

His cries brought the attention of Detective Glass and Mistress Baine. The women watched in frustration while their army was defeated despite their weapons and numbers. While her minions were subdued by the officers, the Mistress reached for a discarded harpoon and rushed toward Laird Brummel. Just as she was about to release the weapon, the pod leader aimed his trident, impaling her through the chest. Baine fell back onto the sand, blood bubbling from her ruby lips.

Detective Glass was only a few yards away when her lover collapsed. Running toward her Mistress, Fiona fell to her knees.

During the chaos, Detective Boyd discovered the disgraced officer weeping over the body of her deceased leader. He removed his trench coat and quietly placed it on the shoulders of his ex-partner. He allowed her to pay her respects before handcuffing the broken woman. He led Detective Glass away into the night, the light vacant from her ebony eyes.

While the officers busily chased down the remaining Hunters, the selkie mothers quietly transformed back to seals. Once their metamorphosis was completed, they picked up their pups by their scruffs and dove into the frigid waters. When the final mother transformed, Laird Brummel gathered Arabel in his arms and headed toward the pounding surf. The friends watched with heavy hearts. Before the pod leader returned to the dark depths of the sea, he turned back toward their group. Jade bowed and her friends followed her lead.

A grey-haired officer noticed them and headed over. He glanced at Marcail leaning against Mrs. Flannery. The distraught teenager held tight to her adopted mother.

"Hello, I'm Chief Constable Rivers. My department is relieved to see Marcail Flannery safe and sound. This case is one for the books. You should know that Detective Fiona Glass has been arrested as a co-conspirator in the Hunters' secret society. She is being booked as we speak. Detective Boyd uncovered their hideaway after discovering Marcail's abductors. He called in for backup. He's the reason we were able to find you tonight."

"This case has a lot of moving pieces. You'll need to make official statements at the precinct tonight. Seeing what you have all endured, my officers will try to make it as brief as possible. I've taken the liberty to call an ambulance for Miss Flannery, so she can get checked over before she goes home," Constable Rivers said.

An ambulance arrived shortly afterward. The paramedics determined Marcail was dehydrated and in shock. They gave her fluids and bandaged her injured hand prior to taking her to a local hospital. Her mother kept vigil, along with the medical staff in attendance. Before they left, Donavon checked on her in the back of the ambulance. Noticing the groom's boy, Marcail reached for his hand.

The exhausted teenager sat up on the gurney and smiled. "Thank you, Donavon. I'm sorry we missed our movie night."

He moved closer, taking her cold hand in his. "No worries, lass. We'll have our date whenever you're ready."

She gazed into his brown eyes and smiled. "I'm looking forward to it."

Mrs. Flannery sat by her daughter's side, watching them both with a soft smile. Marcail looked over her shoulder. "Sorry, momma, I guess I should have asked you first. Is it all right if I go after I'm feeling better?"

"I think it sounds like a lovely idea." Her mom nodded. "Lord knows you deserve some time off after everything you have been through. Things are going to be different from now on." Marcail looked into her mother's loving eyes and smiled.

❦

AIDAN AND HIS GROUP TOOK SEPARATE CARS AND HEADED TO THE PRECINCT to give their statements.

Once the police finished their questioning, Aidan, Jade, Uncle Brodie, Mrs. Flannery, Donavon, Lady Roland, and her two boys made their way back to the parking lot. Jade stifled a yawn; the evening's stressful adventure began to catch up with her.

Before saying their goodbyes, Aidan's uncle turned to him. "Nephew, I think the Hunters will be out of commission for the time being. It's been wonderful having you both in town.

"Hopefully, your next visit will be under better circumstances. I believe you're safe to go back to the States when you're ready, but Molly and I were wondering if you're staying until Saint Andrew's Day on Sunday?"

Aidan and Jade glanced at once another. It was difficult to believe it was all over.

"Thank you, Uncle Brodie. We'll most likely head back in a few days." He locked gazes with his uncle. "If you can, try to keep your schedule open. We'd love to have a get-together before we leave. Saint Andrew's Day will be the perfect holiday to celebrate."

"Sounds good. nephew." Uncle Brodie glanced over at Lady Roland. "We'll see you off in style."

❦

ONCE THEY SAID THEIR GOODBYES, THE COUPLE HEADED TO THEIR CAR. JADE laid her head on her boyfriend's shoulder on the way home, her mind and body exhausted. He kissed her cheek, relieved their troubles were finally over. When they arrived at the castle, Aidan escorted Jade to her room.

Dougal spotted them across the hallway and hurried over. Jade reached down and scratched the terrier's head while he thumped his stubby tail.

"You're a good boy, Dougal," Jade said sleepily. The dog sat up on his hindquarters, his tongue hanging out the side of his ebony muzzle. She laughed, enjoying his silly puppy grin.

Aidan reached for her hand and brought it to his lips, kissing the back of her fingers. Despite being exhausted, his touch sent an electrical current through her body. She blinked in surprise, feeling herself suddenly awake.

"You were amazing tonight, lass, and I couldn't help notice how natural you were helping the mothers with their pups."

"I was happy to help." Jade blushed, gazing into his vivid blue eyes. "I'll never forget the way the pod supported one another. It was incredibly moving, and now it appears we might finally be free from the Hunters. It's crazy to think Detective Glass was helping them the whole time. Can you believe it?"

Aidan kissed her cheek before opening her bedroom door. Dougal trotted inside and made himself comfortable on top of the bed. "Why don't you get some rest, darlin'? There's something special I have planned for tomorrow."

"Oh?"

"If it is not raining when you wake up, please meet me in the garden. I'll have the staff serve our coffee outside," Aidan said.

"Sounds wonderful. It will be nice to finally get back to a new normal."

They kissed goodnight, and Jade closed the door behind her. Once she took a hot shower and changed into pajamas, she powered up her laptop on top of the bed.

She sent a short email to Mary, letting her know they'd be returning in a few days. Snuggling beneath the covers, Jade closed her eyes, listening to the sounds of a thunderstorm rage over Tobermory. Perhaps she could finally start a peaceful life with Aidan after all. She was suddenly homesick, yearning to be back in her tiny cottage in Pacific Grove. The logs popped in the fireplace while she drifted into a peaceful sleep, with Dougal curled against her back.

Chapter Eighteen

JADE AWOKE TO THE SUN STREAMING THROUGH HER BEDROOM WINDOW. SHE was drowsy and craving a strong cup of coffee. While the memories of the previous night flooded her mind, she prepared her bath. Once she finished choosing her outfit, she set her garments by her vanity. The mirrors in the room steamed over and she closed her eyes, trying to make sense of the day. Aidan suggested taking their coffee in the garden. She looked forward to a peaceful morning enjoying the fresh ocean air. As the warm jets soothed her tired muscles, she yawned and stretched, hoping for a quiet day of doing nothing.

After leaving the warmth of the bath, she dressed in a pair of jeans, t-shirt, and a periwinkle blue cardigan. She slipped a pair of black boots over her pants before turning toward the mirror.

She blow-dried her sandy-blonde waves and let her golden tresses fall around her shoulders before applying a light application of makeup. She smiled at her reflection. Her cheeks were rosy, and her steel-grey eyes sparkled in the soft morning light. When she left the bathroom, she was surprised to see Dougal and Morrigan missing from their usual resting spots. Jade imagined Aidan or Mrs. Flannery must have set them up for breakfast in another room.

Jade left her bedroom and made her way down the spiral staircase. When she was outside the castle, she sighed, breathing in the scents of autumn. It was a surprisingly warm day considering the previous night's storm. A faint aroma of honeysuckle lingered in the dewy air. She followed the mossy trail leading to the garden. Once she reached the entrance, curiosity filled her at the sight of rose buds strewn along the path. She bent down and picked up a bright red petal. Puzzled, she held it to her nose and breathed its sweet scent. When Jade looked up, she saw Aidan standing in the middle of the garden. He was wearing a formal kilt and a matching navy-blue Jacobite shirt. An embroidered sash crossed his chest, displaying his family seal crest.

His knee-high boots and matching sporran completed the formal highlander look.

She followed the rose-covered trail, her heart beating faster with each step. Aidan's aqua-marine eyes brightened at the sight of her. He offered his lopsided grin when she stood before him.

Jade blinked in surprise, seeing Morrigan perched in a tree laden with ripe, golden apples. The raven cawed, pearly feathers ruffling in the branches. Dougal sat at his master's feet, pounding his stubby tail against the mossy ground. Off in the distance were two horses, saddled and ready.

"It looks like a beautiful painting," she whispered to herself. For a moment, she wondered if she might be dreaming. "Aidan?"

He bowed. "Good morning, Lady Mackenzie." He took her hand and kissed the top, gazing at her beneath his thick lashes.

"What on earth?" Jade asked.

His eyes were so full of love, her heart skipped a beat. To her amazement, he lowered himself on one knee. Reaching into his sporran, he retrieved a velvet case. Aidan lifted the top, and she gasped, eying a beautiful diamond ring encased with sapphires and gold.

"Lady Jade Mackenzie, I've loved ye from the first time I saw your stunning face. You are my destiny, my family, and my best friend. I want to spend my days with you, cherishing and loving my bonnie lass. Would you do the honor of being my bride?"

Tears streamed down her shocked face while she gazed into his hopeful eyes. Her mouth trembled, trying to find her voice. "Yes, Laird Aidan MacFie. I would be honored to be your wife."

The skin around his eyes crinkled, and the dimples rose in his cheeks. Gently, he slipped the ring on her finger. "You've made me the happiest man in the world!"

He lifted her in his powerful arms, and they kissed under the shade of the apple tree. Beneath a sunny sky, the ocean waves glistened, and seagulls flew over the rising tides.

They held each other in happy silence, listening to the birds sing their morning harmonies. Aidan took Jade's hand and led her toward a marble table. He poured her a cup of coffee and offered a blueberry scone on a porcelain plate before taking his seat. "Lass, you've truly made me the happiest man on earth."

"You've made me the happiest lass," she said, grinning.

"Aww, that's my bonnie Scottish bride. Already talking like one of the locals." He winked, regarding her face softly. "I figured since we're already here at the castle, we might plan our wedding ceremony in Scotland."

She set her cup down, afraid she would drop it. "You're thinking about getting married here?"

He smiled and took her hand. "Yes, I realize it's short notice, but I have a couple of more surprises."

Jade's mind was racing, trying to make sense of everything. "Another surprise, Laird MacFie?"

"I called your friends last night. Mary and Katie agreed to fly over for the wedding. Also, we can arrange travel for anyone else you'd like as well. You just let me know. I already scheduled your best friends' travel plans with our pilot, Johnathon. Of course, this was on the condition that you'd say *yes*." He wiped his brow. "Aye, your answer was such a relief." He chuckled, reaching for her small hands. "So, they are just waiting for my call. I also arranged for the family priest to officiate the ceremony in the garden. The MacFie clan have been generous benefactors to the parish for centuries. Father Bradley moved some things around and will be available. Of course, if you prefer, our wedding could take place in the church, or if you need to push the date back to allow more people to attend, I completely understand." His brow furrowed. "Maybe this is too short of a notice, but I just figured since we're already here…"

Jade put her finger to his lips, stopping him in mid-sentence.

"Oh, Aidan," she whispered, her grey eyes filled with tears. "You've thought of everything. It all sounds so perfect. I wouldn't change a thing. Except, I don't have a dress, or anything prepared."

"I knew you'd be worried, but I spoke to Mrs. Flannery earlier. Can you believe I found her puttering around the kitchen making coffee and scones this morning? Pretty much shooed me out of the kitchen." Aidan pushed a loose curl from Jade's forehead and smiled. "Even after everything she has been through, she's still worried about keeping to her duties. She is a darlin' woman. Well, anyway, I told her about my plans to propose and she already knows the perfect dress shop. She happens to be good friends with the owner. Mrs. Flannery is so excited to help with the arrangements. And the girls can assist you when they arrive in a couple of days."

"Oh, that's so kind of Mrs. Flannery. Do you suppose everything can be ready on such short notice?"

"No worries, lass," Aidan said. "Do you remember when I mentioned the staff arranges special events to supplement the castle's expenses and upkeep?"

"Yes, you mentioned that the day after we arrived." Jade said.

"Right. So, many of our employees deal with wedding venues on a regular basis. Most of the bridal shops and caterers are just a phone call away."

Jade sat back in her chair and lifted her mug to her lips before blowing away the steam. Taking a sip, she closed her eyes. "Oh, it sounds like a dream, Aidan. I completely forgot that the castle hosts special events. All I need to do is figure out what to do with my antique shop, since it sounds like we're extending our vacation."

"That's right, and there's some more good news. Your psychic friend, Madame Garnier, has been helping Mary at the shop. She offered to watch your antique store until you get back. According to Mary, she already sensed her services would be needed. Guess she really is psychic after all."

"Oh, Aidan!" Jade rose from her chair, throwing her arms around his neck. "You thought of everything!"

Aidan leaned in for a kiss. They heard footsteps behind them and turned to see Mrs. Flannery and Marcail walking down the rose-petal covered path. Mother and daughter smiled at the young couple.

"I'm imagining the lady said *yes,* Laird MacFie?" Mrs. Flannery asked.

"Aye, she did! And made me the luckiest man on earth!"

"Well, I was hoping for some happy news."

Marcail looked down, glancing at Jade's ring. She beamed. "Lady Mackenzie, it's absolutely beautiful."

"Thank you so much! I'm so thrilled you're back home! We've been terribly worried."

To Jade's surprise, the teenager rushed over, wrapping her arms around her waist. "Thank you for helping to get me home. My mom told me how you and Laird MacFie worked tirelessly trying to find me. Lady Mackenzie, it sounds like you're a regular Nancy Drew!"

Jade beamed at Marcail. "Seeing you safe and sound is all the thanks I need. Thank God, you're back." Jade put her hand on her shoulder and smiled. "Well, actually, there is one thing you could do for me, if you feel up to it, of course."

Marcail nodded. "How can I be of service, Lady Mackenzie?"

"Would you do the honor of being in the wedding? I'd love to have you as my bridesmaid."

"Oh, yes! Of course, I will. It would be my honor. Thank you for thinking of me."

Mrs. Flannery smiled, relieved to see the tension in her daughter's face lift. "Well, we will leave you two lovebirds alone. We'll have a celebratory brunch in the great hall in about an hour."

"Thank you," Aidan said, watching his housekeeper and her daughter walk back to the castle with their leftovers.

After finishing their coffee, Aidan led Jade to the horses. She gazed into her mare's dark brown eyes before stroking her mane and velvet-soft muzzle.

"Would you like to go for a ride down by the beach?" Aidan asked.

"Oh, I'd love to!"

"Wonderful." He handed a riding helmet to his fiancé, before helping her into the saddle. His fingers grazed over her thigh for just a moment. He glanced up, grinning from ear-to-ear. "Aye, you look like a natural rider, lass. It suits you."

"Thank you."

Although it had been over a year since she rode, sitting on her new pony was like coming home. It was still difficult to imagine Bonnie truly belonged to her. Although she'd always dreamed of having a horse, it seemed unfathomable during this stage in her life. She watched Aidan mount Blackjack.

The stallion snorted and struck the ground, before settling into a cantor. With a soft voice and firm hand, her fiancé communicated exactly what his horse needed to hear. Within minutes, the animal relaxed under the weight of his master.

The sight of Laird MacFie riding a powerful steed, while dressed in his formal kilt, made her heart race. He reminded her of a handsome highlander from one of her favorite romance novels. Jade hoped Aidan would continue wearing Scottish attire back in the States.

Together, they followed the trail down to the sandy shore. With the wind against their backs, the young couple raced along the tides, their horses splashing through the frothy waves. They rode for over an hour before heading back to the stables.

Donavon was inside mucking stalls when they arrived. The couple's faces were flushed from their beach adventure. The groom's boy said his congratulations before taking their horses. Aidan thanked him for his help in bringing their animals to the garden. They chatted a moment before heading back to the great hall for brunch.

Jade noticed the staff sneaking peeks, the news of their engagement spreading through the castle like wildfire. The pair exchanged secret glances throughout their meal. Once brunch was over, Mrs. Flannery met them at the table.

"Well, there's the happy couple. Just imagine, the MacFie Castle will have a new lady of the house. Aye, it warms my heart." Her eyes glistened with tears as she studied them.

"Lady Mackenzie, I am ready to go flower shopping whenever you are available. Laird MacFie arranged a driver."

"Oh, thank you, Mrs. Flannery. The honor is all mine. Will Marcail be joining us?"

"Thank you for asking. Well, as you can imagine, she is exhausted. I told her to go back to bed and take a nap. I checked on her a few minutes ago. She's fast asleep in her room. The rest will do her good."

"I am so relieved Marcail is back home. She's a lovely girl with a bright future ahead of her."

"Aye, she's a fine lass." Mrs. Flannery smiled and patted her hand. "Thank the Heavenly Father my daughter is safe and sound."

"It is such a relief, Mrs. Flannery," Aidan said, setting his napkin on the table and standing from his chair. "I should let you ladies plan your day. I'm going to iron out some details for the wedding." He kissed Jade's cheek before taking his leave. "See you later this afternoon, darlin.'"

Jade smiled, watching her fiancé exit the great hall. Aidan's formal Scottish attire took her breath away. Once he was gone, Mrs. Flannery turned toward Jade.

"Laird MacFie instructed me to let you know the estate will be covering everything for the wedding, so you get whatever your heart desires."

"Oh? Wow, that's so kind. I truly feel like this is all just a beautiful dream, and if it is, I don't want to wake up," Jade said.

"You're a breath of fresh air, Lady Mackenzie. It is about time the MacFie Castle had a young lady's touch. I sensed you were special the moment I met you."

"Thank you, Mrs. Flannery. I'll do my best to earn your respect as lady of the house."

"You will do fine," she said, eyeing the young woman before her. "I'll go fetch my handbag and coat, so we can go shopping."

"Lovely. I'll meet you outside," Jade said.

A few minutes later, the women were on their way to the flower shop. Storm clouds replaced the earlier cerulean skies.

"Oh, looks like we arrived." Mrs. Flannery said.

They parked in front of a brick-covered historical building. A large bay window displayed a variety of colorful flowers and plants. Their driver opened the doors for the women. Mrs. Flannery escorted Jade inside, introducing her to the owner, June McGrady. The Tobermory native was barely five feet tall, with a shock of curly white hair and dark eyes. She pushed a pair of thick spectacles to the bridge of her nose and flashed a warm smile. Jade noticed the elderly woman's crooked back when she turned to lead them toward the back of the shop. Despite her infirmary, the shopkeeper was eager to assist her clients. Mrs. McGrady pointed out several display booths before offering them a seat at a table by the register.

Several binders piled together, filled with floral arrangement samples. Jade breathed in the scent of fresh flowers and cinnamon potpourri. After pouring the ladies a flute of champagne, the owner offered a stack of bridal books for Jade's consideration. She marveled at the photos of luxurious bouquets and table settings. Afterward, Mrs. McGrady gave a tour of the shop. Jade admired the vast variety of flower arrangements and crystal vases. With the help of Mrs. Flannery, she chose a mixture of lilacs and roses for her bridal bouquet and the wedding party's corsages. Considering Aidan's sapphire blue family crest, she decided to pair the color with matching ribbons and lace.

163

AFTER LEAVING THE SHOP, THE REST OF THE DAY FLOATED BY LIKE A DREAM. Once the women arrived home, Mrs. Flannery escorted Jade to the garden area. They discussed final details for the wedding venue. With her mind buzzing with ideas, the bride-to-be hurried upstairs and knocked on Aidan's bedroom door. When she entered, her fiancé gathered her into his arms. Jade breathed in his light cologne and closed her eyes.

"I missed you, love." Aidan whispered in her ear. "I believe supper will be ready soon.

Are you hungry?"

"I am, but I better feed Morrigan. Poor bird is probably upset. I keep leaving her alone."

"Sounds good. I'll bring up Dougal's kibble and meet you in a moment." At the sound of his name, the terrier rushed over, flopping on his back by Jade's boots. Before heading back outside, she gave the pup's belly a pet. After dinner, Aidan escorted Jade back to her room. "I want you to get plenty of rest. You have been through a lot the past week."

"Goodnight," Jade said, watching her fiancé turn to leave down the hallway. After getting ready for a good night's sleep, she flopped herself down on the bed, realizing her dreams were finally coming true.

Chapter Nineteen

WEDNESDAY MORNING ARRIVED WITH HAZY SKIES ON THE HORIZON. JADE and Aidan waited at the bottom of the stairs for their friends' arrival. When Collins pulled up to the MacFie Castle, Katie O'Brien and Mary McClain's eyes widened in wonder. They spotted Jade and Aidan, along with a long line of attending staff.

Unable to keep to formalities, Jade broke away from the group and ran toward her friends.

Aidan smiled while the women hugged beneath the white sky.

Mary whispered in Jade's ear, "I had no idea you were royalty, Miss Mackenzie." The friends laughed as Aidan walked over, greeting his guests.

"It's wonderful to see you." Katie pushed back a lock of auburn hair. "My fiancé is in Kinvara this week, but he's flying in for your wedding on Sunday."

"Yes, my boyfriend will be here the night before." Mary smiled. "He is so happy for you both."

"Great." Aidan grinned. "Looking forward to seeing Paul and meeting Daniel. We really appreciate you dropping everything last minute. I know it's short notice."

"Not a problem. And we were more than happy to fly private," Mary said with a smile.

"Glad you liked it. Are you ready to meet the staff and have a tour of the castle?" Aidan asked.

"Absolutely," Katie said.

"Good, why don't you follow me."

The staff members stood at attention while Jade's friends were introduced. Katie and Mary tried their best to remember everyone's names. It was not an easy task, considering how many people were in attendance that day.

Once introductions were made, Aidan ushered the group inside his ancestral home. Dougal followed, vying for the guests' attention. After a condensed tour, Laird MacFie promised Katie and Mary a more detailed look at the castle once the women were rested and unpacked.

After viewing the ground floor, Aidan turned to Jade. "I should let you have some alone time with your friends. Katie and Mary, your bags will be brought to your rooms. If you are not too tired, Mrs. Flannery has made arrangements for dress shopping this afternoon."

"We both slept on the plane, so we would love to," Katie said.

They turned the corner to discover Mrs. Flannery and Marcail waiting at the bottom of the spiraling staircase.

"Ladies, we'll show you to your rooms, so you can unpack. I arranged a dress fitting at three o'clock. And we have a lovely formal supper prepared afterward," Mrs. Flannery said.

"Wonderful," Mary said.

The group followed mother and daughter upstairs. Katie and Mary's rooms were down the hall from Jade's. Although smaller, both suites were decorated with antique furniture dating back to the eighteenth century. Each bedroom offered views of the ocean, along with a roaring fire. To their astonishment, Mrs. Flannery helped unpack Mary's suitcases, while Marcail assisted Katie.

Once the women were rested and showered, Jade knocked on their doors to see if her friends were ready. Katie and Mary grabbed their purses and followed Jade to her bedroom.

They exchanged glances when they entered.

"I could get used to this luxury," Mary said, flopping down on her king-size bed.

Jade laughed while Dougal smothered her best friend with kisses.

"Everything is magical," Katie said, sitting across from Mary.

Jade agreed. "I feel like I went to bed and woke up in a fairy tale."

"So, tell us everything." Mary smiled. "What's been going on with the Hunters?"

"You might as well sit back and get comfortable. It is a long story."

For the next hour, Jade explained everything which transpired since arriving in Scotland, ending with the *Great Birthing* and the arrests of the Hunters. Halfway through, Mrs. Flannery brought in a tray of tea and scones. The women thanked her as they helped themselves to their refreshments.

Mary moved to the window when the tale was over. "I can't believe this all happened in the past week. Strange, Madame Garnier sensed her services were going to be needed."

"Really?" Jade said.

"Yes, a couple of days before Aidan called, she visited the antique shop. She's been volunteering her time since you left for Scotland. And I must say, she is quite wonderful with the customers. They seriously love her. She dresses the part, too. Madame Garnier shows up every day with a different Victorian gown."

"That's so kind of her. I want to pay you both for your hard work."

Her friend shook her head. "No, flying us up here is more than enough."

"I'm so excited my fiancé will be able to attend the wedding." Katie pushed a strand of Auburn curls from her forehead. "But I was curious about something."

"Oh?" Jade asked.

"Well, I've been planning my wedding for nearly a year. I've been a nervous wreck trying to arrange everything in time. How on earth are you going to manage to pull this off in just a few days?"

"You've got me." Jade shrugged her shoulders. "Aidan said not to worry. Sounds like most of the employees at the castle are pitching in and working around the clock, getting everything prepared. I've already made arrangements with the florist. Mrs. Flannery has been incredibly helpful with planning the event."

"She's a lovely woman," Katie said.

"She really is," Mary agreed, nodding her head while running her manicured nails through her perfectly coiffed hair. The dark edges swept around her curved neck. "Just can't believe you have an entire staff working for you."

"I don't know if I will ever get used to being waited on. I've always been independent. Don't get me wrong, everyone's been wonderful. It's just I'm feeling so spoiled. How will I manage preparing my own tea and coffee when I get home?" Jade asked, rolling her eyes and fanning herself.

Mary and Katie laughed.

"You'll survive somehow, Lady Mackenzie." Mary said.

Jade turned toward Mary. "Has it been quiet at the cottage?"

Her friend hesitated a moment before answering. "Yes, but Paul's been checking on me."

Jade studied her vibrant brown eyes for a moment, feeling like she was holding something back. "How is your police officer boyfriend these days? I noticed Paul couldn't take his eyes off you the last time he visited."

"He's been an absolute gentleman. We've been spending time together almost every evening after work. He's been taking me out to the movies, dinner, and even enjoyed some quiet time back at the cottage. Your fireplace is lovely on a rainy night..." Mary trailed off, blushing. "Jade, I hope you don't mind me bringing Paul to your house? I probably should have asked first."

"Of course, I don't mind. He saved our lives the night the Hunters held us hostage at the beach. Their leader would have killed Aidan if he hadn't shot him. He's welcome to stop by anytime he wants. Aidan considers him a close friend, and he is thrilled you two found each other."

"I've never met anyone like him." Mary sighed, throwing herself backward on the mattress.

"I'm so happy Paul is going to be able to attend your wedding."

"That's wonderful. Who knows, we might be attending yours before you know it," Jade said.

"I can't wait for my fiancé to meet Paul and Aidan. I think the boys will get along famously." Katie said.

"I think they will," Mary said. "As far as marriage goes for me, though, we've only been dating a few weeks. I think we'll need to spend a little more time together before we walk down the aisle." She shook her head and wiggled her eyebrows. The women giggled like schoolgirls.

A light knock at the door made them turn.

Jade ushered Mrs. Flannery and her daughter into the bedroom.

"Ladies, are you ready for some dress shopping?" Mrs. Flannery asked.

"Absolutely," Jade said.

Marcail had changed into a pair of jeans and a light denim jacket, noticeably less formal than her usual working attire. She smiled at the women before following her mother into the hallway.

Jade was happy to see she was in good spirits after her ordeal. The group walked downstairs and waited outside by the roundabout. Marcail and her mother took their own car while Jade and her friends were chauffeured in the Rolls Royce. Gazing out her window, Jade noticed the skies darkening overhead. Ten minutes later, the group was escorted into a lavish wedding boutique overlooking the Atlantic Ocean.

The ladies sat down on velvet chairs while two salesclerks offered them crystal flutes brimming with champagne. Jade eyed the store's impressive displays while she sipped from her glass. "There's so many lovely gowns. I don't even know where to start."

"Do you know what kind of style you're considering?" Katie asked.

"Good question. This is all happening so fast, but you know how I adore antiques…" Katie and Mary nodded.

"I'd love to find an old-fashioned dress with lace and long sleeves, something along the lines of a Victorian style."

A petite woman with thick glasses and a silver-toned pixie cut walked over to the group.

"Hello, ladies. My name is Claire Marchbank. Welcome to my boutique."

"Thank you for arranging a last-minute appointment, Claire." Mrs. Flannery slipped her arm through Jade's and smiled. "This is Lady Jade Mackenzie, soon to be Lady Jade MacFie." Jade held her breath at the sound of her soon-to-be last name. It took her by surprise.

"Aye, it's an honor to provide for your wedding today. The MacFie Clan has been held in high regard in our village for centuries. We will help you pick the perfect dress for your special day, and please don't worry, lass. We will make sure to have everything ready, even if we need to work night and day."

"Thank you so much. It's all happening so fast. I really haven't had much time to think about a dress. Let alone prepare for the wedding."

Deep creases formed around the boutique's owner's eyes when she smiled. "No need to worry. We will help you with all your wedding needs. Do you have a style in mind, Lady Mackenzie?"

"Well, I own a modest antique shop in Pacific Grove, back in the States.

I'm fond of the Victorian era. I don't suppose you have anything resembling a nineteenth century style?"

"How lovely." The woman's green eyes glowed with purpose. "Aye, it is rare these days to find young people interested in the past. I happen to have created three dresses which are designed with the Victorian era in mind. Although they are not authentically antique, I humbly say they are close."

The seamstress ushered the ladies to the back of the boutique. Jade smiled while she studied the collection. Each piece was authentic, down to the antique silk and lace.

"These are incredible! Truly, Mrs. Marchbank."

"I am so happy you approve," said the shop owner. "The Victorian wedding dress should present an hour-glass figure and fitted sleeves. I imagine you already know, considering your knowledge of antiques. Victorian wedding dresses came in a variety of colors, although the wealthier members of society wore pure white. Queen Victoria's pearl-white wedding dress started the trend. Being of means yourself, I think this would be quite suitable."

"Well, I don't really consider myself wealthy." Jade smiled.

"Ah, Lady Mackenzie, you should." The shopkeeper patted her hand. "For don't ye know you're marrying into one of the wealthiest families in the village?"

Jade bit down on her lower lip in surprise. "I guess...I haven't really thought about it that much."

"Well, I'm sure it's just one more reason Laird MacFie loves ye, lass." Mrs. Marchbank slipped one of the gowns from the rack and turned toward the bride-to-be. "Would you like to try one on?"

"Yes, please."

The shopkeeper escorted Jade to the dressing room. "We will take your measurements today. And, of course, you'll need a corset. We will give you a proper fitting and we can make any adjustments needed. The original Victorian gowns were fitted with many layers. Are you interested in having an authentic feeling?"

"Yes, I think it would be extraordinary, if it's not too much trouble," Jade said.

"No trouble at all. It has been some time since we have had a request for a formal Victorian wedding gown. I am so excited to help you. It will be elegant. Go ahead and undress. My staff will bring everything you need, so make yourself comfortable." Mrs. Marchbank smiled and drew the curtain closed.

Jade noticed the chemisette which was set on a hanger by the mirror. While Jade undressed behind the velvet curtain. The shop owner and assistants gathered their supplies together. Several minutes passed before they returned.

"May I come in?" Mrs. Marchbank asked, holding a satin corset in her arms.

"Yes, please," Jade said.

"Well, we will start with a cotton shift for your first layer, stockings, and garters. We'll follow this with cotton drawers and petticoats. Then, I will fit your corset over these layers, and of course, a lovely corset cover to complete the look. I think a hoopskirt is the best choice to add volume to your gown. Back in the day, multiple petticoats were used to create the same effect, but often tangled uncomfortably. For your dress, we will use fewer petticoats and add a hoopskirt to allow for easier movement. Finally, the wedding dress will be placed over all the undergarments. I also have a selection of lovely Victorian-style shoes you may choose from."

Jade's eyes bulged when she tightened the strings around her waist. "Oh, my, now I understand why fainting couches were so popular in the nineteenth century."

"You should count yourself lucky. You have a tiny waist, dear." The shop owner marveled at Jade's hour-glass figure. "Appears we won't need too many alterations if you choose this gown. It's almost as if I designed this dress with you in mind."

After measuring and fitting Jade's corset, she removed it and set it aside to make room for the undergarments. A young assistant entered the room with a set of petticoats, shift, stockings, garters, corset cover, and a hoop skirt. Once Jade slipped into the multiple layers, Mrs. Marchbank and her employees guided the wedding dress over the bride-to-be's head.

"Would you like to try a veil to go with it?" Mrs. Marchbank asked.

Jade blinked. "Yes, please."

"I have one that matches perfectly." Once she finished, the boutique owner stood back, admiring the result. "Oh, my, Lady Mackenzie. This gown was made for you. Are you ready for a peek?"

"Yes, please." Jade said.

Mrs. Marchbank opened the door of the fitting room while her employees helped carry the floral-embroidered train. The shop owner led Jade out toward the raised platform. Her friends waited in anticipation, sipping champagne while eagerly waiting for the bride-to-be. When Lady Mackenzie arrived, the women gasped in awe.

Jade studied herself in the gold-framed mirrors, steel-grey eyes glowing with excitement. Her gown was covered in delicate lace and embroidered roses, continuing down her flowing train. For a moment, it appeared she'd fallen back in time, embracing the Victorian era with all of its beauty and grace.

"Jade, you look like a fairytale princess. You were born in the wrong era. This suits you so much," Katie said.

"You look stunning. The most beautiful bride I've ever seen. I know the dress is the first you tried, but it's perfect," Mary said.

Jade blushed, tears stinging her eyes. "I'm so happy you're both here to share this moment. I can't believe how flawless everything is coming together. I think I'm going to say yes to the dress!"

The women clapped, rushing toward the bride-to-be. Mrs. Flannery and Marcail grinned, watching the friends celebrate.

"Lady Mackenzie, it's an honor to have you as our lady of the castle. You are glowing in your gown," Mrs. Flannery said.

"Thank you for everything. You've made me feel so at home. I wish I could take you back with me to Pacific Grove!" Jade said, locking eyes with Mrs. Flannery.

"Maybe I'll have to visit one day. I hope you'll spend more time with us in the future. I realized you were special the minute you arrived at MacFie Castle."

"Thank you, Mrs. Flannery. You're so kind. If it wouldn't be too much trouble, I wondered if you might help me get ready on the wedding day? I always imagined my mom…" She trailed off.

"Of course, dear. I already think of you as another daughter." Jade hugged Mrs. Flannery in a tight embrace. The women chatted excitedly while Mrs. Marchbank waved to the staff, and they escorted the bride back to the fitting room area. Once Jade changed back into her street clothes, the shop owner led the women over to the bridesmaid area.

After considering several options, Jade decided on floor-length sapphire blue bridesmaid's gowns for her friends. The women talked over one another, expressing their enthusiasm for the dresses. A couple of more hours passed while the ladies' measurements were taken.

Satisfied with their arrangements, the women were driven back to the castle. The next three days were a whirlwind of planning and rehearsal. The days passed by in a series of stormy, grey days. The night before the wedding, Jade lay in her bed, listening to the storm rage outside. The weather report predicted a lull in the rainy weather for her wedding day. She meditated to the sound of thunder, imagining her new life as Lady MacFie.

Chapter Twenty

JADE AWOKE TO SUNLIGHT STREAMING THROUGH HER WINDOW. WITH HER heart racing, she took a shower and changed into her chemisette and satin robe. By ten o'clock, Mrs. Flannery, Marcail and her friends arrived at her room. They all took turns helping the bride-to-be. Katie applied a soft application of makeup, mauve lipstick, and a dusty rose blush to her high cheekbones. Mary helped with the bride's hair, styling it in Victorian fashion, with golden ringlets framing her face. Afterward, Marcail and Mrs. Flannery adjusted the wedding gown over her many layers of silk and damask.

The bride smiled at her friends in wonder.

"Lady Mackenzie, I was wondering if you have something borrowed?" Marcail asked.

"Oh, I actually don't. Guess I should have brought something." Jade said.

The teenager reached behind her neck and unclasped her string of pearls.

"If you'd like, you may wear my mother's pearls."

"Oh, Marcail, are you sure? I know how special they are to you."

"I know she would be proud for you to wear them on your special day, seeing how you helped her people during the *Great Birthing.*" Marcail held out the pearls to the bride.

"I'm truly honored." Jade put her arms out and gave her a hug. "I'll take good care of them. I promise."

Mrs. Flannery smiled at her daughter. "So, Laird MacFie arranged for something blue." Surprised, Jade turned toward the housekeeper.

"Oh?"

"Yes, dear. Your betrothed asked for me to give his gift to you. He understands it's bad luck to see the bride before the wedding."

"Of course," Jade said.

"He wanted me to tell you the earrings belonged to his mother. A gift from his father on their wedding day." Mrs. Flannery presented Jade with a velvet box.

With trembling hands, Jade pushed aside the ribbon and peered inside. Her eyes filled with tears gazing at the beautiful sapphires. After she secured the earrings in place, her friends sighed.

"They look stunning," Mary said.

"Now you have something borrowed, something blue, I believe you will need something old and…"

"Something new," Mary finished her sentence. "Katie and I thought you might like a comb to help hold your veil in place. We purchased it in Carmel before we left. And for something old, I thought you might enjoy my great-grandmother Mara's bridal garter. It dates to 1870, so I think it qualifies for something old!"

Jade eyed the antique-style pearl-comb and silk garter. "Oh, they're perfect! Thank you, ladies."

Together, Katie and Mary helped Mrs. Flannery set the veil and comb atop the bride's sandy-blonde ringlets. Once Jade moved the garter in place, the ladies picked up their bouquets and helped carry the back of Jade's train. In nervous anticipation, they made their way down to the garden area. A large crowd had gathered. Uncle Brodie and Lady Roland waited along with the entire staff of workers from the MacFie Castle. Several villagers were also in attendance, longtime friends of the groom's family.

Once the wedding party arrived, a quartet of violins started to play. Aidan's cousin, Molly, watched proudly as her twin daughters tossed rose petals along the trail leading to the garden. Their fiery auburn curls glimmered beneath the soft autumn light. Shortly afterward, Donavon escorted Marcail across the rose-covered path. She blushed as he admired her beneath the cloudy skies. A tall, dark haired gentleman took Katie's arm before walking behind the young couple. She smiled up at her fiancé and he winked. Mary followed alongside Deputy Paul Rheinstein. Every man in the wedding party wore traditional Scottish kilts, including the ring bearer, Donavon. Aidan stood beneath the golden apple tree, dressed in his formal dress kilt and sapphire blue Jacobite shirt. The MacFie crest was embroidered on his matching sash.

Dougal sat by his master's feet while Morrigan the Raven perched from the branches, patiently waiting for her mistress. Her pearly feathers reflected the afternoon light. Once the wedding party was in attendance, the string quartet played the wedding march.

Aidan stood at the end of the petal-strewn path. He was the most beautiful sight she ever witnessed. The light scent of honeysuckle and lilacs filled the autumn air. The embroidered lace on Jade's gown fluttered in the breeze while her long train swept over the mossy earth.

The sky darkened as storm clouds passed over the wedding party. The smoky hue of the sky matched the intensity of Jade's steel-grey eyes. A soft blush spread over her face. She smiled, seeing the love in her fiancé's aquamarine eyes. The young couple lost themselves in the moment. Time ceased and two worlds became one. A light sprinkling of rain washed over the bride and groom while they repeated their sacred vows, committing themselves before God.

Jade felt Aidan slip her wedding ring on her finger, realizing her dream was now her reality. A single tear slipped down her husband's face when the priest announced them man and wife. They kissed beneath the stormy sky, thunder rolling overhead. When the storm clouds released, they laughed, hurrying back to the protection of the castle. The next several hours blended into an endless dream.

The grand ballroom was transformed into a Victorian-themed world of roses and crystal finery.

The newlyweds enjoyed their first dance to the song of *Moon River*. Afterward, the ballroom filled with dancing partners, including family and friends and their significant others. Uncle Brodie proudly escorted Lady Roland toward the throng of celebratory guests. The couple moved gracefully in time to the music, making sweeping turns as they waltzed in perfect synchrony.

Jade noticed Donavon leading Marcail out onto the marble floor. The teenagers gazed into each other's eyes, losing themselves in the moment.

Mrs. Flannery smiled, watching her daughter from the sidelines. Butler Jacob Allen asked Mrs. Flannery to dance, and they joined in the merriment.

By the early evening, a heavy storm pounded the castle walls. Aidan took Jade by the hand and kissed her rosy cheek.

"Ye made me the happiest man on earth, Lady MacFie. I have one more surprise for you this evening, my love."

She gazed into his loving eyes. "Another surprise? You are spoiling me, Laird MacFie."

"Well, you better get used to it, darlin'." Aidan kissed the nape of her neck before leading her down a long corridor.

They passed several staff members along the way, each employee smiling and offering their blessings for the newlyweds, referring to the couple as Lady and Laird MacFie. The sounds of torrential rains strengthened while Aidan led his bride toward the castle's library. Once inside, Jade marveled at the floor-to-ceiling shelves of books towering above them.

"Oh, I could spend hours here reading," Jade said, gazing at the dizzying array of literature.

"I want you to enjoy the library to your heart's content. It belongs to both of us now. Although, as much as I love a nice story, I had something else in mind this evening." Aidan bit down on his lower lip, his aquamarine eyes glowing with desire. "Darlin', I know you love a good mystery," Aidan said, placing his hand over hers. He pushed the tips of her fingers against the binding of a thick novel at the end of the stacks. As soon as Jade touched the cover, the wall of books opened into a secret room. Soft light illuminated a grand bedroom full of antiques, including an eighteenth-century fireplace, glowing in the corner. The bride gasped. Aidan took her lace-covered arm in his. "Shall we?"

When the couple entered the bridal suite, the door closed behind them. Jade's heart thrummed with anticipation. They followed a trail of rose petals along the marble floor which led to a massive bedroom. The antiques appeared to be centuries old. A fire burned in an ancient-looking fireplace, along with expansive windows opening to the tides.

"I know you have questions, and I promise to answer every one. I will say that this castle holds many secrets, including a hidden master's chamber. This room is normally closed, and only our most trusted staff knows about it.

Mrs. Flannery was kind enough to help prepare the room for our wedding night. For once, we will have no interruptions."

Through an opening in the velvet drapes, a flash of lightning streaked across the sky.

Aidan lifted Jade in his powerful arms and brought her to the king-sized bed. She leaned back against the satin pillows while he drew the curtains closed.

Jade breathed in the aroma of the wood-burning fireplace. She watched Aidan make his way toward the bed, admiring his formal Scottish attire. He slid off his boots and set them against the wall by the window. He came around the side and gently eased the ties from her gown. His fingers grazing over her skin, the electricity between them undeniable.

"I love you, Lady MacFie," Aidan whispered while kissing his bride's neck.

Jade felt her husband's hands on her shoulders, gently unbuttoning the back of her dress. Carefully, he untied each ribbon, allowing her to release a full breath. His hand moved through her long tresses, and then down her back, slipping over the soft material. She maneuvered her way out of the wedding dress and gazed up at his hopeful face. Aidan removed her corset cover and turned her around, carefully untying the satin ties binding her waist. Once he loosened the corset, he carefully removed it, placing it on top of the velvet-backed chair by their bed. He turned her back around, eyeing her remaining layers.

Jade tried her best to hide her amusement, watching her husband's eyebrows lift.

"Lady MacFie, you're going to make me work tonight, aren't you?" he said, his hand grazing across the petticoats. "Aye, but don't worry. I'm up to the challenge, lass."

Jade laughed when he kneeled on the hardwood floor, carefully easing her stockinged foot over another layer of silk and damask. She held her breath as he gently removed the silky material, revealing her shapely legs.

Aidan's fingers grazed over the velvet garter, smiling in anticipation.

Layer after layer, he eased from her trembling body until she was down to her cotton shift and stockings. Her breath caught in her throat, waiting for the secret to be revealed. He smiled down at her hopeful face. With the back of his hand, he gently grazed her cheek.

"I love you, Lady MacFie."

"I love you, Laird MacFie."

When the last of the undergarments were accounted for, Aidan admired her in the glow of the firelight. His hand moved through her long tresses, and then down her shoulders, slipping over her curves. He lifted her into his arms again, moving her across the satin comforter. For a moment, they simply gazed into each other's eyes, enjoying the final moments before the next reveal.

"Now, it's your turn," Jade said, eying her husband's formal kilt.

His mouth turned up in the corners as lightning danced across the inky skies. Listening to the logs crackle, Aidan removed his kilt while Jade's fingers eased his Jacobite shirt from his washboard abs.

By the glow of firelight, his agile fingers explored her eager body, while his tongue flicked over the curves of her breasts and belly. Aidan raised himself on his elbow, gazing down with fire in his eyes.

"Well, lass, it appears there will be no more interruptions this time." He smiled wickedly, his hand following the curve of her hip. Aidan gathered Jade in his arms, lowering her down against the silky sheets.

She looked up into his loving face. Her breath caught as she watched his aqua-blue eyes turn a dazzling shade of sapphire. Looking into their depths was like gazing into the sea itself.

"Aidan?"

He offered his familiar smile before kissing her fully on the lips. His tongue darted against hers while his hands explored her velvety skin. In turn, her fingers slid down his shoulders and arms, sweeping across his powerful muscles and chest. Her nails grazed over his hips, and she felt his manhood awaken. Every touch was intense pleasure, an electric pulse sending an explosion of sensations throughout her body.

"I want you so badly, lass," he said with a husky voice.

Jade's fingers ran through his thick waves. "I want you, husband."

His eyes glimmered an unworldly blue. He pulled her closer, their bodies becoming one in the glow of firelight. Outside, the thunder rolled across the heavens while Aidan and Jade became man and wife.

Chapter Twenty-One

JADE AWOKE TO AIDAN GAZING DOWN AT HER FACE, HIS LIPS MOVING OVER her own. Her body was glowing from the night before.

"Good morning, Lady MacFie."

"Good morning, Laird MacFie."

"How are you feeling?"

"Wonderful. Last night was so magical."

"I couldn't imagine loving you anymore, darlin', but last night, you took my breath away. You are the most beautiful woman I have ever encountered, lass. God, you are my heart and soul." He leaned down, giving her a soft kiss on the lips.

"I love you, Aidan. Thank you for being so tender and gentle. You made our wedding night a dream come true." She bit down on her lower lip, looking up through her long lashes. "I can still feel your touch on my skin. It was electrical. And your eyes, love. They were glowing, I swear. I've never seen them do that. It was unworldly."

"Well, let me just say you bring out the wild side." He chuckled. "We may have to give you some swimming lessons soon. Just wait."

Jade's grey eyes flickered in the soft light. *If he could transform in the sea, would a bath work as well?*

"Can you change during…"

He took her hand, kissing her palm. "I don't know. Truthfully, I have never tried, but I imagine together anything could happen."

She stretched back on her pillow with her mind brimming full of ideas.

A roll of thunder echoed in the distance.

"I could stay in bed with you all day, but I suppose we should probably go down to breakfast," Aidan said.

Jade held her breath while her fingers combed through his wavy hair. "Oh, I wish we could too, but breakfast does sound wonderful. I'm starving this morning."

"I am not surprised, love. We had quite the workout last night!" He chuckled and kissed the tip of her nose. "Appears Mrs. Flannery set two outfits for us in the closet when she prepared the room."

"Oh, that's so sweet."

"Figured we could just dress here and go down for breakfast. She's going to feed the pets this morning."

"Oh, wonderful. I seriously don't know how we'll manage without her when we go back home."

Aidan smiled and gently grazed Jade's cheek with the back of his hand.

"I suppose I should take my lovely wife to breakfast, but first, would you do me the honor of joining me in the shower, Lady MacFie?"

"Mmm, I think I'd like that, Laird MacFie."

Aidan handed Jade a terrycloth robe. "I woke up earlier and discovered his and hers robes hanging next to the shower."

"Aww, Mrs. Flannery thought of everything."

Once Jade slipped on her robe, Aidan took his wife's hand and escorted her over to the clawfoot tub and shower combo in their spacious bathroom. When the water warmed, the couple slipped their discarded robes over the towel rack and stepped inside the porcelain tub. Aidan pulled Jade close, feeling the thrumming of her heart against his. She met his desire, wrapping herself around his muscular body. The mirror in the bathroom steamed over as the newlyweds enjoyed their alone time before breakfast.

WITH FLUSHED CHEEKS AND BRIGHT EYES, HER HUSBAND ESCORTED JADE downstairs. They were surprised to see their friends waiting at the dining room table. The group tapped their flutes of champagne with their spoons, signaling to the newlyweds.

Aidan and Jade kissed before taking their seats across from one another. The group clapped and took a sip of their mimosas.

"Good morning, everyone! Thank you for joining us for breakfast. Looks like we're in for a storm today. Hope you don't mind staying inside," Aidan said.

"Oh, that sounds really nice. I've been a little on the tired side since we arrived with jetlag and all," Mary said.

Paul moved his arm around Mary's shoulder. "We're just excited to spend time with you in Scotland. I wish we could stay a little longer. Hate to leave tomorrow, but things are busy right now in Pacific Grove."

Katie turned to her fiancé, Daniel. He was well over six feet with auburn hair and piercing blue eyes. He addressed the group with a heavy Irish accent.

"It's nice to be able to finally meet everyone. Katie's been talking nonstop about you these past few months. Feel like I already know ye. Aidan and Jade, your wedding was truly lovely, and we're both looking forward to having you visit us in Ireland when we say our vows," Daniel said, taking Katie's hand. She smiled up at her fiancé, eyes shining with love.

"Jade and I are looking forward to it as well." Aidan grinned. "I believe she said you're from a town called Kinvara, Daniel?"

"Aye. I'm from Kinvara, Galway. It is a sea-side town, much like your Tobermory. I think you will feel right at home when ye visit."

Aidan took Jade's hand. "We are both looking forward to it. Thank you for inviting us." He raised his glass. "I want to thank you for coming together at the last minute for our wedding. You all made our day so special, and I want you to consider the MacFie Castle your home away from home. Make yourself comfortable. We will be enjoying a special dinner tonight. Our chefs are preparing some traditional Scottish dishes with a vegan twist. If the weather permits, we will be flying out at eight tomorrow morning."

The friends enjoyed their breakfast, catching up on all the news while they were away. Jade and Aidan took turns describing their adventures while their friends listened in astonishment.

Marcail was heading to the kitchen when she felt a gentle tap on her shoulder. She turned to see Donavon standing behind her with a bouquet of daisies. She took the flowers in her arms. He gave her a peck on the cheek before disappearing around the corner. The soft sound of their laughter rang out like tiny bells.

Aidan and Jade exchanged amused looks.

"So sweet," Jade whispered.

"It's good to see her smiling again. Poor girl's been through it. Glad she can enjoy being a kid again," Aidan said.

A few minutes later, the teenagers headed over to their table. Marcail deposited a tray of warm blueberry muffins before disappearing back into the kitchen. Donavon walked over toward Aidan. Jade noticed a lipstick stain on the boy's flushed cheek and tried to hide her amusement by taking a sip of her mimosa.

"Laird MacFie, I'm sorry to interrupt your breakfast, but thought you should know I've checked the horses this morning and they're doing fine. A little nervous with the storm but eating well. I made some calls like you asked. Sounds like everything's in order concerning their travel papers."

"Travel papers?" Jade asked.

Mary and Jade exchanged curious looks.

Aidan reached for Jade's hand and gave her fingers a gentle squeeze before wiping his mouth with his napkin. "I was going to speak to you about it later, but since it's come up, I have one final surprise."

Jade laughed. "Oh, my gosh, husband, another surprise?"

"Aye. So, this is totally up to your discretion, but seeing you already have a stable on your land, I figured you might agree. I remember you mentioned your great-grandparents housed their horses near the cottage after crossing the Oregon Trail. I noticed the old barn on your property during my first jog over."

"Oh, yes. That tired stable is in sad shape. Hasn't been used in decades. My family hasn't owned horses for years."

"Figured as much. I've made a few phone calls and found some workers who would be happy to set it right again. And if ye approve, I thought I would have Blackjack and Bonnie flown to the cottage. I imagine we will spend much of our time there and figured you might enjoy riding horses on the beach. Of course, we have the penthouse, too, but imagine we can keep that as our vacation house. Whatever you prefer, lass."

Jade's eyes glistened with tears. She jumped out of her chair, rushed around the table, and threw her arms around her husband's neck.

"Oh, Aidan!"

"Is that a yes?" he asked.

"Yes!"

Katie and Mary laughed, thrilled to see her friend's dreams coming true. They spent the rest of the day exploring the castle and enjoying their accommodations. Mrs. Flannery and Marcail took turns packing up the ladies' wardrobes, preparing for their return home.

Before they left, Jade took the mother and daughter aside.

"I can't thank you enough for all of your kindness. You made me feel right at home the minute I arrived."

"Lady MacFie, the pleasure is ours," Mrs. Flannery said.

Marcail grinned. "Lady MacFie, it's sad to see you leave, but we look forward to your next visit."

"Thank you! I can't wait until we return, and I want you to know you always have a place with us if you would like to visit the States. It would be our pleasure to host you both."

Marcail exchanged excited looks with her mother. "Oh, that would be a dream come true! Donavon is always talking about visiting California."

"Well, he is certainly invited!" Jade said. The ladies chatted while they packed, looking forward to their next visit together.

ॐ

LATER IN THE EVENING, AIDAN BROUGHT HIS SUITCASES INTO JADE'S bedroom. "So, I finally get to join you in the master suite, Lady MacFie."

"Finally! "Jade said, smiling up at her husband.

They cuddled up to the fire and readied themselves for another romantic evening as newlyweds.

Chapter Twenty-Two

AIDAN AND JADE READIED THEMSELVES FOR THE LONG DAY AHEAD OF THEM. They met their friends on the steps of the castle beneath charcoal grey skies. The staff waited in line to say their goodbyes. The storm had tapered off, with a light dusting of fog kissing the sea. Dougal followed Jade's heels, while Aidan carried Morrigan's cage. They loaded themselves into two cars and arrived at the landing strip surrounded by fields of purple heather. Once the private jet was loaded, the group took their seats inside. Mrs. Macleary offered champagne to the guests before takeoff.

They sat back, readying themselves for the twelve-hour flight.

"Hopefully, we will have a smoother ride than last time," Jade said.

Mary and Katie exchanged glances.

"Don't worry. We'll be fine," Jade said.

For the next several hours, the group enjoyed their flight by catching up, eating, drinking, and sleeping. Before they realized, they were back in the States. They said their goodbyes, promising to get together soon. After their driver dropped them off, Jade and Aidan took turns carrying their luggage and pets to the cottage.

"I'm dying for a hot shower," Jade said with a deep yawn.

"Good idea, love. Why don't you get started, and I'll get Dougal and Morrigan's supper ready?"

By the time she left the warmth of the bath, Aidan had lit a fire and fed the pets. Jade headed to the kitchen but turned suddenly when she heard Dougal growling beneath the fireplace. She joined her husband in the living room. In disbelief, the couple stared at the portrait above the hearth.

"Oh, my God, Aidan."

The lone man, who once stood by the sea, had vanished. In his place was a grey lady surrounded by a shroud of Monarch butterflies.

"What does it mean?" Jade asked.

"Seems like we have another mystery to solve."

Jade pushed a golden curl from her forehead and yawned. "Looks like it's time to get back to work. I guess our vacation's over."

"Don't worry." Aidan smiled down at her. "I promise we will unravel it. It's not the first time we've had a mystery to solve, and it may not be our last. But for now, let's go to bed. We will figure out everything in the morning."

Jade sighed, gazing into her husband's aquamarine eyes. "Hmm, that does sound nice."

He lifted her in his arms, carrying her to the bedroom. Gently, he laid her down atop the quilts, kissing her soft lips. Outside, the storm pounded the sandy beach. Lightning lit up the bedroom windows. Aidan moved Jade against his eager body, and they created their own rumblings beneath the satin sheets.

The End

Don't miss out on your next favorite book!

Join the Satin Romance mailing list
www.satinromance.com/mail.html

THANK YOU FOR READING

❧

Did you enjoy this book?

We invite you to leave a review at your favorite book site, such as Goodreads, Amazon, Barnes & Noble, etc.

DID YOU KNOW THAT LEAVING A REVIEW...

- Helps other readers find books they may enjoy.
- Gives you a chance to let your voice be heard.
- Gives authors recognition for their hard work.
- Doesn't have to be long. A sentence or two about why you liked the book will do.

About the Author

AnneMarie Dapp is a graduate of San Francisco State University, where she studied Studio Arts and Art History. She lives and writes on Sock Monkey Ranch, her and her husband Dale's vegan farm in Prunedale, California.

https://sockmonkey.live

facebook.com/AnneMarieDapp68
twitter.com/AnneMarieDapp
instagram.com/annemariedapp
pinterest.com/duckmomma1

Also by AnneMarie Dapp

White Raven Series

Prairie Ghosts

The Phantom Portrait

Selkies of Scotland

www.ingramcontent.com/pod-product-compliance
Lightning Source LLC
Chambersburg PA
CBHW02095818062
46814CB00003B/1147